THE
VINTAGE
TEACUP CLUB

THE
VINTAGE
TEACUP CLUB

VANESSA GREENE

BERKLEY BOOKS, NEW YORK

THE BERKLEY PUBLISHING GROUP
Published by the Penguin Group
Penguin Group (USA) LLC
375 Hudson Street, New York, New York 10014

USA • Canada • UK • Ireland • Australia • New Zealand • India • South Africa • China

penguin.com

A Penguin Random House Company

Library of Congress Cataloging-in-Publication Data

Greene, Vanessa.
The Vintage Teacup Club / Vanessa Greene.
pages cm
Previously published as "Sphere trade paperback edition / October 2012" — Title page verso.
ISBN 978-0-425-26558-1 (pbk.)
1. Female friendship—Fiction.   2. Sharing—Fiction.   3. Life change events—Fiction.
4. Domestic fiction.   I. Title.
PR6107.R4443V56   2013
823'.92—dc23
2013021376

PUBLISHING HISTORY
Sphere edition / October 2012
Berkley trade paperback edition / November 2013

PRINTED IN THE UNITED STATES OF AMERICA

10 9 8 7 6 5 4 3 2 1

Cover photo by Lee Avison/Arcangel Images. Cover design by Leslie Worrell.
Interior illustrations copyright © iStockphoto.com/mubai.

For my mum and sister.

Acknowledgments

Thanks to Caroline Hogg, for making this novel happen and for her creative input at every stage.

To the outstanding team at Sphere, in particular to Manpreet Grewal and Rebecca Saunders for their dedication, skill and enthusiasm from day one, and to Andy Hine for believing in the power of teacups. Thanks also to Andy Coles, Jen Wilson, Carleen Peters, Madeleine Feeny, Kate Hibbert, and to Sian Wilson for the cover.

I'm extremely grateful to Emma Stonex and Sheelagh Alabaster, whose feedback on early drafts was invaluable, and to Caroline Hardman at Hardman & Swainson, for her expert guidance. Thanks also to Kim Lines, Becky Bradley, Ellie Jacob and James Gill—and in particular to my niece Eloise—for their insights and support.

To the lovely brides who supplied tales of their wedding day joys and hiccups—thank you!

Finally, thanks to James—for the laughter, inspiration and Yorkshire tea.

How We Began

(May–June)

Prologue

Jenny

Gold-edged, delicate, almost translucent—four perfect teacups sit on four perfect saucers and a small and shapely teapot gleams in between them. The tea service seems to light up the open trunk of the bottle-green Morris Minor, and as I reach out a tentative hand to touch the china I'm pretty sure I can hear a gospel choir singing out. *Yes.* Here, in the hum and bustle of Charlesworth's flea market, the Saturday bargain hunt that brings the residents of our old market town together, we've found each other at last.

"Anything in particular you're after, love?" comes a gentle, welcome voice over my shoulder. My *lord*, is that a matching creamer and sugar bowl I can see nestled among the yellowing newspaper? I peel a corner back to check. I'm right, and they all have the same pretty forget-me-not pattern below the gold rim. I'm transfixed.

I wrestle my gaze away from the teacups and turn towards the voice, warm smile already in place—less a charm offensive to kick off the negotiations, more that I simply can't stop grinning like a fool. I meet the stallholder's world-weary eyes, gray-blue under unruly brows. I expect my hazel ones look a bit manic—because in my head I'm desperately trying to decide on a maximum price for something I've fallen budget-defyingly in love with. Then, before we've even exchanged a word, I see the old man's gaze drift over my shoulder. Hang on . . .

"Well now, not a customer all morning and then along come three lovely ladies at once."

I swivel round and see that two pairs of elegant hands have crept onto my tea set—touching the precious cups that, once I'd bought them, would make everything in my life just right. The women look up in surprise, drawing back from the open trunk in unison, still clasping a teacup each. One cup is held protectively by a willowy redhead in a cream silk vest and khaki slacks, the other by a curvy brunette in a gingham dress and red lipstick, her hair pinned back in 1940s victory rolls with just a few curls escaping.

"But . . ." I start. *I was here first*, I long to protest. But then I see the expressions on their faces and I can't bring myself to say the words. They both look every bit as forlorn to see me as I am to see them.

"Listen," the redhead says, composing herself and fixing the stallholder with an assertive glare. He's clearly

about eighty, and I worry he might faint if a conflict esca-
lates. "It looks like you'll be going home with less stock
and fuller pockets when you leave this car park today."
Her green eyes sparkle, and I flinch—how on earth can I
compete with this cream-silk-clad professional? She's a
crockery *tiger.* Retro brunette seems to be losing her
nerve, she's fiddling with her chunky red necklace and
glancing around—though something tells me that she
might have the cold hard cash to come up on the inside.
And me . . . I look down at my worn jeans and Converse,
suddenly aware of the girlishness of my blonde ponytail
and petite figure, complete with blink-and-you'll-miss-it
cleavage. I feel twenty-six going on sixteen. Jenny Davis
the amateur; my art deco engagement ring the only sign
I've even dipped a toe in the antiques market before. But
I do have *passion*—and that's supposed to count for something, isn't it? Even so, I can't help fearing that neither my
purchasing prowess nor the contents of my purse are going
to be hefty enough to land me this tea set of dreams. I
hope, at least, that the others can't see that my heart is
breaking a little bit.

"But ladies," says the redhead, her auburn waves catching the light as she turns to face us, "something tells me
that taking this set home would mean really quite a lot to
each one of us. Am I right?"

I'm so shocked by this curveball from the tiger, I just
nod dumbly—tears prickling at my eyes. Instinctively I
look back at the set. Yes, the sugar tongs need a good

polish, but that somehow makes the whole thing even more perfect.

"Yes, it looks like we're all keen," I finally pipe up, turning towards the bemused pensioner. "Could you put a hold on the tea service for an hour?"

That was how our summer started.

Chapter 1

Maggie

"Two hundred bunches of cornflowers—yes, two hundred, ten blooms in each bunch." Maggie Hawthorne rested the phone against her shoulder, tipping her head slightly as she tied her auburn hair back with a band.

"And I'll also need a lot of wicker . . . Oh, you know a good supplier—great! It's for giant croquet hoops, woven round with daisies . . . and matching oversized mallets. Yes, I know, but this isn't an ordinary wedding—OK, I do know it's Sunday . . ." She breathed out slowly, trying to stay patient. "Shall I send you an email and you can look at it tomorrow? Right, no, no, I understand. Let's speak then."

Maggie sat back in her garden swing seat, settled her gin and tonic on the side table and brought her Netbook onto her lap. She tapped out an email to the Dutch supplier with the key points from last Friday's meeting with her new clients, Lucy and Jack. Finding the tea set yesterday at the flea market had sparked off a lot of ideas and she could now picture exactly how the wedding would look. She just wanted to get started. But although she had the whole of today stretching in front of her, empty time, it seemed she'd have to wait for the start of the working week until she could get the details she needed.

She knew—her friends and family were always telling her—that she should give herself the weekends to relax, but she couldn't fight the urge to use the time to get ahead on her business projects. There was always a last-minute rush with weddings. Even after fifteen years in the flower business she hadn't mastered the art of avoiding eleventh-hour panics—but the meticulous preparation she did ensured that, in her clients' eyes at least, everything flowed seamlessly.

The sun was warm on her face as she put the computer aside and took another sip of her drink. Pressing down the toes of her black suede pumps she set the swing seat in motion and leaned back. On a spring day, sitting out here was hard to beat. Friends were always surprised when they saw her garden—the layout was simple, with an emphasis on color, rather than intricate design; the lawn was well kept, with azaleas blooming around the edges. It was a world away from the exotic wedding flowers she often favored, and a contrast to the way she had furnished the house indoors. But the classic blooms and uncluttered symmetry put her mind at ease. Out here, twenty minutes' drive from the high street, the only sound was birdsong.

She fiddled with the wide gold bracelet she'd put on to complement her fuchsia dress that morning. Today, even here, surrounded by nature at its loveliest, Maggie felt restless. What was it about weekends? Sometimes the pressure to relax, to just be yourself, felt immense. Why was relaxing so important anyway?

Friday's meeting had unsettled her, and even two days afterwards her garden couldn't calm her like it usually did. She was used to doing big events—she'd been arranging flowers for them for years—but even by her standards the Darlington Hall wedding was quite something. When she'd driven through the gates in her convertible VW Beetle that first time, the sight of the stately home had taken her breath away. It was even more impressive than it looked in photos. The house itself was Georgian, with pillars by the door and stables off to the side in a nearby block, and the grounds seemed to spread out for miles around. However, it was the bride, not the place, who had really knocked her for six. Lucy Mackintosh's wedding vision was an *Alice in Wonderland* theme—with croquet on the lawn and a Mad Hatter's tea party laid out next to toadstools. Money, it seemed, wasn't a big consideration—Lucy was the only daughter of a self-made millionaire, and Maggie knew Lucy's father was as keen to impress his friends as the bride-to-be was to raise the stakes for the exclusive photo rights.

Hovering in Lucy's shadow as she led Maggie around her father's grounds had been the groom-to-be, Jack. In baggy jeans and a pair of scuffed trainers he had looked every bit the fish out of water. But with his chiseled good looks and gentle warmth (neither were lost on Maggie, despite the ten-year age gap) it was easy to see why Lucy had fallen for him.

"Where do you get your flowers from?" Jack had asked, looking over at Maggie and then quickly back at his shoes. He seemed genuinely curious.

"From all over, really, Jack," Maggie had replied. "Holland is an important supplier, and we get our roses from South America . . . but I tailor things for each wedding, and with this being the biggest one I've handled it's likely I'll be sourcing flowers from all over the world. Did you have any specific ideas?"

"Umm, no, no," he stumbled, "I'll leave that to Luce, she's good with that stuff, not me . . . I was just wondering, you know—what it's like to run your own business."

Beyond the shyness and beneath the sweeping brown fringe nearly resting on his eyelashes, Maggie wondered if there might just be a budding entrepreneur. As she went to respond, Lucy cut in.

"What I was thinking is we could have the tea party here, so when the guests arrive they'd be greeted with a cup—from some gorgeous vintage set. Did you get that, Maggie?" As Lucy spun around to face her, the emerald on her necklace glinted in the sun. "I mean, where you come in really is that I'd like to see that look echoed with cups filled with flowers all around. I don't mean shop-bought, I mean proper *bona fide vintage* teacups. God, the wedding planner I started out with didn't understand my vision on that at all." Lucy rolled her eyes and turned to Maggie, fixing her with a stare that ensured her point was crystal clear. "Dropped her like a bad habit. But you see things my way, don't you, Maggie?" Maggie nodded, then listened as her client continued. "You'd be sourcing the crockery, the wicker . . . Well, let's just say that I expect the very best . . . If Bluebelle du Jour don't wow me then we can't expect my guests to be impressed either, can we?"

Lucy was talking through her plans ten to the dozen now, twirling a strand of her immaculately highlighted hair, walking swiftly around the garden, pointing and gesticulating all the while. By the time they arrived back around at the front of the house Maggie was a little out of breath from rushing to keep up.

"You have some really original ideas, Lucy," Maggie remarked, tactfully, biting her tongue before saying any more, something her years of experience had taught her. She couldn't help glancing with sympathy at the young man who was about to sign up for a lifetime of not being able to get a word in edgewise. "I'll get onto it right away, challenges like this are my speciality. Just one thing, though . . ."

She hesitated. God, it went against every instinct she had to admit weakness, especially to someone so clearly used to getting their own way.

"Your vision is fantastic, like I say, but these are fairly big plans, aren't they? I mean, you know that I'll deliver, at Bluebelle we *always* deliver . . . but things like big toadstools aren't exactly my speciality—my experience is in the flower business, first and foremost."

Lucy let out a high-pitched laugh and threw her head back, shaking her hair-envy-inducing mane. Maggie waited for her client to calm down—the laughter didn't seem very kind—and when she did, Lucy had her hand on Maggie's arm. "Oh no, Maggie, darling." Maggie looked down at Lucy's tanned wrist and pearl bracelet against her own pale Irish skin, conscious of a physical closeness that she hadn't invited.

"Jack's friend Owen is handling all that. He's a landscape gardener—isn't that right, Jack?" Jack nodded and smiled, shifting from one foot to the other.

"Yep, that's right—Owen's just set up his own company too, you see that's what got me thinking . . . But yes, Owen's a great—"

His fiancée interrupted with a whispered aside to Maggie. "Only qualified a year ago so he's dirt cheap too."

"Ahh." Maggie said. She didn't like what Lucy was implying, but her relief was genuine. She'd been wondering how on earth she was going to manage it all by herself. "That's great. Look, I have to head off now, but it's been wonderful to talk with you today. When I've got a few things firmed up perhaps we could schedule in a meeting? So that Owen and I can brief each other—and you—on our plans, I mean. Lucy, Bluebelle du Jour is going to make this day perfect for you. Trust me. Bespoke weddings are what we do best."

Standing next to Maggie's car, they'd shaken hands and

air-kissed. When Jack's mouth briefly touched Maggie's cheek, his stubble brushing against her skin, she had not been able to stifle a smile. He was such a genuine guy. Lucy would have to work hard to train him out of that.

In her garden, Maggie shivered. A cloud was starting to block out the sun, and without a wrap over her pink dress she felt the sudden cold. Gathering up the phone, her Netbook and her empty glass she headed back inside through the French doors of her two-storey 1920s cottage. Mork, her Burmese cat, snaked his way between her feet before dashing inside ahead of her. There was a Mindy, too, her sister Carrie's cat from the same litter—Mork had the cushier deal, as Mindy had to endure quite a bit of tail pulling from toddlers.

Maggie closed the doors carefully behind her and switched on the stereo. Billie Holiday's soothing tones started to fill the room. The notes started low and wove upwards. They seemed to reach out to each of the magnificent orchids that filled the living room and the adjacent kitchen. Maggie picked up the plant spray and began her daily routine, singing along to the melody and spritzing each orchid in turn. From fragile white petals to delicate pinks and bold purples—each bloom had her full attention for a moment as she assessed its position, movement and coloring, and looked out for any flaws or damage.

Maggie wondered what would happen if she ever took the time to assess her own body in the same detail. At thirty-six she was still looking pretty good . . . but when she stepped out of the bath each night the steps that followed were hasty. She'd rub on body moisturizer in swift strokes and dodge the view in the wide mirror. She questioned now why she'd ever thought that mirror was a good idea. Linger too long and she knew what she'd see—dimpled skin, thread veins and stretch marks, her life's adventures mapped out across her thighs, stomach and bum. She knew how to dress her figure well; in fitted but forgiving jeans, and linen, silk and cottons in cool shades; but the naked truth was another story—wasn't it for every woman?

The orchids, however—young and old, perfect and flawed—were all beautiful to her. She stepped up on a little wooden stool and spritzed her favorite of all—a bright pink bloom that she'd placed in a gilt birdcage she'd bought years ago in Islington. Maggie was a London girl. She'd lived just off Camden Passage once, the cobbled street that every weekend became an antiques heaven. Back then, she'd been learning the ropes at a friend's flower shop nearby and singing with a band in bars and clubs most evenings. With time things had changed though, and apart from the birdcage, very little from her previous life had come with her to the Charlesworth house.

Maggie's mind snapped back to the music playing— the iPod plugged into her stereo was flicking through the Bs, from Billie Holiday to Blondie, and something told her that her orchids weren't going to respond as well to "Atomic" as they did to "Summertime." She chose one of her favorite Aretha songs instead. As she put the iPod down, a memory nagged at her; there'd been a day when half of her music collection had been quite different; once upon a time her flowers had listened to the Strokes and old Led Zeppelin tracks, whether they liked it or not. She forced the thought away—that had been a lifetime ago, and each month that passed she felt more distant from the woman she'd been back then. She'd thrown away the photos; her early thirties weren't a time she needed to revisit. Bluebelle du Jour, exhausting as it could sometimes be, kept her busy and energized, and Charlesworth had really begun to feel like home. The best thing of all was that she had complete control over everything in her life, from the timing of her breakfast coffee to the way her flowers framed the lawn. When she plumped her cushions they stayed that way. Maggie had worked hard to find the balance she had now—and while it looked like Lucy Mackintosh was going to be a tough customer, it would take far more than her demands to unsettle that.

She bent over her Netbook one last time, unable to resist checking if the supplier had been able to reply to her message after all.

There was a new email, but not the one she'd been expecting. From: *Dylan Leonard*. Maggie sat down in her wicker chair, to steady herself. A cool chill rushed over her skin. Christ, she thought. Some things just won't stay buried.

Chapter 2

Jenny

"'*A Vintage Affair . . . retro accessories, mother-of-the-bride outfits*'? What's this, eh, Jenny?"

Oh crap. I looked up from my screen to clock my boss Zoe leaning down over me, our faces nearly touching. The eyebrow she'd raised had disappeared under her blunt-cut black fringe. I'd watched her go out for a cigarette five minutes ago but must have missed her come back in, darn it. I clicked to minimize the wedding fair website, silently cursing the open-plan layout in our office. I took in a lungful of the familiar cloud of tobacco and Chanel that clung to Zoe.

"Sorry, Zoe . . ." I said, turning to face her again. Why did she always manage to rumble me like this? "I've finished the stationery order, so I was just . . ." My sentence trailed off when I realized she had a wry smile on her face.

"Oh chill out, Jenny," she said dismissively, standing

back up to her full height. "I'm only teasing." She smoothed an untidy strand of her shiny hair back into place. "God knows you give enough of your life to this place. Focus on marrying whoever this man is who's been keeping you sane."

And *breathe*. It was a good mood day.

Zoe was the advertising manager, and her look was hard-edged, all *Pulp Fiction* hair and tailored trouser suits that gave her a terrifying sleek silhouette. She was notorious for her steely front while keeping the ad sales guys in line and the unpredictable, fierce temper that could leave even the MD trembling. But sometimes, like today, I caught a hint of something more human about her.

The pressure had been on at our magazine, *Sussex Living*, to start generating more cash through advertising—the lifeblood of the regional glossy—and with another sales target approaching most of us were tiptoeing past the advertising department—and *especially* around Zoe. Somehow, to date I'd dodged the bullets. As an office manager I wasn't closely involved in ad sales, and I certainly wasn't a threat. I also had a little ammunition of my own: a while back Zoe had drunkenly confessed to me about sleeping with Ryan, the nineteen-year-old post boy, after a night out. I'd never dream of using it against her, but she didn't know that. I noticed that he still gave her a wink when dropping off her letters in the morning and more than once I'd seen her shrink behind her computer screen. Although Ryan *had* proven his initiative by speeding around the office in a swivel chair—halving his delivery time—he was still just the teenage postboy and shagging him wasn't something you'd really want to shout about.

"Tangfastic?" I reached for the bag on my desk and offered it up to Zoe. She peered into the bag and pulled out a sugar-frosted ring and some cherries.

"Mmm," she said, chewing, her heavily lined eyes squinting a little at the sourness. "I'd forgotten how good these are."

I pushed my chair back and straightened out my red skirt. "I think it's time for a tea. Fancy one?"

"Why not," Zoe replied, reaching past me to retrieve a couple of sugary cola bottles before sitting down at her desk and turning her back.

As I waited for the kettle to boil, I unfolded the little list I'd drafted over breakfast that morning while Dan was in the shower.

Dan and Jenny Get Hitched—eleven weeks to go!

- _Invite ideas—show them to Chris_
- _Grandma Jilly—don't want a repeat of cousin Rosie's wedding. Get someone (Dad?) to be on booze-diluting duty?_
- _White lace basque for wedding night. Too Playboy? Am marrying Dan, not Hef, after all. Ask Chloe_
- _Wedding favors??_

The kettle clicked off and I filled two mugs. That reminded me, at least I was starting to make headway with one of the most important things: the teacups.

Despite the shaky start, my weekend bargain hunt had actually worked out quite well. After asking the stallholder to put a hold on the tea set, Maggie, the willowy redhead, Alison, the retro-styled brunette, and yours truly had ducked into the refreshments tent. With 99 Flakes in hand, we'd talked through our plans for the crockery. I told them about my wedding in August, the vintage tea party theme, and my plans to collect enough teacups for all the guests to drink out of.

Alison had loved the idea; Maggie nodded along positively too, but a wedding reception at the old schoolhouse can't have seemed much compared to the lavish do at Darlington Hall she was arranging flowers for. Alison wanted the set for a different reason—to make the gorgeous teacup candles I'd seen for sale in the boutiques in town. It was Maggie who came up with a solution to our predicament. It was a very English agreement; we'd buy the forget-me-not tea set together, and take it in turns to use it.

I'd have the tea set for my wedding first, then Maggie would use the cups for her *Alice in Wonderland* garden. She'd then pass the tea things on to Alison, who'd keep the cups to turn into candles. All in all, it wasn't a bad compromise. And it was more than just that—we decided we would join forces, scouring charity shops and auction sites, to find more teacups that we could all use. An hour later, a little untidier for ice-cream drips, we were handing over a tenner each to the stall owner with smiles on our faces and each other's phone numbers noted down. Alison had offered to store our finds in her studio, and we arranged to meet for lunch at hers next Saturday to catch up.

Dan had laughed when I'd first broached the tea party theme. "I always thought weddings were supposed to be about getting drunk?" he'd said, only half serious, his warm brown eyes crinkling at the edges. But once I'd put together the scrapbook to show him what I had in mind he seemed to warm to the concept. Though perhaps that was because I was blocking the screen when he was in the middle of playing Grand Theft Auto. Eventually he put the controller down and pulled me onto the sofa for a hug. "Jen," he'd said, holding me close. (He was wearing that old Rolling Stones T-shirt—the one I could have sworn I'd chucked out.) "I couldn't care less what people are drinking, or eating, or wearing. This is going to be the most important day of my life because I get to marry *you*. That's what makes it the big one for me." He'd then pinned me down and covered me in playful kisses in a way that was both rough and tender, his stubble leaving patches that felt pleasantly raw—it was a bit like being mauled by a koala. Once I'd stopped laughing I held him close to calm him down again, and also because I loved taking in the smell of him, even in that old T-shirt—it said home to me in a way no other smell could. He was a little chunkier now than when we'd met, but it suited him. I kissed him on the mouth and pulled him close.

Dan had made me smile every day since we first got together at uni. We'd both lived on campus back then and he and his friends used to play football on the grass in front of my flat in halls when I was writing essays. One July day, when the ball hit the window above my desk particularly hard, he'd come close to the glass, mouthed "sorry," and smiled. As our eyes met my heart was thudding in my chest. I couldn't focus at all on what I was writing for the rest of the afternoon. When his friends started getting their stuff together to go, he came back over to my window, gave me a wink, and stuck a piece of paper to the pane: "Dan" it said, and then he'd written his phone number. After a few ciders at the union bar with my flatmate the following evening, I'd got up the courage to call him. And the rest? Well, the two of us have been hard to separate ever since.

That night, as I got into bed beside him, placing the engagement ring we'd scoured Brighton's South Lanes to find on the night table, I thought: men don't always get it, do they? I mean yes, Dan wanted me to be his wife, but did he really get the importance of beautiful events,

VANESSA GREENE

memories to treasure in forty years' time? I wanted a perfect picture on my shelf to remember the perfect day. The
details were part of creating that.

I thought of the empty mantelpiece at Dad's. As a little
girl I used to pick flowers from the garden and put them
in a little vase to fill the space where Mum and Dad's
wedding photo used to be. Dad said he wasn't bitter about
Mum leaving us, and my brother, Chris, had found his own
way of coping. Me, I'd started putting the flowers there.
I was six when she left, but over time my flower-loving
heart hardened. It had toughened a little more each time
I walked past other mothers waiting at the school gates;
or when I'd had to summon up all my courage to buy
tampons on my own that first time, my cheeks red hot. I
had tried to understand Mum's reasons, but I never really
managed—leaving just isn't something mothers are meant
to do.

Anyway, I had my own life now, and mine and Dan's
wedding day was going to be just right. I'd make those
photo-frame memories, even if I had to organize some of
the things that mattered to me on my own.

"Hey, dreamer," said Chloe, nudging me out of my
thoughts and back to the reality of the office. "Enough in
that kettle for one more?"

"Hello!" I said, giving her arm a squeeze. "For you,
chief bridesmaid, anything," I laughed, getting another
mug out of the cupboard.

Seeing Chloe, even for an instant, was enough to light up the magazine office. When she'd come in on work experience two years ago, with a glint in her eye and brown ringlets springing in all directions, we'd become friends almost immediately. She'd been so enthusiastic about the work, taking on even mundane tasks with gusto. The long commute from her village to Charlesworth didn't seem to bother her, even though she was getting paid nothing but expenses for the privilege. To look at her bright eyes after the MD finally offered her a paid role you'd have thought she was coming to work at *Vogue*. Perhaps inevitably, the scales had fallen from her eyes a little since then.

"How's your day going, Chlo?" I asked as I filled her cup.

Her wide, mascaraed eyes met mine—a flash of barely concealed irritation there. "Slow start today . . . Gary's got me working out a spreadsheet of his expenses that is taking an age. He said he needs it, but I feel like he's just monopolizing my time; he knows how much I want to be writing features. Do you know what I mean?"

"I guess so," I said. But I didn't understand her frustration, not really. The truth was I liked spreadsheets. There was nothing better, I thought, than creating order from chaos—the only big project I wanted was my wedding. It made me feel happy knowing everyone in the office had the resources they needed, and reliable, efficient admin systems. Of course I knew that most of the junior staff couldn't wait to get assigned to feature writing, or build up their skills in design and page layout; but for me the joy of letting someone know that their stack of neon-colored Post-its had arrived was sometimes enough.

I did my best to put myself in Chloe's shoes: she was smart, dedicated, aimed high and anyone could see she'd be more than capable of overtaking Gary given half a chance. "Chloe, you'll get there—I reckon he's just testing you, don't you think?"

"Yep, you're probably right," she replied. "But enough about me, Jen." She waved her hand, changing the subject. "I'm just in a Monday mood, you know how it is, brilliant weekend and then reality bites. Cheer me up—how's Dan? How's the wedding planning going?"

It was pathetic really but just the mention of Dan was enough to make me smile. Chloe had always been surprisingly tolerant of my soppiness. "Dan's great—we spent most of the weekend at home, mainly deciding on the table plan."

To be honest Dan had done a lot of this on the sofa with his eyes closed—but his company had still meant something and, well, I was motivated enough for the two of us. He was putting in so many hours at the travel agency at the moment, plus there was his commute, and when it got to the weekend he just needed to crash. That Sunday I'd happily stuck Post-it notes labeled with people's names onto paper plates and then shuffled them around until exes were separated and embarrassing relatives were out of harm's way. The invites hadn't even gone out yet, but with the family politics we both had going on I was getting an early start; I was not going to leave anything to chance. Dan opened a sleepy eye, nodded and smiled his appreciation at the end result.

Dan had been working so hard because, as we found out pretty quickly, sugared almonds cost cold hard cash. Even with our salaries combined the wedding we wanted was going to be a stretch, but he knew how important it all was to me and he was going all out to do overtime and boost our funds.

I stirred a heaped teaspoon of sugar into Chloe's tea and as I passed it to her saw she was smiling.

"It's great to see you so happy, J," she said, taking the mug. "You deserve this, you know. And I know your wedding's going to be spectacular." She pulled me into a warm hug.

As we separated she spotted my to-do list on the counter. "White lace basque?" she exclaimed, then saw her name and looked up, brow furrowed.

"Hold on, am I the official wedding-night underwear adviser?" I watched as a smile spread across her face. "Brilliant! You know I have to say I *hate* white lace, Jen, far too Bunny Girl . . . but you, Mrs. Yates-to-be, are going to look fantastic in this retro corset I spotted online . . ."

Chapter 3

Alison

Alison Lovell frowned in concentration as she mixed wax for the candles she was making—trying to ignore the fluffy gray muzzle pressing against her side and letting out little whines in an attempt to distract her. George, the family's wolfhound, nudged his scruffy head under her arm until she finally shooed him away, readjusting the pencil that tied her wavy dark hair up. Newspaper covered every surface in the studio and Joni Mitchell sang out from her wax-spattered stereo.

Alison had just mixed a golden yellow wax when soft-skinned arms hooped around her waist from behind and she jumped as her daughter Holly gave her a squeeze. She turned to see a grin on Holly's freckled face, her messy brown curls clipped back with sparkly hairclips.

"Woah, you gave me a fright, sweetheart," Alison said, smiling. "I didn't hear you come in."

"Sorry," Holly said, with a shrug. "Bye, Mum."

"Bye, darling, have a good day," Alison said, giving her a kiss on the head. She heard her elder daughter, Sophie, shouting out from the hallway, "Come on, Dad, you're taking ages!"

"Bye, Sophie," Alison shouted out. The front door slammed, her goodbye unanswered. She did not miss the school run. This was usually the last distraction before the day was all hers: a quiet, productive, peaceful Tuesday. She loved her two daughters to bits, but work could never really get going until they were out of the house.

Alison had put on a linen apron to protect the 1950s floral dress she'd put on that morning. Impractical, yes, but it suited her, flattered her curves, and she couldn't resist wearing it now spring had finally sprung after what had felt like an endless winter. Ten identical blue teacups stood near the edge of her table ready to be filled with wax; by next week they would be sold as candles in the upmarket boutiques on Charlesworth High Street. She took a ladle over to the first cup and carefully filled it, then moved on to the second one. The golden yellow wax contrasted nicely with the blue—but something wasn't quite right. She looked up at the mood board next to her studio window— color swatches with delicate lilacs and bronzes, intricate embroidered lace, 1940s wedding photos and newspaper clippings giving a visual reminder of the brand identity she wanted to capture in her work. She added to it whenever she found a new scrap and looking at it always lightened her mornings. Not a teenager on there—just the beautiful things that had always inspired her. But the problem remained—something about the new cups didn't quite fit.

George, spotting a coal tit on the windowsill, leapt up from the blanket where he'd been feeling sorry for himself and launched himself towards the open window by Alison's worktop. The bird made a good getaway but the table, just a section of wood balanced on books and paint cans, wobbled and shifted—Alison reached out to stop anything sliding off, her heart racing as she pictured the teacups crashing down, but broad-based and sturdy, they hadn't even flinched. In the garden, the blossom on her cherry tree quivered from the coal tit's hasty exit. She'd picked out the cups from an online homeware shop. Totting up prices and calculating the profit margin had put her out of her comfort zone—the figures had made her head spin—but she knew they were cheap and clicked "buy" on twenty items before her head took over. Since last Christmas, when Pete lost his job in communications for the NHS, things had changed; with only one of them working now she had to be practical where the business was concerned.

But this morning she couldn't see past the fact that these plain teacups weren't delicate or pretty enough. They'd withstand an earthquake. She glanced from their cheerful matte blue back to her mood board—what she needed were fragile, soft tones that conjured up a different era, when people would make do and mend and a precious set of china would be cared for and cherished. What could be more indulgent than enjoying a bath surrounded by her upcycled teacups—candles with history? The flea market tea set she had fallen for was The One, no question—the fact that Jenny and Maggie had felt the same only confirmed it. Jenny's glowing face, the look of love at first sight as she touched the cups, had made her smile in recognition. Nothing else would compare—but it wasn't hers to use yet. As they'd agreed, Alison would keep looking for similar cups and if she was going to fill the new order she'd received that morning, she'd better find something soon.

Alison knew that there had to be more genuine vintage cups that would delight her customers without breaking the bank, and Charlesworth's charity shops were the natural place to start her search. Sophie and Holly would be at school all day, if Sophie didn't get sent home for winding up her teachers again, that was; and Pete, well . . .

Pete was a trouper. He was dropping the girls off now and wouldn't be back till at least midday, with his arms full of Sainsbury's bags, a half-smile on his face, trying to dodge a rogue baguette threatening to poke him in the eye. With his dark eyebrows, untameable brown hair and gangly limbs, Pete was one of those grown-ups who'd never really stopped looking like a guitar-strumming teenager. He still played with his band when they got a local gig, and when he did, Alison caught a glimpse of the eighteen-year-old boy she'd first met. That day Pete had had sun-bleached stubble and tanned skin, just back from interrailing around Europe, and Alison was wearing a T-shirt and cut-off shorts, sitting out with her friends on the green, enjoying her first summer after O levels. He'd brought his guitar over as dusk drew in and, smiling and half drunk, played U2's "With or Without You."

It was about six months ago, twenty-five years into their marriage, that her mind had started to regularly drift elsewhere when she and Pete made love. Last night, as he'd lain beside her, holding her in a loose embrace and beginning to snore softly, she had wondered whether this happened in all marriages, after decades together, or whether she should be doing something about it. Perhaps it was enough that they were still doing it?

Her thoughts were never of other men. During the throes of passion, she'd think of grocery lists and dentist's appointments, parents' evenings and invoices. Did that mean there was nothing to feel guilty about, or—and this was what really nagged at her—was it somehow even worse?

Anyway, she thought, drifting back to the present, Pete had the shopping under control, no one needed her right now and she could afford to take some time out of the studio and pop down to the high street. Her friend Jamie at the hospice charity shop would probably be able to help her in her search, and there were a couple of other errands she could run at the same time. She undid her apron and hung it over the chair.

Standing at the hall mirror, tidying her hair and putting on a slick of red lipstick, she considered her reflection for a moment; not too bad for forty-two, she thought. She didn't go in the sun much nowadays, and pilates kept her pretty toned. She heard George galloping down the corridor towards her. She ruffled his head and slipped a lead onto his broad leather collar, forgiving his earlier impulsiveness in an instant. She glanced first at her beloved red kitten heels—they'd look so perfect with the floral dress—then back to the dog. She opted instead for green battered DM boots; it was a look of sorts. "Join me on the hunt, George." She unbolted the door and with a backward glance down the hall saw the empty space where Pete's briefcase used to be. When he had put it away in the hall cupboard at the start of the year, after his redundancy was confirmed, something in him—and perhaps also between them—had shifted.

She climbed into her battered Clio and started up the engine. Having two cars was an extravagance really, she supposed, now that Pete wasn't using the Volvo for work. She ought to find out how much the car cost to run and talk to Pete about whether they really needed it.

The drive to Charlesworth's pretty, shop-lined high street took less than fifteen minutes, about as long as George would tolerate staying put on the back seat without trying to leap over and join her in the front. She listened to the news on the journey, and when she arrived she opened the door to get George out and tied his lead to the railings outside the hospice charity shop before heading inside.

A jangle rang out as she opened the door. "Hello, darling Ali!" the man behind the counter called over. Jamie was gruff-voiced but kitten-soft in character, a far cry from the quiet blue-rinsed ladies who volunteered on the other days. When he was at work, forties and fifties jazz and jive were never off the stereo. Jamie lived his life as if every day were a glittering event, and he didn't even realize he was the real star, center stage. He and Alison went way back. They had been swing dancing partners for some years, and when Jamie's partner Seb had been diagnosed with cancer it was Alison he'd go to when he needed to let his defenses down. Two years after Seb's death Jamie was still pouring his energy into raising money for the hospice that had cared for Seb during his final days. Jamie had transformed the shop into a vintage wonderland. There wasn't an old Next shirt with yellowed underarms or a dodgy toast rack in sight—he trawled through the donation bags, picking out only the very best, and sometimes even sourcing clothes and bric-a-brac from elsewhere so that the shop glowed with glamour and the promise of a bargain.

"Hi, Jamie," Alison said, walking over to him and being welcomed into a warm hug.

"How are things?" he asked, pulling back to look her in the eyes.

"They're fine," she started, hesitating before going on. "You know how it is. Sophie, it's a bit of a battleground there . . . but the business is going well, really well—in fact I've got a bit of catching up to do. Anyway, I could go on,

Jamie, but I'm actually on a bit of a mission today. I've got a new order for my candles and I need to make this lot *dazzling...*"

As she talked, she was scanning the shelves—soundtrack LPs, a 1960s Monopoly board, veiled bridal hats, oversized chrome ashtrays on stands, petticoated dresses and bolero jackets. Where did he find this stuff? But not a tea set in sight. Alison's heart sank.

"Tea . . . cups?" she ventured.

"Oh, sorry, Ali—you know how that stuff is flying off the shelves at the moment. We sold a cracking little set last week but that was all we had."

"Darn." Ali snapped her fingers. "Ah well, I'll have to be quicker on the draw next time." She fiddled with the chunky red beads strung around her neck as she mulled over what to do next. "I guess there's always eBay. That's got to be worth a shot, no?"

"Of course, petal." Jamie's eyes crinkled as he smiled. His stubble was gray and his hair was thinning out, but he was still one of the most handsome men in Charlesworth—and in his perfectly cut jeans, a crisp shirt, waistcoat and tan brogues he was the best dressed by a long shot. She stood beside him in her flowery, full-skirted dress and DMs. Ali imagined the sight of the two of them together. Improbable though the pairing was, they *worked*; and she silently savored the moment.

"But where are my manners, Jamie . . . How have things been for you?"

He laughed and ruffled Alison's hair. "I'm fine, hon, ticking over, more than that actually. There's something I'd like to talk to you about. Maybe we could go for coffee next week and I'll catch you up properly?"

Alison could hear George's barking through the shop window and it was getting louder. As she turned around she saw him leap out at an elderly lady who'd been trundling along with a walker.

"Oh God, George—GEORGE." As she fled the shop, her full skirt whirling, she turned to look back at Jamie, who was starting to laugh. "Ooh—but yes, Jamie—absolutely, sounds good, yes, let's do it—I'll call you!"

In a jangle of bells Ali was back out in the high street and apologizing profusely to a rather dazed-looking lady who was frozen to the spot. "Oh, don't worry, dear," she began, still plainly startled. "He's just so, well, *big*, isn't he? I'm sure they're bigger now, than in my day." She smoothed down her gray hair, then steadied herself so that she was holding the walker with both hands again.

"I really am sorry," Alison said, quickly casting an eye over the lady to check for any damage. "Are you sure you're OK? He just gets so excited when he's out." Alison hauled George back and shortened his lead. He protested with a bark. So much for the quiet trip out, she thought to herself. She watched the old lady take halting steps away down the street and walked George back to the car. She left him in the back while she ran a few errands—leaving the other charity shops for another day and instead picking up the

THE VINTAGE TEACUP CLUB

shampoo and toiletries that she was ashamed to admit she didn't trust Pete to get right—and then drove back home. She was determined to turn her morning into a productive one by sketching out some new hand-embroidered cushion cover ideas she'd been meaning to get round to.

As she pulled into the wide gravel drive in front of their tumbledown-but-pretty cottage, with its wonky front door frame and peeling paint, her mobile rang. She pulled the hand brake on and fished the phone out of her bag.

"Hello?" she answered, turning the engine off with her free hand.

"Mrs. Lovell?" came the shrill inquiry.

"Yes, yep, speaking." She rearranged herself in her seat. Damn, she'd recognize the headmistress's voice anywhere.

"It's . . ." Alison filled in the blank: *Sophie*. She had set someone's lab coat alight . . . was holding a sit-in protest about regulation skirt length . . . had been caught snogging in class again . . . Alison pictured her elder daughter—dyed black hair and bangles, that new, defiant expression. They were all plausible scenarios.

The headmistress carried on, "Mrs. Lovell . . . it's Holly."

Alison let the phone fall away from her ear for a moment. *Holly?*

"Sorry, yes, Mrs. Brannigan—what is it?" There was silence on the line for a moment.

"I think it's best if you come in to the school so that we can talk this through."

Chapter 4

Jenny

"How about Devon?" I asked Dan, spreading the holiday brochures out between us on our blue and white checkered sofa. He'd brought a pile of them back from the travel agency where he worked and we were spending Saturday morning having a browse through, deciding where to go for our honeymoon.

"Hmm . . . Devon," Dan said, trying to work out how he felt about it. He pushed down the plunger of the cafetière. "We could surf there, right? That could be fun." His eyes lit up at the thought.

"Yes. *Or* we go for cream teas and gentle strolls along the beach instead?" I replied, as he passed me a mug of hot coffee. "I'm not sure spending the week in wetsuits that smell of wee is the sexiest start to married life."

Dan laughed. "You'd look scorching out in the waves, Jen, even if you do smell odd."

We'd spent a couple of months after uni traveling in Central America and for part of that time we'd learned to surf. The water was so warm over there that I'd been in a bikini. I'd loved every minute, but two months had been enough for me and I'd liked coming home to Dad and Chris. I hadn't wanted to leave it too long before looking for a job, but Dan had stayed out there and discovered a passion for travel that had been with him ever since—climbing volcanoes, horseriding in the Andes, exploring temples, you name it. He'd brought me back souvenirs, taken photos at every destination. I liked that our cozy living room was filled with small framed prints of our photos; Mexican beaches, cityscapes, sunsets, a journey round the world. He'd written me emails almost every day he was away. I'd read them in the little flatshare I'd found above a shop on Charlesworth High Street, feeling as if I was right there with him.

After eight months Dan's money had run out and he'd come back. He had been at loose ends for a while until we'd spotted a job at the student travel agency in Brighton. It was perfect for him. He really enjoyed advising people about where to go and what to do when they got there. The cheap flights he got working there were a big bonus too—we'd been on a fantastic trip to visit Dan's sister Emma in Australia when she was living in Melbourne. In the last couple of years Dan had organized a few trips abroad with the boys, muddy adventures like multiday hikes and high-altitude cycle rides, and I was happy to leave them to it. I loved hearing the stories when he came home, though. A year ago when he'd finally paid off his credit card bill, we'd rented a small but perfectly formed one-bedroom flat on the second floor of a terraced house. And we've been here ever since.

I drew my eyes back from where they'd drifted, to a panoramic photo of Rio we had propped up on the mantelpiece, and returned to more practical considerations.

"Dan, are you *sure* you don't mind?" I asked, turning to look at him.

"What, seeing you dressed up like a seal in your wetsuit?"

"No, don't be silly, I mean the budgeting. I know this is our honeymoon—but like we said, even if you get us a good deal on flights our cash just isn't going to stretch that far."

Dan moved the brochures onto the coffee table, nudging a copy of *Brides* magazine out of the way. I'd been reading it earlier that morning, but had put it down when I got to yet another feature about mother-of-the-bride outfits. Why were all wedding magazines so obsessed with her role in things? Dan pulled me closer, putting an arm around me. "Jen, I thought we'd already talked about this? The money that we have is going to go to our wedding, so that it's the day you've always wanted it to be. We only

THE VINTAGE TEACUP CLUB

get married once, after all. We'll have time further down the line to save and go on another trip." With those words, he brought back my smile.

"And you know what," he said, reaching for a brochure about Scottish Highland breaks, "I'm into this stuff— there's so much we haven't seen that's close to home. We're going to have a great time, trust me." He flicked open the page and pointed to a little hotel room with a balcony overlooking a vast lake, the scenery lush and green. "It does look pretty nice there, doesn't it?" I nodded, it did.

"See," he said, holding me closer and kissing the top of my head. I looked up. His warm brown eyes had a way of making my worries disappear. "Being with you is adventure enough, Jenny. I mean, quite honestly, it's downright exhausting sometimes . . ." I grabbed a cushion and thwacked him around the head with it. He laughed. "Dan Yates, it's not too late for me to pull out of this marrying-you deal, you know."

I left Dan doing the laundry and got to Alison's house just before one, resting my bike up against the wall. The house was built from old gray stone and the front garden was untamed, with long grass that crept over the front wall, and blue and purple wildflowers everywhere I looked. Nature was spilling over into the gravel drive, so the boundaries weren't clear; it was a world away from the carefully tended window boxes in town. A light rain had started to fall and while I'd been cursing it on the ride over, it brought out the smell of the flowers and made everything fresh. Paint was peeling away from Alison's window frames and the door frame was a bit wonky, but it all added to the place's charm.

I'd put a biscuit tin into my bike's wicker basket before setting out, and at some point along the way it had got jammed. While I was trying to wrestle it free I heard heels on the pathway and a woman's voice call out. "You all right there?"

I turned to see Maggie, serene in indigo jeans, a linen jacket and an amber necklace. Her auburn hair was swept up into a French braid, highlighting her high cheekbones and the delicate line of her jaw. One hand was holding up a turquoise Japanese parasol, fragile but just perfect for sheltering from the gentle rain. In contrast, my hair was clinging in damp strands to my forehead, I had on the old Reeboks I always wore for cycling and the leggings under my checked shirt dress were splashed with mud. "Hi, Maggie," I managed, just as the tin came loose from the basket, nearly sending me off-balance. The contrast between us now seemed complete. She smiled kindly at my wobbling and then looked down at the tin I was clutching to my chest. "What have you got there?" she asked. As she put the parasol down she reached out for the brass door knocker and brought it down with a loud thud.

"Some fuel for our brainstorming session," I said.

"Aha," Maggie replied, with a wink, "I like your style."

"Ladies, welcome!" Alison said, opening the door wide while trying to hold back a tall gray dog with one arm. "Come in, come in."

I put a protective hand over my tin; bitter experience has taught me not to trust dogs where baked goods are involved. Alison led us down a hallway filled with enticing cooking smells, to the open door of her bright living room. There was a grandfather clock in the corner and generous sofas scattered with patchwork cushions. A teenage girl was stretched out on one of the sofas reading a copy of *Twilight*, her black hair tied up in a rough top knot, and a younger girl with freckles sat at the other end squashed against her sister's feet, playing on a small pink games console. She was the first to look up when her mum stepped in to introduce us.

"Hi, girls, here are some new friends of mine. Jenny, Maggie," Alison said, motioning to us, "meet Sophie and Holly." Sophie, the elder girl, nodded her acknowledgment blankly and went back to her book.

"Hi," said Holly with a smile, resting her game down on the arm of the sofa. "Are you all going to have lunch now?"

"Yes," Alison said, "but no, that doesn't mean you can go on the Internet as soon as I'm out of the room, Hol. You know the rule on that." Sophie gave her little sister a kick, and Holly pinched her leg back.

"Right, grown-up time," Alison said, turning to us with a weary smile, "and not a moment too soon." She walked me and Maggie into her open-plan kitchen and dining room. Once inside, Alison went over to the oven and took a lasagna out, and the room filled with the mouth-watering smell of it, the windows steaming up with the heat. Everywhere I looked there was color—bright seat cushions, a large canvas hung on the wall, an abstract painting in oranges and reds. A vase of cut wildflowers, the same ones I'd seen growing out in the front garden, sat in the middle of the chunky wooden table.

"Wow, it's beautiful in here," I said, looking around.

"Oh, thanks," Alison said, dishing up. There were tiny personal touches everywhere my eyes fell; even her oven gloves had sunflowers stitched on them. "I suppose I do like making stuff."

Maggie raised her eyebrows at the understatement, still taking in the details of the room, and Alison continued, "I used to make a lot of clothes for the girls— pinafores, skirts, blouses." Alison passed them a plate of vegetable lasagna each and put a big salad bowl on the table and then a jug of cordial. "Tuck in," she said, sitting down.

"I mean, it's hard to imagine now, isn't it?" She nodded in the direction of the front room, and loaded up her fork. "But they used to be so happy wearing those things." I served myself some of the salad, full of avocado and red peppers—there was definitely more of my five-a-day here than in the bacon sandwiches Dan and I had made for breakfast.

"I bet they looked adorable," Maggie said, spearing a slice of pepper.

"Yep," Alison replied, mid-mouthful. "But then secondary school came—and wearing stuff your mum's made didn't seem that cool anymore. So now, well. We had a clear out and I started making things for the house and for friends instead. The business I have now just grew from there—one day I was making bunting for my sister-in-law's fortieth, the next I was selling the candles, cushion covers, oven gloves and tea-party things online and through the local boutiques. The painting's just for fun," she said, waving vaguely at the bright canvas hanging next to us. "I don't really get time for that nowadays."

While Alison glowed as she told us about setting up on her own, Maggie, with one eye on the large kitchen wall clock as she ate, silently revealed the downside of managing a business. She seemed to be struggling to relax.

"How old are the girls now?" I asked Alison, switching the subject away from work.

"Sophie's fifteen, Holly's twelve," she answered, scooping another heap of salad onto Maggie's plate.

"I keep forgetting Holly's nearly a teenager, that she's not my baby anymore," she added, shaking her head slightly.

"Are you and her dad friend or foe right now?" Maggie asked, intrigued.

"Good question," Alison said, "and I'm not entirely

sure." She took a deep breath and continued, "Holly might look like butter wouldn't melt, but she was caught stealing last week." Alison covered her face with her hands and peeked out from between her fingers to show her mortification. "The school caretaker found bags of brand-new clothes in her locker at school—she and her friend Chrissy had bunked class and gone on a shopping spree with Chrissy's mum's new credit card. It turns out Chrissy had nabbed it when the post came in and knew the pin number was her own birthday.

"Anyway I had to deal with the headmistress yesterday—Pete and I have already had a few run-ins with her about Sophie's behavior and the marks she got in her mocks, so it wasn't great." The light went out of Alison's eyes for a second and I noticed for the first time the fine lines around them. "But it was the fact that she kept it from us that was the hardest to take. The girls felt too guilty to even wear the clothes. When we asked Holly about it she told us the whole story right away. Tears, tears, tears," Alison's face softened at the memory.

"That's something at least," Maggie said sympathetically, "that she realizes it was wrong."

"Oh, yes," Alison continued. "And to be honest even though we were both furious, we still felt for her. She'd clearly wanted to put things right but didn't know how. Anyway, none of this changes the fact that over a month has passed and we're now stuck with hundreds of pounds' worth of clothes it's too late to take back."

It was the kind of thing that had happened at my school, but Chris and I had never really rebelled as teenagers. Even then we both knew that Dad had enough on his plate.

"Does that mean it's down to you to pay this girl's mum back?" I asked.

Alison nodded. "Yep, it looks that way . . . But enough of this stuff, you two didn't come here to listen to my moans about being a mum." Alison started to collect our empty plates together.

"Luckily I've got something that might cheer you up," I said, bringing the biscuit tin up onto the table and prising off the lid.

Alison tidied the food away and laid my homemade flapjacks out on a gold-trimmed plate and before long the table was liberally sprinkled with oats.

Maggie got a little Smythson notepad out of her bag and opened it. "So I was talking to a supplier in London," she started, "and I'm going to go up there for a meeting in a week or so—I thought it would be a good chance to check out some of the vintage shops, perhaps go around Brick Lane, pick up a few bargains."

"Great," I said, before taking a big bite of my flapjack.

"Alison," Maggie started, "are you still happy to look at the charity shops round here and maybe go to a couple of the local flea market?"

"Sure, of course," Alison said. "I'll ask my friend Jamie

to keep a lookout too." Maggie was noting this down neatly in her book and I realized it was my turn to say something.

"I've been looking online, at the specialist suppliers and then auction sites like eBay—there are some beautiful things out there, but the prices are pretty high. The experienced sellers seem to have clocked the trend and marked all their stuff up. I reckon that for the real bargains we're better off sticking with the stalls and flea markets, just like on Saturday. It may be slower progress but we'll be able to afford some nice items, and there's still plenty of time."

"OK, sounds sensible," Maggie said. "Shall we just meet up again in a couple of weeks and see where we are?"

There was a faint knock at the door behind me.

"Mum." The door creaked open and Holly's freckled face appeared around the side. Their dog dashed under Holly's arm and through into the kitchen and began to hoover up flapjack crumbs from the floor.

"Come in, Hol," Alison said, as her younger daughter shuffled through the doorway. I noticed she'd doodled on the backs of her hands in pen like I had done at her age.

"I got a bit bored in there," Holly said. "Sophie's hogging the phone and there's nothing on TV. I know I'm grounded, and I understand about the Internet, but . . ." I caught her eye and she gave me a shy smile.

"OK, come in," Alison said, "take a seat. We're just

finishing up. Do you want one of the flapjacks Jenny brought?"

Holly sat down on the bench next to me and wriggled around to get comfortable, reaching for the plate. "You're hunting for teacups, aren't you? Because you're getting married? Mum told me," she said, looking at me, her wide eyes sparkling.

I nodded and smiled.

Alison squeezed her daughter's arm gently and said, "Perhaps when we find them, we should hang on to them for when you and Sophie meet your Prince Charmings?"

"Awesome!" Holly said, letting a giggle escape.

Alison rolled her eyes then, turning to me and Maggie, "Or at least someone who can turn these two frogs back into my lovely girls . . ."

"Keep the teacups for our weddings!" Holly called out, still giggling, her shyness gone.

As Alison joked with her daughters I realized that one day they'd probably be having this conversation about weddings for real. As Holly and Sophie planned their celebrations, their mum would be there, to go to dress-fittings, visit venues, and help them work out the table plan. On the day, Alison would be there, proud and more than likely a bit tearful, as she saw her daughters off into married life.

"You're looking for others like that tea set, right, more old stuff?" Holly asked me.

I nodded, but my mind was foggy. Thinking about

Alison being there for her daughters' weddings had made me realize that however I looked at it, there was going to be a gap at mine.

"Yes, that's right," Alison said. "But not just any old stuff, Hol, beautiful things—like the set Granny has at her house."

"As much as I'd like to stay here all day," said Maggie, again casting a glance at the wall clock, "duty calls. I really should get back to the shop." She picked up her linen jacket and got to her feet with a smile. "It's been lovely, Alison, thanks a lot for lunch, and sorry I've got to dash." Catching sight of my empty flapjack tin on the counter, she picked it up and passed it over to me.

"Yes, thanks, Alison," I said, taking the tin from Maggie. I thought for a moment about staying, but realized I couldn't shift the mood I'd sunk into. I got up to leave. "I should really be off too."

Alison was stroking Holly's hair absentmindedly as her daughter chewed on a flapjack. "Of course," she said, looking up. "You're very welcome. I'll see you out."

I cycled back to the flat, pedaling fast down the country lanes, the wind whipping through my hair. While lunch had been nice, I'd been grateful for the excuse to leave Alison's house; seeing her with her daughters was hard, it had reminded me of what I would never—and could never—have. It would always seem as if there was an empty chair at our wedding.

Thoughts rushed through my mind just like the scenery whizzed by, a blur of green. I knew I was lucky, really lucky. I was going to marry Dan, who I loved to bits, and who made me happy. I also had my dad, and Chris, who were both amazing.

So why did I feel so empty?

Chapter 5

Maggie

"Maggie, ah, hello—you're back!" Anna called out.

Maggie stepped in through Bluebelle du Jour's shop doors and her eyes met with chaos. The florist's was normally immaculate—clear surfaces leading the eye to tastefully arranged flowers against a backdrop of Parisian street signs, framed art nouveau prints and French film posters. Today, though, the counter was overflowing with notes for orders and the shop floor badly needed a sweep—there were petals everywhere. Maggie scolded herself for taking time out for lunch at Alison's. The state of the shop confirmed all her misgivings about leaving the shop on a Saturday. She couldn't expect things to be OK without her.

Anna was bright, but she was only nineteen. Maggie cast an eye over her assistant—dressed in a frilly shop pinny and Nike Air trainers with a flush to her cheeks and her bleached blonde curls spilling out of an untidy bun, she looked even younger. Yes, the customers adored her, but sleek and professional she wasn't.

"Yes, hi, Anna, here I am," Maggie said, picking up a few of the notes on the counter and tidying them into a pile. "Wow," she continued, "it was so quiet earlier this morning, wasn't it?"

Anna nodded. "I know—but the sun came out and, whoosh! All the shoppers came in. We must have sold twenty bunches of tulips, then three of those orchids we've had in the window for a while. A lot of freesias and lilies too. Isn't that great?"

"Yes," Maggie replied, distractedly, and continued with her work, ensuring the orders had been processed properly before filing them away, then greeting the new customers who had stepped into the shop. She was so wrapped up in the moment she failed to notice Anna hovering by her side.

"Oh, Anna—you're still here . . . sorry, take a break."

She needed support, yes, but she didn't want Anna getting burned out with the springtime rush starting. As Anna walked out of the shop door and into the bustling high street, Maggie spotted two young women who were looking at some of the arrangements in the window. She took a deep breath and walked over to the front of the shop to join them. "Ladies, welcome to Bluebelle—what can I help you with today?"

*

Maggie got back home at seven, after she had finished some paperwork and locked up. There was a postcard on her doormat, a beach scene of St. Ives with a cartoon in the corner of a woman eating a Cornish pasty. She flipped the card over and smiled as she saw the familiar signatures at the bottom—Kesha, Dave, and a big handwritten scrawl from their daughter, Evie, who'd written her little brother's name, Oscar, too.

> *Dear Maggie, So sorry we couldn't make it over for your birthday. We're having fun in the sun down in Cornwall and hope to see you soon.*

Maggie had been friends with Kesha ever since they were at school together in north London. Along with their friend Sarah, they had been as close as girls got. There had been a time they'd all known what the others ate for lunch and who had a crush on whom—but nowadays it was hard enough just to keep up to date on what jobs they were doing, or when babies were due. Maggie tucked the postcard into the side of the hallway mirror and felt a pang of nostalgia, then went through to the kitchen.

She fixed herself a Pimms, slicing oranges, mint and lime, and opened the kitchen window. She pulled up a stool and settled at the breakfast bar, and in a linen-bound sketchbook started drawing out some ideas for the Darlington Hall wedding. Would the bride accept a simple bouquet of cornflowers? As much as it irked her to admit it, Lucy's eyes were a spectacular blue, and cornflowers would set them off perfectly. Maggie did a bird's-eye view sketch showing which floral displays would go where, and what direction the guests would approach the garden from, to maximize the impact of the flowers. It all began to take shape. She added more details, notes and color until the pages were full of lively plans. The grand venue and generous budget meant her imagination could run more freely than it had in months. While she'd been daunted by the idea of arranging the non-floral features when Lucy had first mentioned them, she now found she had lots of ideas for those too. She'd be making the landscape gardener's work easier, she reasoned.

While she wasn't the easiest woman to get on with, Lucy had a knack for party planning, and she was business-minded. She'd made it clear that she wanted to use the wedding to raise her profile and bring in some more modeling work, and she'd hinted that with a bold enough floral concept some of that same publicity could come Maggie's way too. Maggie's spirits had leapt at this; while she was generally down-to-earth in her aspirations, she knew that getting a few key mentions in the right glossies could be transformative for Bluebelle du Jour. If she could hook a couple of A-list clients, or better yet another investor, she'd be one step closer to her dream of setting up a London branch. Maggie's heart might now be in Charlesworth, but she was increasingly aware that her friends and family weren't. Having a shop in the city would not only mean expanding the business; it would also allow her to spend more time with her mum and sister Carrie, her niece Maisy, and to keep in touch with Kesha and Sarah. And if she was being really honest, success on that scale would also prove that her dad had been wrong in declaring, before he died, that she was wasting her time and her language degree by setting up the business. She'd always been the apple of his eye, and ever since that day she had been determined to demonstrate that setting up on her own had been the right move.

Maggie finished up her final sketch, and got some pesto, spaghetti and pine nuts together for supper. As she waited for the pasta water to boil she wandered into the living room, Pimms in hand. She flicked through the DVDs on her shelf—*Gone With the Wind, Casablanca, It's a Wonderful Life*—but she didn't feel like watching any of them. Except maybe . . . right at the bottom were a few eighties classics she'd hidden away before her last dinner party . . . *Pretty in Pink, The Breakfast Club, St. Elmo's Fire*. She pulled out the last one; Rob Lowe might cheer her up just a little bit. She put the movie on top of the TV to watch with her meal.

There was something on her mind, and she couldn't put off dealing with it any longer. With the water still far off boiling, she opened her Netbook, sat on the sofa and scrolled past the last few days' worth of business emails.

There it was: Dylan's message. She took a deep breath and reread it, thinking this time of what to reply.

To: Maggie Hawthorne
From: Dylan Leonard
Subject: Long time

Dear M,
I know it's been a really long time, but I've been
thinking about you lately.
I heard from Andy that you left London a couple
of years ago, but he didn't know where you'd gone.
How are you?
Can we talk?
Dylan

Maggie felt a lurching in the pit of her stomach as she looked at Dylan's words again. Pimms schmimms. What she needed was a gin.

"Have I interrupted bathtime?" Maggie asked.

"No . . . no . . . I mean, well, yes, sort of," Kesha's warm voice was a comfort, even if it was nearly drowned out by the sound of splashing water, "but it's great to hear from you, sweetie. How are you? Did you get the postcard?" she asked.

"I did, it was a lovely surprise," Maggie replied, "and

Evie's handwriting—I'm impressed. It's even better than mine now, Kesh."

"Isn't it? She's getting really big, Maggie. It's scary. But anyway, did you have a good birthday?"

"Yes, lovely thanks," Maggie said, and it was sort of true. She'd had a nice massage and had been happy to stay in on her own. "But listen, Kesh, I'm actually calling about something else," Maggie said. "It's Dylan."

Maggie twirled spaghetti strands around a fork and caught them in her mouth while keeping the phone at her ear. A little bit of pesto hit the leg of her cream satin pajamas.

"Damn it," she muttered, "I mean, not Dylan . . . but I suppose maybe—yes, damn him too."

"Christ, Maggie," Kesha said, "talk about out of the blue. What did he say?"

"I don't know, Kesh . . . that he was thinking about me, wants to talk."

"Too late," Kesha said, firmly. "Far too late. But it sounds like maybe he's finally realized what he's lost. That's something."

Maggie thought about it. Yes, it soothed her still-bruised ego a little that Dylan had got back in touch, but part of her wished he would disappear again, just crawl back underneath whatever stone he'd been under for the past four years.

"Sort of," Maggie said. "And at least it's happened now,

when I know I'm finally over him. I guess what I'm wondering is, should I, do you think I should—"

"Oscar, *stop* that!" Kesha shouted. "Stop splashing Evie in the eye—right now. That's it, I'm confiscating that water pist—sorry, Maggie. I'm sorry about this—I really am—but I'm going to have to call you back."

"OK, sure," Maggie said, taking the phone away from her ear as the line went dead. She knew from past experience that Kesha's call back wouldn't come tonight, and that, despite her best friend's good intentions, it probably wouldn't come at all. She put the receiver down and went upstairs to run a bath.

Maggie had just started watching *St Elmo's Fire*, on her second gin and tonic, when she remembered she'd left the bath running.

"Oh *bugger*," Maggie said, pressing pause and leaving Demi Moore and her crimped hair frozen in time. Maggie dashed out of the living room and up the stairs to turn off the taps and take the plug out. She'd caught it just before the water spilled over the sides. At least she hadn't lit any candles yet—perhaps tonight wasn't the night for that. She sat down on the edge of the bath as she waited for the water to drain away, and spotted her BlackBerry on the bathroom shelf. Drying her hands and picking it up, she scrolled down to Dylan's email, hit "reply," and started to tap out her response.

Dylan,

I'm not sure why you're writing to me, now, after so long. But if you really want to talk, you can call me one evening next week. My number's at the bottom of this email.

Maggie

No kiss.

Before she could stop herself, she pressed send.

Chapter 6

Alison

Alison woke up to a knock at the bedroom door and Holly's voice.

"Mum, the woman from next door is here. She says she wants to speak to you or Dad."

What time was it? Alison squinted at the alarm clock, it was just gone half-eight. Surely that was a bit early on a weekend to be paying your new neighbors a visit?

"Can you tell her I'll pop over to hers in half an hour, Hol?" Alison called through the door from bed.

"Not really," her daughter yelled back. "She's a bit cross, Mum, I think you should come down."

Pete was dead to the world still, he'd rolled away from Alison and was now sleeping on.

"OK, hang on a sec." Alison walked to their ensuite and splashed her face with water. She heard the bedroom door creak and then Holly appeared near the bathroom doorway.

"Holly—you know what I said about barging in," Alison said quietly. "Dad's still asleep, you know."

Considering she was almost a teenager, Holly was pretty perky for a Saturday morning, already dressed in cut-off jeans and leggings with a loose black Beatles T-shirt. Holly lowered her voice to a whisper. "Mum, she's waiting downstairs. She was pretty shouty."

Alison came back into the bedroom and replied, "I'm pretty sure whatever it is can wait until I'm dressed."

Holly glanced around the room as Alison slipped on underwear, jeans and a long-sleeved top. "Mum . . ." Holly was staring at her mother's dressing table, tugging distractedly at her messy ponytail, bangles gently jangling. "Why do you have all these pictures of olden-days dead people getting married?"

Alison looked over to where Holly's eyes had come to rest. She'd never thought of the photos like that before. She'd been collecting them for years, black-and-white photos of couples on their wedding days, the more awkward-looking the better. Her friend Carla had sent her one she'd picked up in Portobello market, a very young bride with too-large shoes, who looked like Olive Oyl, her chunky older husband looking down at her adoringly. She'd framed each photo in a junk-shop frame and mounted them around her mirror. There was no way of knowing whether any of the couples were still alive now, but if they were they'd certainly be very old.

"I just like them," Alison said. "Don't you think they're interesting?"

Holly didn't pause for a second. "No, Mum. I don't—I think they're creepy. Are you ready yet?"

Alison and Holly walked downstairs and there was Janet from next door, still waiting on the doorstep, the front door open. Janet was a stout woman of about fifty, with ruddy cheeks and carefully curled ash blonde hair; in Alison's view she was no match for Sally, her old friend and neighbor who'd moved out the previous summer.

"Hi, Janet," Alison said, clipping the front part of her hair back with a kirby grip. "What can I help you with?"

"Your dog," said Janet, her flush deepening as she struggled to even get the words out. "Just come and look at what he's done."

Alison and Holly followed Janet as she marched back towards her house in her high heels, sending bits of gravel flying. She led them down the side passageway between their two houses, past her living room window with its ruched coral curtains, into her back garden. Alison hadn't seen the next-door garden since Sally had left—but Janet and her husband had manicured the lawn to suburban perfection, with neat rows of matching pansies filling each flower bed up to the back, except for . . .

Janet thrust out a sturdy arm to indicate the damage

where the fence had been torn down, flashing her fuchsia-painted nails. There really wasn't any need, it was hard to miss. George must have powered through the back panel of fencing, and he was presently having a whale of a time digging a big hole in the once-pristine lawn. Muddy laundry, pulled from the line, lay scattered around and about. And cowering under the garden bench was Janet's cocker spaniel, Cassie, a quivering wreck.

George had taken to barking at Cassie through the fence the moment she arrived—but it looked like he might have taken things a step further today.

"Ah," Alison said, Holly next to her, shaking with suppressed giggles. She drew on all her strength to stop her own emerging. "I see. Oops," Alison said, biting her lip. Then she put two fingers in her mouth and whistled loudly. The wolfhound's head bobbed up from the muddy hole. "Party's over, George," she called out.

Janet's lips were pursed so tightly she looked as if she might pop.

"Oh Christ, she's awful, Jamie," Alison said, her head in her hands, weeping with laughter. "So prim. And after she woke us up at half-bloody-eight in the morning I was dying for her to be the one in the wrong . . ."

Jamie was cooking up pancakes in the kitchen of his little thatched cottage. "Do you live next door to Hyacinth Bucket?" Jamie asked with a laugh, giving the first pancake a flip.

"Yes, yes, I do. She *is* her, Jamie. And God help us George had only gone and chosen her frilliest nighties to rip into shreds. They must have been her very best."

"Here you go, tell me if this doesn't make you forget all about it," Jamie said, passing Alison a pancake and a bottle of maple syrup. He ladled more mixture into the pan to cook up a second.

"Yum," Ali said with her mouth full. "Outstanding, sir."

Jamie slid into the seat opposite and put slices of chopped up banana in his pancake before covering them in chocolate sauce.

"Ali, you know I mentioned I had something to talk about with you," he said, folding the pancake over.

Alison nodded, then swallowed the mouthful of pancake. "I do indeed, and that's exactly why I'm here. So what's the big mystery?" she asked.

"It's good news, I think," Jamie said, a hesitant smile on his face. "A big step, but an exciting one. It'll be a totally new start for me and a potentially interesting opportunity for you."

Jamie had Alison's full attention now. He could gossip with the best of them, but when it came to his own life he tended to be private, so she knew this must be something he had given serious thought.

"Ali, I've decided to start up a new business. It's something I've been thinking about for years, but with one thing and another . . ." Jamie's attention drifted briefly.

For a moment Alison could picture Seb with them in the kitchen at the worktop, he would have been making tea while Jamie flipped the pancakes. They had been one of the strongest teams Alison knew.

"You know that estate agent on the high street that went quiet and eventually closed?" Jamie looked her squarely in the eye, as she tried to remember. The shops on the high street seemed to be changing so often nowadays. "The one opposite your friend Maggie's flower shop?" he prompted.

"Oh yes," Alison said, "I saw it was empty. It's a nice space inside, wasted on an estate agency really."

Jamie nodded. "That's right. Well. It's up for rent."

"And this affects us how?" she asked, trying to guess what Jamie had up his sleeve.

"A café, Ali," Jamie said. "But I'm not talking about just any café. Great cakes, fresh coffee, a wide selection of teas, yes, all that. But more than that. This would also be an inspiring place to be, with gorgeous vintage furniture and retro styling and a gallery space. BLITZ SPIRIT," he said, raising a hand to indicate a sign above the shop.

Alison tilted her head, as if viewing the imaginary sign, slowly letting the idea sink in.

"I just think we all deserve something a bit funkier than Joey's, don't you?" Jamie said, and Alison laughed. Joey's café on the high street had been around since she was a little girl, but longevity didn't always equal charm. The service was awful and the food wasn't much better—everyone in Charlesworth went there occasionally, for the simple reason that it was the only place where you could sit down and eat. What Jamie was suggesting was something very different though, a café that would be the social hub that their old market town needed.

"So I'm thinking that as well as being a chic hangout, it could bring out the town's creative side—with top-notch art and crafts for sale inside."

"It sounds great," Alison said. "I can already picture you running it actually."

"Thanks, hon," Jamie said, smiling, the creases around his eyes deepening. "But look, this doesn't have to be all me. If you like the idea, you can be part of it too." He continued, "I'm just putting this idea out there, no pressure. But I was wondering if you'd like to come in as a partner, Ali."

Alison sat back in her chair and listened as Jamie went on.

"So the idea is that you'd make a contribution to the rent, and get a share of the profits. In addition to that, you'd have a space of your own to sell the candles, your embroidered cushions and homeware, plus any new craft lines you might want to start. You'd have the benefit of café customers lingering long enough over their cups of Earl Grey to fall in love with the stock."

Alison smiled, mulling it over.

"I'd run the café, and organize everything to do with the food, including baking, so your time would remain devoted to the crafty side of things. But ultimately the space would be shared and I'd want for us to decide on the art and any events together. You mentioned you still had quite a bit left over from Pete's redundancy payment," Jamie said. "So perhaps this could be a good investment?"

"OK," Alison said. "This all sounds . . ." she continued, grinning, a wave of excitement building. "I mean, you know better than anyone, Jamie, that this is what I've always wanted to do."

Jamie reached over and gave her hair a ruffle. "Good," he said, "because you're the only person I can imagine doing it with."

"So what would the costs be?" Alison asked, sitting up straighter in her chair and clasping her scarlet-nailed hands together.

Jamie went over to the counter and brought her a sheet of paper with his calculations on it. He ran his finger down the right-hand column. "How about if you paid three hundred pounds a month towards the rent at the start," Jamie said, "and then we could adjust that up later if you wanted? You said you had about half of Pete's lump sum left, didn't you?"

Alison nodded and looked over the figures on the sheet.

"Anyway," Jamie said. "It's a big decision, I know. And you'll need time to think about it and talk to Pete. So just come back to me when you're ready."

Alison nodded, knowing that despite what Jamie said, he'd need to put a deposit down soon in order to make sure no one else rented the space.

"You're really making this happen, aren't you?" Alison said, giving Jamie a hug. "Your very own café. Of course I want to be part of it."

Chapter 7

Jenny

"Chloe, come on, not that tight!" I called out, giggling and reaching behind me to still Chloe's hand. Chloe and I were crammed into a toilet cubicle at work and she was lacing me into my wedding-night corset.

When the parcel arrived on my desk that lunchtime, Chloe spotted it from across the office, leapt up from her chair and dashed across the room, ringlets bouncing, shepherding me away from my computer and into the ladies'. I'd liked the look of the underwear on the Blackout Nights website—it was all original 1940s, and the corset promised a waspish waist and a curvy bust. My waist was now tiny—miniscule in fact—but I could hardly breathe, and looking down I wasn't sure I had much of a boosted cleavage for all the effort.

"All *riiiight*," Chloe finally relented. "I'll tie it here. Spin around and show me."

"Spin around, are you kidding?" I laughed. "We can hardly move in here without getting intimate."

"Right, let me get past," Chloe said, "and you can show me properly by the sinks."

"Come out then," she called a moment later. "Don't worry, I've got the bathroom on lockdown." I peeked out and saw she did indeed have her back to the main door, holding it firmly shut. I ventured forward, and took a look in the full-length mirror. I had on my work trousers still, but I looked completely different.

"What a bombshell," Chloe said, smiling.

Actually, I didn't look half bad. While my curves weren't quite dynamite, they were, undeniably, *there*, knocked into my slightly boyish figure by the corset's engineering. Earlier that week I had been to the hairdresser to have some pale blonde highlights added to my shoulder-length hair and a new, sweeping fringe now brought out my wide-set hazel eyes. The overall effect was impressive: it was still *me*, but a more glamorous version of me. A push at the door made me jump.

"*Busy*," Chloe yelled, leaning back on it hard.

"It's not bad, is it, Chlo?" I said, fidgeting with the boning, "although I just can't see how on earth I'm ever going to eat any wedding cake in it."

*

Back at my desk, I kept my head down for the last few hours of the day. While the art director who sat nearby talked through with his team what images were needed for the next issue, I sorted through paperwork, responded to emails and helped Zoe with a gigantic pile of filing that had to be done before the office inspection the next day. The highlight of the afternoon was an email from Maggie with a picture of some handmade wedding decorations she'd spotted—vintage maps cut out into strips and made into heart shapes you could string together. By the time the clock on my computer clicked to half past five, I'd finished everything on my to-do list and emptied my inbox.

Zoe stared at me across the desk, faint shadows visible under her dark eyes. "Well, go on then," she said flatly, tipping her head to indicate the other empty desks. Only Gary, Chloe's manager, was left, tapping away intently on his computer. "No prizes for staying late, you know, Jenny. We're only still here because we have to be." She looked back down at the document she was checking, not waiting for a response. It was Zoe's way of being sort-of-nice. I picked up my gym bag with a goodbye and walked out of the office's wide glass doors.

Chloe met me in reception, leaning on the counter and switching from towering heels to flats. She was shoving her work shoes into her handbag when I arrived.

"Jen," she said, flexing her feet in the ballerina flats as if getting used to the feel of them again. "I know we

70

said we'd go to Zumba tonight," she caught the suspicious look in my eye and geared up her excuse, "but I had to wear these stupid heels for a meeting today and my feet are killing me. Plus it's such a gorgeous summery evening. How about we go for a drink instead?"

I'd been looking forward to our regular Zumba date, there was nothing like a little booty-shaking to latin rhythms to kick the Monday blues; but Chloe's wide eyes implored me to let her off the hook just this once. "I promise we'll go next time," she said.

"OK," I relented. "But I'm going to hold you to that; we're definitely going on Thursday," I said, smiling. "I want to be more toned than this for the wedding—even if I do have the corset to hold everything in now."

"Fox and Pheasant?" Chloe suggested, and together we walked out of the air-conditioned *Sussex Living* offices and into the warm evening air. It was only Monday, but the pavement outside the pub opposite, our regular, was already crowded. Charlesworth's shop and office workers were enjoying the unexpected balminess, white wine spritzers and bottles of Magners in hand. Chloe and I crossed the street and I went into the pub to get a glass of white wine for each of us, while Chloe nabbed an empty bit of bench to sit on.

"So," I said, when I returned from the bar, settling myself on the seat and tucking my unused gym kit under the table. "How was that thirtieth you went to on Saturday?"

"Ahem, yes . . ." Chloe started, wrinkling her nose a little.

I knew that face. "Chloe . . ." I started, in the schoolmarmish voice that I seemed to adopt whenever we had this conversation.

"I know, I know." She held her hands up. "But the men at the party were all such idiots, Jen. It was mainly Nikki's banker friends down from London. It was like they expected us country girls to leap straight onto hay bales with them at the mere mention of champagne," Chloe said, unclipping her hair and raking her hands through her chestnut curls. "So when I got a text from Jon at midnight saying come over, I did."

I raised an eyebrow.

"He was so lovely when I got there."

"Right. Of course he was," I said, before I could stop myself.

"I know, Jen. You don't need to remind me." Chloe looked a little defeated.

Chloe and Jon had been on and off for as long as I'd known her. Jon had swept her off her feet when she met him online dating three years ago, and according to Chloe their first year together had been a dream. From what I'd witnessed, though, he'd spent the following two years breaking all of his promises and breaking up with her. Then, without fail, just when she was getting back on her feet again, he would decide he wanted her back.

"He was really apologetic about missing Jo's wedding,"

Chloe said. "And the thing is, he's not great with weddings anyway, so perhaps it was best he wasn't there after all, like he said." Chloe sipped her wine and smoothed down her peach pleated skirt.

"Jen," Chloe said after a pause, "how do you and Dan make it look so easy?"

"Do we?" I said, genuinely surprised that she thought that. "I've no idea, Chlo—because it isn't, not always. Ask him what it's like going out with someone who alphabetizes his DVDs and 'disappears' items of his clothing she isn't keen on. We have our moments, believe me."

"OK, but you don't have doubts, do you?" Chloe asked, "I mean big ones."

"No," I replied, mulling it over. "Not big ones. I'm pretty sure this time." I thought about how different things had been with my ex—I'd had a catalog of doubts back then. But when I met Dan things just seemed to fall into place, and while it wasn't all perfect, for the most part loving him felt like a lazy Sunday, not a battle.

"Good," Chloe said, cheering up. "Because as it happens I've had some really good ideas for your hen night, so we can't have you bailing out now."

I smiled. "Not a chance."

Chapter 8

Maggie

Hearing his voice was the hardest part, but it definitely helped that Dylan had picked up a stupid-sounding transatlantic twang.

"Hey, Maggie," he said, as soon as she answered the phone. "So where are you living now?" he asked her, once they'd exchanged a few pleasantries. "And what about work, did you start up on your own like you always wanted to?"

Maggie was sitting on the edge of her sofa, her bare feet pressed into the soft blanket and a glass of wine on the table next to her. It was eleven p.m. and rain was battering against the French windows. The hot weather had broken earlier that evening and the storm was still going strong. The branches of her apple tree knocked against the glass. Maggie had been trying not to watch the phone since replying to Dylan at the weekend, but from time to time her eyes would drift over to it, wondering if and when he would call.

"Yes," Maggie answered, trying to keep the tone of her voice even and steady. "I did move. I'm down in Sussex now actually, in an old market town." She was grateful that her voice came out sounding calmer than she felt.

"Ah, right, Sussex," he said. "Nice. But I bet country living hasn't knocked the city girl out of you yet."

"Look," Maggie cut in, steeling herself. "Let's not mess around, Dylan. Why was it that you wanted to speak to me?"

They fell silent.

"OK, Maggie, you're right," Dylan said at last. "To the point." She heard him take a deep breath. "I never meant for it to be so long before we spoke again, but like I said, I needed some time completely apart."

Maggie took a sip of her wine and listened.

"I've been living in New York for the past three years. With my international client list it was easy enough to set up a studio over there. I've been photographing everything from car ads to book covers. I know you always thought I let my work take over, but I suppose there were just some things I needed to do."

Each word about Dylan's success was like a stab to her chest.

"I've got an apartment in Brooklyn," Dylan continued.

"And the city is amazing, there's a real buzz here. I wake up each morning and can't wait to get started."

Hooray for you, Maggie thought. Her thoughts flicked to the adored wedding ring she'd put away in a box a few summers before. Dylan had put so much energy into his career back then that it had felt to Maggie as if there hadn't been any left for their marriage. And now she had to listen to Dylan celebrating all he'd achieved without her? Really?

"But the truth is it doesn't feel right anymore, Maggie." Dylan's voice softened. "None of it does. I don't want a bachelor lifestyle. I want what the two of us had together. Every woman I meet, every flower arrangement I see, every flash of red hair in the street reminds me of you."

Oh. Maggie took a gulp of wine this time.

"I'm ready for something more," Dylan continued. "Something I wasn't ready for when we broke up. I know you never wanted for us to get divorced—I made that happen and, Maggie, I'm so, so sorry."

Maggie mustered up a hesitant "OK," although it really wasn't.

"Maggie, look, this is how it is. I'm coming to London at the end of next week. I want for us to talk face-to-face. Please hear me out. Will you? I hope that what we had is worth that?"

Dylan's words hung in the air.

"Let me think about it," Maggie said.

*

The morning sun streamed in through Maggie's white muslin curtains as she woke to Mork mewing gently for food. She felt as if she'd hardly slept, the storm had been battering at the windows till the early morning and Dylan's words had been going around and around in her head. Barely moving from the position she was in, she lazily reached out a hand to stroke the cat and caught sight of her alarm clock. The numbers glared, reprimanding her. Five past ten. Oh, darn it. She was due at Darlington Hall in twenty-five minutes and it would take her at least that just to drive there.

She'd been in a daze when she'd finally gone to bed last night and now she realized she must have forgotten to set the alarm. She got to her feet quickly and pulled her satin dressing gown off the hook and around her. Sweeping Mork up in her arms she headed downstairs, poured him out some cat biscuits and grabbed a glass of water. Where had she put those sketches again? She found her linen notebook on the breakfast bar and some other loose pages she'd made sketches on, and put them in her leather satchel alongside her Netbook, BlackBerry and diary.

There was definitely no time for a shower. No time at all. But could she really face turning up at Darlington Hall in this state? She ran upstairs, switched the shower on to warm up and tied her hair back in a pink sequined scrunchie her niece Maisy had left on the side the last time she'd visited. She washed in a zingy grapefruit shower gel that made her feel a whole lot more ready to face the world. Back in her bedroom she peeked out of her window—after the storm there were pure blue skies and sunshine. She chose a pale green silk dress with Chinese-style fastening at the top and brown leather gladiator sandals. She pulled on her chunky gold bracelet and headed downstairs, satchel in hand. She got into her Beetle and looked down at the clock. Ten twenty-five. Argh.

As the gravel crunched under her tires she saw there was another vehicle already pulled up at Darlington House—a battered pickup truck with gardening tools in the back. She parked next to it, hopped out and walked, as fast as was dignified, up to the front door of the house. The bell rang grandly and Lucy opened the door.

"I'm so sorry, Lucy," Maggie began. Lucy looked her up and down, unimpressed.

"Look," Lucy began, "you've missed the pastries and we've started already, but come in. We're in the drawing room." Maggie followed her through to a sunny room furnished with a chaise longue and a rocking horse. Two dark red velvet sofas faced each other in the far corner next to the French windows, and Maggie saw Jack and another guy with dark hair—presumably his friend, the landscape gardener—sitting together on one. Maggie walked with Lucy and took a seat beside her on the other sofa.

"Maggie, this is Owen, Owen, Maggie." Owen looked like he was in his late twenties. He was lounging back in a scruffy checked shirt and khaki combats as if he had no need to make an effort even at a manor house. When Maggie shook his hand, his dark eyes met hers, but he didn't smile. His gaze was so steady that it unsettled her. Looking away, she noticed that Lucy's father, Jeremy Mackintosh, was out on the terrace, pacing up and down and talking on his phone.

"Owen's put together some really good designs here," Lucy began, pointing to some papers on the coffee table. "He's planned out where to put the mushrooms and which way the guests will walk."

Maggie opened her satchel and produced her linen notebook and sketches. "Ah, that sounds interesting . . ." she said, not looking over. "Lucy, there's something I wanted to show you both too."

Maggie put her designs on the other half of the table and opened out her sketchbook. She ensured she had all of Lucy and Jack's attention before she spoke. She glanced at Owen too, but got the sense he couldn't care less about what she had to say. It didn't help when his gaze drifted away from her designs towards the garden, where Lucy's dad was standing. Maggie pointed at her first drawing. "I thought we could have the guests walking from this main door—" she pointed to the drawing room door, "down the steps to hit the display like—"

"Oh, no, no, no," Lucy said. "I much prefer what

Owen's done here, with the lakeside rose display and the candlelit area by the herb garden, don't you, Jack?"

Jack nodded, then caught Maggie's eye and stopped. "I like them both, to be honest, Luce. They're just different."

Maggie carried on, regardless. "But you see what I've done here with the wicker hula hoops will make the display a really interactive—"

"Wicker hula hoops?" Owen said, laughing as he turned back to the table and looking at Maggie straight on, his dark eyes resting on hers again. "Really?"

OK, perhaps that had been a step too far, Maggie reflected, but was there any need to be rude?

"Didn't you say I'm doing the garden and she's handling the flowers, Jack?" Owen continued. "I thought that was what we agreed?"

Maggie seethed, a flush of frustration and fury coming to her cheeks. She glared at him in disbelief.

"Actually we did say that, didn't we, Maggie?" Lucy said.

OK, so they had, but after their first meeting she'd realized she was more than capable of doing some of the designing herself. She shouldn't have been so daunted by it. Now Owen was acting as if she was treading on his toes, when it was just as much her event to organize. She wanted the wedding to fit with the Bluebelle brand, and if Owen started to take over too much she knew she could risk compromising that.

"Yes, we did, but I thought you'd still like to see . . ." Maggie started.

She looked from her drawings over to Owen's designs, and was irritated to see that they did look quite carefully thought through. But he was clearly far younger than her, what did he know about planning events of this scale? He drove a pickup truck, for God's sake! Maggie was surely far better suited to working on a wedding of this kind, with this caliber of guest.

"Look. No offense, but weddings really aren't my thing, as you two know." Owen looked from Jack to Lucy. "There's nothing sustainable about one big, blowout day of indulgence, even in the name of love. But like I said, I'm willing to do this for you guys as a favor."

Jack was starting to look a little uncomfortable now, shuffling in his seat.

"But if I'm going to do it," Owen continued, "it has to be my way. Leave the garden stuff to me," Owen said to Jack. "That's what we agreed, and that's what I'm trained to do. And she," Owen waved his hand dismissively in Maggie's direction, "can do the flower-arranging."

"OK," Jack said, hurriedly trying to make amends and placate his friend. "Maggie, we really want your input on the flowers, though, like we said."

When Maggie looked up to argue her case, Owen was staring at her, at the top of her head his brown eyes glinting.

"Nice scrunchie," he said.

*

"Mini pork pie?" Maggie asked, passing the plate.

"That would go perfectly with my bowl of Quavers," Jenny said, with a giggle, putting a tub of ice cream into Maggie's freezer and picking up a pie.

Alison picked up the three full glasses of lemonade, and the women took their plates and a large pizza box over into Maggie's pristine living room.

"Thanks for coming over," Maggie said, getting comfy on the armchair, tucking her legs up under her. "And for bringing the junk food extravaganza." In front of them was an array of comforting carbs, including an enormous pizza. Maggie hadn't really expected Alison and Jenny to be free on a Friday night, but after the day she'd had at Darlington Hall she was longing for some friendlier company and so had invited them round on the off-chance. When she'd answered the door to find them laden down with snacks and smiling with slumber-party glee, Maggie's blues were all but forgotten.

"Pah!" Alison said. "Don't worry, Maggie, we've all had one of *those days*." Jenny nodded and took a mini sausage roll from the pile on her plate, her blonde ponytail bouncing.

"It's been a while since I had a good junk food feast anyway," Jenny said, with a wink. "They're wasted on hangovers, don't you think?"

"Definitely," Maggie said, "and it's the lesser of two evils. It's a good job you came around really, or I'd probably be a bottle of wine down by now. Honestly, Lucy Mackintosh's wedding was sent to test me."

"Is she really that bad?" Alison asked, brushing a crumb off her checked shirt.

"Yes," Maggie replied in an instant. "Only now it's not just her." She paused, recalling the disaster that had been that day's meeting. "She's got this really arrogant upstart on board to do the landscaping and . . . No," Maggie shook her head with determination. "I'm not wasting valuable snacking time even *thinking* about them." A wide smile took the place of her scowl as she took a slice of pizza from the box.

"Anyway, Alison," Maggie said, through a mouthful of mozzarella, "your friend Jamie from the charity shop popped into the shop the other day for some freesias. Said he might be starting up a café over the street. Did you know about that?"

Alison beamed. "Yes, and to be honest I've been desperate to blab about it—I'm thinking of going in with him as a partner." She took in her friends' intrigued expressions. "But there's a lot to think about before then. I've got to talk to Pete first really, but I'll keep you posted." She stroked Mork's arched back as he sniffed at the pork pies. Looking around the room, Alison changed the subject. "Anyway, this place is stunning, Maggie," she said. "White carpets, blimey, the stuff of dreams when you have kids."

Maggie smiled warmly. "Well, I guess there are advantages to living alone."

"You can say that again," Alison said, laughing. "I think every piece of our furniture is practically wipe-clean." She hopped to her feet to inspect the framed photos on Maggie's mantelpiece. "So are you sure there's no one on the scene, man-wise?"

"Nope, no one. I'm absolutely certain," Maggie said, focusing on taking another bite of pizza without cheese dripping on her chin.

"Nosy," Jenny said, directing the comment at Alison.

"Look," Alison said, picking up a photo of Maggie with Kesha and Sarah for a closer look. "Let me live vicariously a little. With two kids and an elderly mum to think about, I need all the kicks I can get."

"I don't mind," Maggie said, smiling. "I only wish I could provide a bit more in the way of entertainment for you. But it's a romantic desert round here I'm afraid."

Alison narrowed her eyes as if she didn't entirely believe what she was hearing.

"Seriously!" Maggie confirmed. "Haven't you spotted all the scented candles and cushions I've got in this place? Single woman's prerogative."

"OK, we believe you—it's true there are a lot of candles. But still, I'm amazed. Well, enjoy it while it lasts, I say. Family life can really take it out of you."

"Does your mum live nearby, Ali?" Jenny asked, lifting her glass to her lips.

"Close-ish, yes," Alison replied. "I'm popping round to see her with my brother tomorrow actually. She's OK most of the time, but she's stubborn as you like and she isn't ready to accept that she's not as strong as she once was." Alison's eyes drifted, then her gaze came back with a smile. "It's a good reminder to enjoy being young and healthy while we can, isn't it?"

Jenny raised a glass of lemonade in one hand, the pizza box in the other. "Ahem?" she said, glancing from one to the other. "We'd better get busy then. I'm not sure how much longer we have."

Chapter 9

Alison

It was Saturday evening, and when Alison got back from her mother's house Pete and Holly were curled up together on the Chesterfield sofa watching *Doctor Who*. Alison's heart lifted at the scene: Pete had one arm around his youngest daughter, the other lazily draped over the dog. Pete was wearing an old checked shirt, one that Alison really liked for its softness. His hazel eyes lit up when he saw Alison come through the door, and Holly acknowledged her with a smile, before her eyes flicked quickly back to the screen.

"Hello, family," Alison said, standing in the living room doorway. "I'll be with you in a second, I'm just going to grab a drink."

Alison poured herself a glass of red wine and rested against the kitchen counter for a moment. It had been a long day. She'd been riding high since her conversation with Jamie the other day, and Pete had been equally excited about the café idea, but seeing her mum again had brought her back down to earth. Her mother was still the fun and feisty character she'd always been, but physically she was getting extremely frail and Alison could see that living on her own was now a challenge for her. A carer came in a few mornings a week, and Alison and her brother Clive dropped in when they could, but they both knew she needed more help.

Alison's eyes drifted to the kitchen table and she noticed that the forget-me-not tea set was out of its box; Holly must have wanted to take a look. She put her wine down and wrapped the cups and saucers back up in their newspaper. The text at the top of one of the yellowed sheets caught her eye: *The Charlesworth Chronicle*, 14 June 1964. She remembered that her dad used to read that paper. It had closed a few years ago, was replaced by glossy magazines like the one Jenny worked for, with features rather than local news. As Alison put the cups back into the box and closed the flaps, she saw the pen scribble on the top: "Mrs. Derek Spencer." Probably a house clearance, she thought to herself with a pang of sadness.

Alison walked back into the living room and over to the sofa, settling herself beside Pete and Holly and taking off her boots.

"So," she said, giving Pete a kiss and squeezing Holly's arm. "How has today been?"

"It's been fun, hasn't it, Holly?" Pete replied, looking for a response from his daughter, who was still caught up in the program. Maggie noted that Pete's stubble was even longer than usual, and it sort of suited him. But then she couldn't help thinking—he's unshaven because he's got nowhere to be, tomorrow or the next day. Or the day after.

"We took George on a really long walk and I bumped into Sally, you know, old-neighbor Sally? She's back in town looking for a new property. It turns out London didn't suit her at all."

"Oh, right, that's nice," Alison said. "I'd been wondering about her. It was a whole lot more fun when she lived next door, wasn't it?"

Pete nodded, then changed the subject. "How was your mum's?"

"Not great, to be honest," Alison said. "She's having real trouble moving about on her own. Clive and I were talking today . . ."

Alison shook her head, as if she could get rid of the problem that way. "Clive can't help any more than he is already, not with the kids and Susan pregnant again. We're thinking about moving mum into a home."

"Granny?" Holly said, looking up from the TV.

"Yes," Alison said to them both. "She's beginning to need more support than Clive and I can give, and if her health gets worse I think it's our only option. There's a good one in Easton, so she would still be very close. It's not cheap, but we'll find the money somehow. I know Clive could cover it, but I don't want him to . . . Anyway, nothing's been decided yet."

Pete looked at his wife, a softness to his gaze. "It sounds wise," he said, "to at least consider it, I mean."

"Yes," Alison said, not wanting to dwell on the topic any longer. "Where's Sophie anyway? Upstairs?"

"Nope," Pete began, brushing his hair out of his eyes. "She's gone to a slumber party at Janie's. I dropped her round there earlier."

Holly started to fidget, rearranging her position on the sofa. "That's not what I heard," she said, glancing up at her mum with a cheeky smile, then looking back at the screen.

"What do you mean, Hol?" Alison asked, her brow furrowed.

"Nothing," Holly said, more serious now, as if she'd had a change of heart.

"Holly." Alison's patience was getting thinner. "It is clearly not nothing, or you wouldn't have said anything. What did you hear?"

"Matt," Holly chirped up at last. "I heard her on the phone to him earlier. He's a new boy at school, plays guitar in a band."

"Sounds cool," Pete said, with a smile and a tilt of his head. Alison gave him a glare.

Holly continued, "He's fitter than her last boyfriend."

"Matt," Alison murmured, letting the sound linger,

searching her memory for some link, a mention Sophie could have made. "So what was she saying to him? I'm guessing he's not at Janie's sleepover too?" She gave a small snort of disbelief.

"That part isn't true," Holly said quietly, wriggling to get comfortable as George made a claim for more space on the sofa. "It was a lie, so Dad would let her go."

Alison drew in her breath and looked over at Pete, who looked startled. "Holly," Alison said, putting a hand on her younger daughter's arm. "It's really important that you tell us what you heard." Holly's face went pale, and she stared down at George's fur for what seemed like minutes. "OK," Alison said, breaking the silence. "I'll just call her then, and—"

"No," Holly said, panicked. "You can't." She paused, taking a breath. "I shouldn't have been listening. She was in her room, but the door was a bit open. She said to Matt that she and Janie would meet him by the old house by the tracks, for the party. When she left she had some other clothes to change into, I could see them in her bag."

For a moment Alison was relieved to know the truth, feeling just slight annoyance at Pete's oversight of something even Holly had spotted, and then the facts sank in.

"She doesn't mean the *old derelict house* on the outskirts?" Alison said, registering, looking from Pete to her daughter. "By the railway tracks? Where the junkies go?" Holly's expression was blank, and it was clear she'd now told them everything she knew.

"Pete, why didn't you call me before you agreed to let her go out?" Alison asked, searching for a way to understand the situation, as she fumbled in her bag for her phone and called through to Sophie's number. As the line redirected, Sophie's voicemail was loud enough for all three of them to hear. Alison cut off the call.

Pete shrugged, but his eyes gave away his anxiety. "I didn't want to bother you, Ali—I know how tough it can be on you sometimes when you go to visit your mum. Anyway, Sophie's slept over at Janie's before, I had no reason to think she would do anything else."

"Oh God," Alison said, hiding behind her hands. "Pete, have you ever seen that house? Have you even been around that area? It's not safe at all."

Alison put her boots back on again, trying to stay calm as she felt panic begin to rush through her. She got up from her place on the sofa and turned back to face Pete. "You stay here with Holly. I'm going to find Sophie and bring her back."

Alison slowed in her car and turned the headlights to full beam as she neared the railway tracks. A fox sped out in front of her, but aside from that the dark road was empty. She heard the party before she saw it, a heavy bassline thudding and the laughs and shouts of teenagers. Alison parked outside the house and looked over at it—the front door was wide open with a cluster of older teenagers beside it, the windows were boarded up with chipboard and sections of roof slate were missing. Alison turned off the car engine. She saw Janie, Sophie's best friend, right away. Dressed in a black-and-white spotted dress with her hair tied up in a thick black band, she was smoking a cigarette outside with two other girls who looked as if they could be in their twenties.

"Janie," Alison called out, as she walked over. Empty cans and cigarette butts littered the yard, and Alison saw a hypodermic needle by the wall. The young girl looked panicked. "Janie," Alison lowered her voice as she took the girl to one side, away from the rest of the group. "Listen, I'm going to presume you have your parents' permission to be here, but Sophie doesn't. Where is she?" Janie bit her lip then said, in a quiet voice, pointing, "She's out the back. Please don't tell her I told you."

Alison walked away from Janie and pushed her way down the hallway crowded with teenagers; it smelled of urine, weed and sweat. Some of the floorboards were missing or broken. Curious eyes tracked her, and the music and shouting got louder the farther into the house she went. Her heart beat hard in her chest as she tried to push away images of what she might find. You can roll up your school skirt and put on as much makeup as you want, Sophie, she thought, tears stinging her eyes, just please be OK.

In the back room she found a couple of old sofas and beanbags strewn about, with dark forms lying on them. Alison could make out about a dozen people. She saw a dark ponytail swing, heard a laugh, and breathed out for what felt like the first time since she'd entered the house. Sophie. She made her way over to the far corner and the girl looked around—she was about the same age, but her eyes were sunken, her expression hard. It wasn't her daughter.

"Have you seen Sophie?" Alison asked, but the girl just shook her head dumbly in response.

"Mum?" came a hesitant voice. Alison turned towards it. There was a girl over there, a dark shape, lying on a beanbag with a trilby-hatted boy. "Soph? Is that you?"

Sophie hastily rearranged her clothes and pulled herself upright on the beanbag. "Mum, what are you *doing* here?" The boy in the trilby got to his feet quickly, gave Alison a nod and then scurried away across the room.

Alison crouched down so that she was level with her daughter. "You know what, Sophie," Alison said in a loud whisper, her relief now swamped by the feelings of anger and frustration it had masked. "I was going to ask you just the same thing." A small crowd of teenagers had gathered at the doorway.

"Oh God," Sophie said almost silently, lowering her head. "I want to die. This is so mortifying."

"You know you shouldn't be here," Alison stood up to her full height and waited for Sophie to get up. "I can't believe you lied, Sophie," she hissed. "Come on, we're going home."

"I'm not coming, Mum." Sophie focused on sliding her bangles further up her arm. "And you can't make me—"

Alison cut her off mid-sentence. "We're going. Now get up."

Sophie slowly got to her feet and as Alison walked out of the room her daughter followed close behind, cowed.

As they went to leave the room a boy with a dark pony-tail and a shark's tooth on a leather thong around his neck blocked their way.

"Mummy come to pick you up, has she, Sophie?" he taunted, his stance wide.

Alison noticed the boy with the trilby from earlier step forward, then, after a sharp look from the boy in the door-way, back away.

Alison's temper flared, but as she struggled to control it she spotted a scar on the boy's eyebrow that triggered a memory.

"Mummy has come to pick her up, yes, Gavin," she said, fixing him with a glare. "Just like I remember *your* mummy picking you up from Sophie's sixth birthday party."

He shuffled a little, and took a swig from his beer bottle. "You may not recall it," Alison continued, "but it was a hot July day and when your mum arrived, you were stark naked and jumping around, waving your willy in the sprinkler. Saying you never wanted to leave."

Gavin blanched, and a small crowd of onlookers formed around them.

"But Sophie and I are less keen to stick around at this party," Alison said, "so could you please move out of our way?"

As Gavin moved reluctantly to one side, a snarl on his lips, Sophie rushed past him towards the front door. Alison strode behind her and they both walked out of the house and over to the Clio.

"Unlock it, Mum," Sophie insisted. "I just want to get in and go home, right now. This is the worst night of my life." Alison beeped the car open and they both got inside. The thumping bass from the house showed no sign of quieting. Mother and daughter sat for a moment in the car, Alison looking at her daughter in profile, the party in full swing behind her. Alison saw that Janie and the boy with the trilby were looking over at them from the doorway. Sophie had her eyes fixed on her feet.

"Sophie," Alison said, casting an eye back at the house before her gaze rested on her daughter. "Do you know what a dangerous situation you just put yourself in?" Sophie's face was turned away as Alison continued. "Aside even from the fact everyone was drinking, and that it looked like there were drugs around too, the house itself . . . the structure's totally unsound! If even one of those candles had got knocked over that place could have gone up in flames like a tinderbox." Sophie didn't say anything. The boy in the trilby took a step towards the car and Sophie looked over. He gave a little wave and Sophie raised her hand and waved back. Alison started up the engine and they drove home without saying another word.

"I'm going to make us both some hot chocolate," said Alison, going over to the kettle, "and then let's go and sit in the den." She'd called Pete to let him know that everything was OK, and had insisted he go to bed. She told him there was no point both of them losing sleep, but the truth was that she couldn't help blaming him for what had happened. Whether or not that was fair, she just wanted to handle things on her own.

The den was a hideaway next to Alison's studio that they'd turned into a makeshift office for Pete. There were postcards pinned up on one wall and piles of books leaning against another; it was scruffy, but it was cozy with an old red sofa in the corner. Alison came into the room with two steaming mugs, to find Sophie perched on the sofa's edge, looking like she'd rather be just about anywhere else.

Alison sat down next to her daughter, this girl who it seemed like only yesterday had been trampolining in the back garden, helping her sister make a flower press. Her eyes were dark pools now, devoid of any expression Alison could read.

"You know what hurts most, don't you?" Alison said.

Sophie fiddled with a hole in her jeans.

"That you lied to us." Alison heard her own voice, accusing, but inside she felt something different, a sadness that left her raw; a sense that she had lost control.

Sophie nodded, and tears began to well up in her eyes. "But everyone else was there, Mum. They were all allowed to go. I knew you and Dad would never let me." As she rubbed her eyes roughly, her voice hardened. "Anyway, now they've all seen me leave with my mum, I'll probably never get invited to any parties ever again. It's going to be awful at school on Monday."

"You certainly aren't going to get what you want by lying to us, Sophie," Alison said. "We need to be able to trust you if we're going to give you freedom."

Alison reached out for her daughter's hand. For a moment she felt it, Sophie's skin as soft as when she was just a little girl. Then she pulled her hand away and turned her face towards the wall. Alison felt a tightness in her chest, the daughter she knew had gone.

Chapter 10

Jenny

Evening sun cast the streets in a bronze glow as I walked from work over to Dad's house. The girls playing out by our row of cottages brought back memories—that was me and my friend Annie once. Her with her pink Raleigh with decorated spokes, me in my rainbow Rollerblades. We used to get up early to play before school and drive the milkman mad by crisscrossing in front of his float. Chris hadn't been able to join in, but he'd wait on the doorstep, chatting with the boys next door and calling out to us. We'd always try and bring him back some sort of treasure left in the road or a skip—a discarded cassette, a Tic Tac box, a comic someone had chucked out. It was amazing what you could find on our street, and because Chris was only little then it was all precious to him.

I got to Dad's green front door and unlocked it, calling

out hello. I heard Chris before I saw him. "Hey, sis!" he shouted, coming through from the living room in his wheelchair. He looked like he'd caught the sun, his light brown hair was flecked with blond and his skin had the beginnings of a tan. I reached down to hug him hello.

"Hi," I said, "you're a nice surprise. How are things?"

"Good thanks, Jen. I just got back from Brighton and thought I'd pop by and say hello."

"Is that why you're brown?" I asked, pointing at his tanned forearms. "I thought you were supposed to be glued to a computer screen all day?"

Chris laughed. He worked freelance as a website designer, and had a little office set up at his flat around the corner. He was usually so busy that he often joked about rarely seeing daylight. Chris was born with spina bifida, so he had to use leg braces, or sometimes the wheelchair; but as long as the place he was in was accessible there wasn't much he couldn't do—and he'd proved through his success at work that there was a lot he could.

"Yeah, I had a couple of meetings with a clothes label this week and we decided to have them at a bar on the beach." I looked at him with envy. "I know," he said. "Sweet setup, eh? Anyway," Chris continued, "I thought I'd see how you and Dad were doing."

At that moment Dad appeared in the doorway to the kitchen in a dusty apron. He must have been out the back in his carpentry workshop when I arrived.

"Hello, sweetheart," he said, his eyes crinkling, wiping

a stray bit of sawdust from his brow. "Come and give me a hug."

I went over and hugged him, stray woodchips and all. Dad smelt of soap, and new tables and chairs, just like always. He wasn't much taller than me, but he was stocky and strong, and I think secretly proud to have quite a bit of brown, albeit graying, hair left on his head.

"Good to see you, love," he said, pulling away to look at me. It must have been all of a week since I'd seen him last. "Have you got time for a cuppa?"

"Of course," I said, putting down my handbag. I followed Dad through into the kitchen, where Chris flicked the kettle on while I got three mugs out and put some Jammy Dodgers on a plate for us. "What are you working on out there, Dad? More shop fittings?"

"No, not this time, Jen, it's a bed for your cousin Angie's attic room. It's a small space so she needs something customized." He pulled out a chair and sat down, then returned my questioning look with a firm stare. "And yes, she is paying me for it, Jen."

My dad thinks I'm too money-minded, I know—but he'd do all his work for free if it were down to him.

"Dad was over at the old schoolhouse all weekend, you know," Chris said. "Measuring up for his mysterious creation for your wedding. The caretaker just gave him the keys—they're all big fans, isn't that true, Dad? They remember him from when he'd go and do DIY there."

The place where Dan and I were going to have our

wedding reception had once been our primary school, and Chris and I both had some happy memories of it. "Oh, Dad. I hope you're not going to any trouble—" I started.

Chris interrupted. "Jen. You know he likes using the old carpentry skills when he gets the chance."

Dad nodded. "I'm enjoying it, love," he said.

"And while I haven't inherited Dad's way with wood," Chris went on, "I have just finished the final design changes on your invites, so I'll send them over to you tomorrow. If you're happy with them now, then we can get them over to the printer."

"Thanks, both of you. I'm really grateful." I took a bite out of one of the Jammy Dodgers. "Everything is looking good, I think. Although as things stand it does look like Dan and I might be going back to Bognor Regis for our honeymoon." I wrinkled my nose.

Chris laughed, "I'm sure it'll be glorious that time of year."

When Dad, Chris and I had been able to go away as a family, we'd always gone to Bognor with some of Chris's friends from his Saturday club who had discounts on some specially adapted cottages down there. We would have a great time; I think Dad secretly used to like showing off his barbecue skills to the single mums. But I had no wish to hurry back there, and Chris knew it.

I pushed the plate of biscuits over towards Dad in case he wanted one. "Actually, come to think of it, we're so strapped for cash we might need a tent," I added, smiling.

Dad was staring out of the window. On the wall next to it, he still had up pictures I'd done when I was a teenager, sketches of him, Chris and Grandma Jilly.

"What was that, Jen?" he said, trying to catch hold of the conversation again. "A tent, did you say? Yes," Dad looked back towards the workshop. "I'm sure we'll have something out there."

Chris looked at me and raised his eyebrows. It was official then: Dad was acting really weirdly.

"Dad, are you OK?" I asked, puzzled.

"Yes, love, I'm fine," he said. He put down his mug as if he was about to say something, but he didn't.

It was getting dark, and I'd been about to leave Dad's when I remembered Maggie's text that morning, asking if I had copies of *Alice's Adventures in Wonderland* and *Through the Looking-Glass*. I left Dad and Chris in the living room watching a repeat of *Only Fools and Horses* and went upstairs to my old bedroom. This house was so tiny I almost felt like Alice myself. I had to duck my head as I neared the top of the staircase. My old bedroom was just as I'd left it: S Club 7 stickers on the door, Letts revision guides stacked on the desk, candy-striped curtains Mum had sewn for me when I'd decided my favorite color was pink. Everything was still there. I guess Dad didn't need the space.

I walked over to the wooden bookshelves and touched my old picture books. There was shelf after shelf of them—*The Wind in the Willows, What-a-Mess, Where the Wild Things Are*—and that was just the Ws. All my books, here and at the flat, were in alphabetical order by title, something Dan had always teased me about. I glanced up at the other shelves, *The Hungry Caterpillar, James and the Giant Peach*, Babar after Babar . . . I'd always liked the bright, bold pictures and lively line drawings as much as the stories, which was why I'd kept them all through my teenage years. I could still remember the funny voices Dad used to put on as he read and Chris and I drifted off to sleep. When I was younger Dad and Mum used to do the voices together, laughing as they competed to be the most booming and dramatic, but that was before Chris came along, one of those faint memories that slips away if you try to catch hold of it.

If I tried hard enough, I could still picture Mum, coming out of the bathroom next to my bedroom wrapped in a yellow towel, her hair sticking up from having been dried roughly. "You still up, chicken?" she used to say with a smile, when she found me on the landing waiting for her, rather than tucked up in bed where I should have been. I remember her cuddling me and carrying me back to my room. "No, you're the chicken," I'd protest, night after night, laughing, our regular game. "You've got chick hair and you're yellow."

I found the Lewis Carroll books, early hardback editions in good condition, and put them in the cloth bag I'd brought, ready to give to Maggie.

"Are you OK up there, love?" Dad called up the stairs.

"Yes, Dad, I'm fine. I'll be down in a bit."

I pulled out a copy of *The Enormous Crocodile* and flicked to the page where the crocodile pretends to be a palm tree, balancing on his tail and holding up a couple of coconuts. I'd always liked that bit. I closed the book and put it back on the shelf and as I did so I spotted the side of a thin cardboard box stored vertically on the shelf.

It was years since I'd last looked at it.

I slid the box out and sat cross-legged on the floor and lifted the lid, then smiled as I took out the contents. There were chunky card pages with bold pencil drawings and pasted-on sections of typed text—it was a pretty crude production process, but I hadn't wanted to use a computer. On the front, the title—*Charlie, Carlitos and Me*.

Here's the story: Charlie is a chinchilla, but not just any chinchilla. Charlie belongs to a little boy called Jake—the "me" of the title—who loves his new pet because he is impossibly soft and bounces from sofa to carpet like a pom-pom. One night Jake creeps downstairs and out into the garage where Charlie's cage is kept, and it's here he first meets Carlitos—or *Carleeeeeetos*, Charlie's Latin alter ego. He greets Jake up on his hind legs, in a Peruvian hat, playing the pan pipes.

Carlitos explains that he's from a far-off mountainous land called the Andes, and that he feels a little out of sorts in a cul-de-sac in Blackpool. He likes Jake and his sister but, truth be told, he misses the mountains and his alpaca

friends, and he really misses his family, the Pelu-
dos . . . Jake vows to help him get back home.

I looked through the pages, remembering all the hours
of late-night scribbling. The sketches were simple line
drawings of Jake and Carlitos—a fluffy ball in a patterned
Peruvian hat. I hadn't worked out the logistics of getting
Carlitos home at the end—that was a tricky one—but it
was pretty funny, on reflection, and the drawings actually
weren't half bad. I turned to look at the first page again
and felt a little flush of possibility that mirrored the feeling
I'd had the day I'd come up with the idea. I'd started it for
fun, because I'd always enjoyed writing and drawing and
had wanted a project to work on. But then I'd hoped to
finish writing the story and get the drawings colored up,
and I'd even wondered if maybe I'd be able to get a publisher interested. But somewhere along the line I'd shelved
my dreams.

Perhaps it was due to that nagging voice of doubt I had
always heard but was only just beginning to recognize:
the voice that made me believe that if I were *really* any
good Mum wouldn't have left.

But, these days, I was getting better at shutting it out.
I put the book pages into their box and tied it back up
with brown string. This time, it wasn't going back on the
shelf.

Chapter 11

Jenny

The three of us stood on the seafront, the first weekend in June, leaning up against its painted blue barrier. Alison and Maggie were laughing while their hair whipped around their faces and Maggie's skirt was swept up by the wind. I took the Flake out of my ice cream and licked it.

Our Sunday so far had passed in a heady, laughter-filled daze. It was the first really hot weekend we'd had and everyone's spirits were high. I had called Maggie and Alison that morning to suggest we spend the day antiques-hunting in Brighton, just the three of us. They'd both leapt at the idea and just over an hour later, we were scouring the stalls and vintage hideaways of the north lanes. Luck was on our side, we'd found four 1950s cups with richly colored anemones on the sides, another full set with tiny primroses on them, and a trio of identical tiny creamers that were going to look perfect on the tables at my wedding.

We'd walked through the cobbled streets, looking around the shops, Maggie driving a hard bargain as ever. Jugglers and musicians competed for attention on street corners, distracting passersby from their shopping and entertaining families with young children.

When we'd finished our shopping, Alison, Maggie and I had walked down onto the pier. "Look at this," Maggie had said, picking up a giant souvenir lollipop. "I'm getting one for my niece Maisy." We'd walked along the wooden boards, looking out at the expanse of sea, the sun glinting off it. Alison decided to have her fortune read, but came out of the little cabin a fiver down and none the wiser. "I thought they were meant to tell you about abundant riches and your tall, dark stranger?" she said. "But all she told me was to tread carefully, that there was a big change coming. Do you think she means the menopause?" She bit her lip, then smiled. "I didn't pay to hear that . . ." After a round on the dodgems in which Maggie swore I'd given her whiplash, we'd wandered back here, to the seafront.

I took another mouthful of sweet white ice cream and laughed at Maggie's attempts to stop her skirt blowing up. Down on the pebbled beach in front of us an old man threw a tennis ball for his golden retriever and two colorful kites intertwined in the air.

"How about we grab a bottle of wine and head down

there for a picnic?" I suggested, pointing down towards the pebbles.

"Good idea," Maggie said. "Let's stop by the car and I'll get the blanket."

We'd set up camp at the far end of the beach, complete peace apart from the distant noise of the fairground on the pier and the squawking of seagulls. I'd opened a bottle of white and was pouring large cups for me and Alison and a more modest one for Maggie, who was going to be driving us home.

"Maggie?" Alison said.

"Yes?" she replied, taking a sip.

"I've been thinking, are you interested in dancing at all?" Alison asked hopefully. "It's just, I've been taking a break from swing, but we could go together, there are some really nice men there I think you might enjoy meeting."

"Ahh," Maggie said, "I see where this is going. Thanks for offering, Ali, I appreciate it. But work takes up most of my time." Alison raised an eyebrow at that. "And anyway . . ." Maggie's voice suddenly became more businesslike. "Well, seeing as I have you two here, can I pick your brains about something?" She rearranged her position on the blanket, hugging her legs to her. "I've got a bit of a dilemma."

"Of course," Alison said with a warm smile, and I nodded. "Step into the surgery. What's up?"

"It's a man thing, unsurprisingly," Maggie ventured,

her cheeks coloring a little. "I wasn't always the weird scented-candle-cat-lady, you know," she said, smiling.

"For a woman like you, I'd say a glamorous romantic past is a given," Alison encouraged her.

"Agreed," I said, "and as for the cat thing, I've really only heard a couple of kids call you that."

Maggie gave me a good-natured push.

"So I was married once," she said, her voice gaining strength now. "When Dylan and I tied the knot I thought that was it, happily ever after." Maggie took a sip of wine and her brow creased as she searched for the right words.

"Anyway, after three years he changed his mind." She shrugged her shoulders and continued. "He said he'd been unhappy for ages. I hadn't realized at all, perhaps I'd had my head in the sand but it felt to me like one day, without any warning, he packed his things and left our London flat. I couldn't afford the rent on my own, needed a change, and so I came to live down this way instead."

"How long ago was that?" I asked. I was still processing what Maggie had said—how could any man leave a woman like her?

"Four years," Maggie said. "Four years, some difficult, some rewarding. I started up Bluebelle and bought my house."

"And what about Dylan?" Alison asked.

"We didn't—couldn't—speak. That was the hardest thing but also the only way the two of us could let go. We never had that many mutual friends, only one or two, and I fell out of contact with them once I'd left London. I just drew a line under the marriage and built a new life for myself."

"But now?" Maggie said. "Something's changed?"

A Frisbee landed in the middle of our blanket, missing the wine bottle by a couple of centimeters. A blond teenage boy in board shorts dashed over to retrieve it. "Sorry, ladies," he said, giving us a cheeky smile. I passed the Frisbee back to him, then listened to Maggie continue her story.

"This week Dylan got in contact and made it clear that he wants to meet up. He says he's sorry, and, I suppose this is my dilemma: I'm wondering whether to hear him out," Maggie said.

"I see," Alison responded. "So he's had all that time to look around, sow his wild oats a bit, get lonely, and now he wants you to forgive him, right?"

Ouch, I thought, that was a bit blunt.

"Yes, maybe," Maggie said, tilting her head.

"Does he deserve a second chance, do you think?" Alison asked, and a flush rose to Maggie's cheeks. She looked as if she wished she'd never brought the subject up.

"How about we look at this another way," I said, feeling for her. "You say you never really understood what happened, and that it came as a surprise when he left. Would it help you to know what his reasons were?"

"Part of me thinks that." Maggie shrugged. "Some

closure might help me to move on with my life. Romantically, I mean."

"In that case, I think you should do it," I said. "Why not?" Alison raised her eyebrows at me. "Give him a chance to clear the air, at least."

"OK, I think I will," Maggie said with a nod. "It's all water under the bridge for me. What he's going through now, doubting the decision he made, wanting to see me again, I went through all of that years ago. I feel sorry for him, in a way, that he's only just at the start of it."

"I bet he's kicking himself for ever letting you go," Alison said.

"I can't say I don't enjoy that idea, just a little bit," Maggie said, smiling. "But how is it that just when everything is going well, when your life is sorted, exes seem to pop up from nowhere and try to derail it?"

"Well I've had no blasts from the past," Alison said breaking the silence. "But I do have a tearaway teenager who's driving me to my wits' end. Might have to start saving to send her to brat camp."

"Is Sophie really that bad?" I asked.

"Yes. But she's a teenager—she's meant to be, isn't she? I found her at this awful party the other night." She held up her hands in an expression of feigned despair. "Ah, if only I could blame the mum and dad, eh?"

"You're both good parents, Ali," I said. "You love Sophie and Holly and they know that."

"Oh, I don't know. We try." Alison shrugged, looking defeated.

"Jenny's right," Maggie said. "And no parent gets it right all of the time."

"I'll say," I said, refilling Alison's glass, then mine, and topping Maggie's with sparkling water. Maggie went to take a sip but squealed as the Frisbee returned and hit her on the leg. Calmly picking it up and standing to her full height, she launched it in a perfect arc—the disc cut a clean line through the blue sky and landed right back where the boys were calling out apologies.

"Not bad eh?" she said, sitting down with a smile and stretching out her legs.

"What was that you said, Jen?" Maggie asked.

"Oh nothing, really." I shook my head to dismiss it. "Anyway, I'd like to propose a toast. To new friends, a port in the storm."

Alison and Maggie raised their plastic cups to that, smiling. "To new friends," they said in unison.

Secret Histories

(June–July)

Chapter 12

Maggie

Dylan looked different. His hair was shorter now, and light brown, with the front swept to the side; his sun-bleached surfer's curls were gone. Without the long hair, Maggie noticed the clean line of his jaw.

He raised his eyebrows at Maggie's porridge and blueberries. "I guess some things do change," he said, smiling, as he tucked into his crisp hash browns. "I remember you as a girl who enjoyed her food, Maggie."

Maggie lifted her coffee cup and brought it to her lips, but the coffee was so hot it nearly scalded her. She put it down and met Dylan's blue-eyed gaze. He was smiling. She wasn't.

"I still do, Dylan. I just enjoy different things now. Anyway, a lot has changed in the last four years." She saw his face fall a little. He looked older, but she had to admit the years hung well on him. There were new creases around his eyes and on his forehead, but his smile was more or less the same. His teeth were whiter maybe, and it looked like the one he'd chipped years ago playing rugby had been fixed, but she could still see the old Dylan there. Was he assessing her appearance in the same way? She felt suddenly self-conscious. Maggie was sitting opposite him in the window seat at Bondi, a cozy, Aussie-run brunch stop in London that had once been their Sunday regular. It was quiet this morning, a Monday with no queue stretching out onto the cobblestoned Islington street like there often was at the weekend.

"I know some things will have changed, Maggie," Dylan said in his smooth drawl, the traces of an American accent softening his London one. "And, for what it's worth, you look fantastic."

Maggie shrugged off the compliment but she was secretly pleased; she'd spent hours choosing an outfit that would show that she was confident enough—*over their divorce enough*—not to have to power-dress. She'd opted for a white Ghost tunic over leggings, with dark gold sandals, and then put on her favorite amber necklace, the one her grandmother had given her. She wore her hair loose and had opted for a muted lip gloss and smoky eyes. When she'd been with Dylan red lipstick and nails had been her trademark. He'd done a double-take when they'd kissed hello.

"I never thought you'd come," Dylan confessed.

"When you didn't answer after a week, I thought that was it."

"I didn't want to see you at first, actually," Maggie replied. "So your instinct was right."

"I know I hurt you, Maggie," he said then, looking her dead in the eyes.

Maggie looked down, scooping up her blueberries, one, then two, on her spoon. "Yes," she said, catching his eye again. "You did hurt me, Dylan." A quiet rage was building but she was determined not to let him see it.

"Maggie . . ."

She shook her head. "No. You know what, I don't want to think about it right now. Let's talk about something else. Tell me about New York, about your studio."

Dylan shuffled in his seat. "Right, yes. It's a warehouse space I converted together with Luca, another photographer. There's this incredible exposed brickwork and a great view over Prospect Park. My apartment's just down the road. Have you ever been to New York, Maggie?"

"No, I've always wanted to, actually. But I never have." It was true that Maggie had often pictured herself wandering in Central Park and shopping in Manhattan.

He reached over to touch her hand. "I think you'd like it. And I'd love to have you there with me."

Her stomach contracted at his words.

"I miss you," he said. He shook his head slightly. "I made such a terrible, selfish, stupid mistake."

Maggie looked over at him. "Did you, Dylan?" she said

softly, after a beat. "You seem happy. Was leaving me really a mistake?" She remained calm. "Tell me—truthfully— would you undo the last four years if you could?"

"That's an impossible question, Maggie," Dylan said gently, not taking his eyes off her. Then he ate the last of the bacon on his plate and broke the yolk in his fried egg with a slice of his toast.

An hour later they stepped out of the café into a cool June day. Right away Maggie saw her favorite junk shop, Violet's, across the cobbled street, and spotted a perfect teacup in the window.

"Look at that little beauty," she exclaimed. "We're going in." Dylan looked bemused, but she tugged at his jacket sleeve, pulling him through the shop doorway. She leaned into the window display and swept up the silver-rimmed cup, tilting it to read the price—seven pounds. Hmm, she wasn't going to get quite the haul they had managed on the seaside trip, but this was a quality piece. A young guy dressed and styled like a teddy boy stepped forward to help. "Got any more like this?" she asked. She could tell from his startled expression that she'd said it a bit more forcefully than she'd meant to.

He hesitated for a moment and then said, "Sure, I think so, let me check out the back."

"What are you up to?" Dylan asked, looking up from the teacup she was holding to her smiling eyes.

"A secret mission," she said, with a wink. "Don't you worry your pretty head."

The teddy boy came out from the back room and put four cups on the counter—two were matching, gold and yellow with a pretty buttercup pattern. The other two looked older, 1930s maybe; one was turquoise and white, Ali would adore that, and the other was Chinese blue and white. Miraculously they were all unchipped and had matching saucers in good condition.

"I'll give you eighteen for the lot," Maggie said. "Deal?"

The teddy boy shook his head. "The owner would kill me. We're doing a nice little trade in this sort of thing at the moment. I could give them to you for twenty-five. How about that?"

"Twenty-two. And that's my final offer. Come on," Maggie said, raising her hands, "they're not even a set."

The teddy boy gave in, "OK, OK. It's a deal. I'll wrap them up for you."

Maggie turned around to see that Dylan had donned a leather cowboy hat and a white feather boa, a long cigarette holder hanging from his lips. She laughed before she could stop herself. He set the cigarette holder down and took the boa off, sweeping it round her shoulders instead, then took off the hat and plonked it on her head. "Perfection," Dylan said, that familiar twinkle back in his eye.

Dylan and Maggie left Violet's and browsed through the other shops. When they stepped out of the last one in the row—Maggie now had a bone china teapot to add to the collection—it had started to rain. Dylan got an umbrella out of his bag, put it up and held it out for Maggie to come under. Tentatively she moved closer to him, the drops were coming so heavy and fast now that her thin white top was in danger of getting soaked through.

Minutes later they were drying off in the Queen of Hearts, the pub where they'd first met and had visited together a hundred times. It was snug inside, with framed movie posters covering the walls and a jukebox in the corner.

"I know it's early, but God, you know I've missed this pub," Dylan said, grabbing them a booth at the back. He motioned for Maggie to sit down on the bench and hung his jacket over a chair. Dylan always used to put seventies rock on the jukebox, while Maggie would choose soul, jazz and blues, the same tunes she'd liked to sing herself. It had been after one of her gigs here, when she was twenty-six—Jenny's age, she thought idly—that Dylan had first locked eyes with her as she sang. He had watched her intently throughout the performance and then at the end come up and given her his number. He'd said the music wasn't his usual thing but that he'd loved watching her nonetheless. At home alone later that night she had pulled the card out of her purse and flipped it over. On the back Dylan had done a pen drawing of a nightingale.

"What will you have? I won't try and guess . . ." Dylan said, his London accent back now.

"I'll have a cranberry juice," Maggie replied. "It's only one o'clock."

"Go on," he said, tempting her with a wink that sent a shiver across her skin and brought a smile to her lips.

"OK, if you are, and if you insist. A Campari soda, please. But I've got a meeting with a Dutch supplier at three, so I'll have to head off soon."

Dylan looked her in the eye and smiled, holding her gaze. "So you're just squeezing me in, are you?" he asked, pretending to be offended.

She watched him leave for the bar and cursed the old feelings that were coming back. Dylan's charm was wearing her down, layer by layer, and she was longing to feel his touch, to feel, just for a moment, the intimacy they'd once had. He took his time, chatting to the barman while the drinks were poured. Maggie found her handbag among the pile of vintage purchases, and checked her phone to see that there'd been no emergencies at Bluebelle. It was the first time she'd left Anna on her own all day and she couldn't shift the nagging worries that something could have gone wrong. She'd resisted the urge to check in, but found there were two new messages. She read the first, from Anna:

Hi Maggie. Everything is fine, REALLY. The shop is
quiet, just a few online orders that I have sorted.
Hope London is fab! Anna x

Then she saw one from Alison:

Soo . . . ? How is it all going with D? We are
dying here. A and J x

Dylan was back at the table before she could reply to
either. She put her phone back in her handbag and looked
up, smiling to thank him for the drink.

"Boyfriend?" he asked.

"No," she said. She'd meant the texts, but realized her
tone had given away far more than that.

On the train back to Charlesworth that evening Maggie
watched the rain-drenched fields go by and felt grateful
to be warm inside. Her supplier meeting had been suc-
cessful, she'd managed to negotiate some really good bulk
prices, but Dylan was still on her mind. When they'd left
the pub he'd walked her to the tube, and her heart had
been thudding harder with each step. When he'd leaned
in to kiss her she felt a rush of adrenaline readying her to
move away. But then came the coolly formal peck on the
cheek and she was left feeling strangely flat. He left to go
back to his hotel alone and she watched him walk away;

while she hadn't known what she'd been expecting, it hadn't been that.

She got up to go to the tiny train toilets, and it was in there that she heard her phone buzz with a new message.

M, can't tell you how great it is to see you after all this time. Dx

As her heart leapt, the last half-decade of her life dissolved; she read Dylan's message and felt a glow she hadn't experienced in all that time. The way Dylan made her laugh, the way he inspired her; she'd looked but hadn't found anything close to that since they broke up. She looked at herself in the train mirror, her reflection juddering slightly as the carriage moved. Dylan had always loved the defined edges of her collarbone, sometimes he'd photographed just that part of her, with a glimpse of pale shoulder and a curl of red hair. She turned slowly around and held her own gaze in the mirror, letting the strap of her white tunic slide down her arm, revealing more of her back. There it was—she hadn't seen it for ages, hadn't looked. On her right shoulderblade, the outline of a songbird, the sketch Dylan had done for her the night after he first heard her sing, before they were even together. She ran her fingers over it now; that part of him she'd never been able to let go.

Chapter 13

Alison

Alison's umbrella blew inside out the moment she stepped out into the car park. The rain dripped down her cheeks, and she knew her dark eye makeup would be smudging. She really needed today to go well, so that she could get a loan approved and get the café started with Jamie.

She'd worked in the studio until midday that morning, filling an order for thirty teacup candles and then starting work on some cushions with outlines of foxes sewn onto them. She'd listened to music, humming as she stitched, and remembered how much she enjoyed sewing; time just disappeared as her needle ran through the material. She smiled to herself thinking of how much craft she'd be doing once she and Jamie had the café up and running— she couldn't wait. When the rain had started, she'd grabbed her chunky knit cardi and pulled it tight around her as she worked. Ah, the English summer. The moment you start to take it for granted it's gone.

It was only a five-minute walk to the bank on the high street from where she'd parked, but by the time she got there she was soaked to the skin. Her umbrella had got so battered she'd thrown it away, and her leather satchel was wet through. Mr. Cavendish, the bank manager, was there to meet her when she stepped inside. "Mrs. Lovell, hello," he said, in a voice no bank manager should really have—it was as comforting as warm buttered toast. Ever the gentleman, he acknowledged her dishevelled state but only smiled gently. "Come into my office where you can warm up." He took her coat from her. "And let's hang this up by the radiator, shall we?"

Mr. Cavendish knew things about her that even her closest friends didn't know. When her clothes shop had foundered a decade ago he had helped her work things out so that her debt was manageable and she'd slowly got back on top of things again. She should have been more honest with other people back then—hers wasn't the only good business ever to hit the rocks after all—but she hadn't wanted her friends and family to think of her as a failure. It was easier to say that she'd wanted to spend more time with the girls while they were still young, and do without the long commute. And of course both those things were true. It just hadn't been the whole truth.

"Mrs. Lovell. It was good to hear from you again the other day. It's been a while." His forearms were resting on the table and he leaned towards her, looking her in the eye. His hair was an attractive salt-and-pepper and his suits were always well cut. Still no pictures of children on his desk, she noted, idly.

"Yes, thanks for fitting me in today," she said.

"From what you've told me, it sounds like your current business is going rather well. Are you looking to develop that further? Or was it something different you wanted to talk about today?"

"A bit of both," Alison said. "What I'd really like to do is sell my products in my own shop, rather than selling them on to boutiques. And an opportunity has arisen for me to do just that." She shifted slightly in her seat.

"Go on," Mr. Cavendish said.

"I know I'm in a good position now," she said, "with a steady stream of customers and no overheads, but I can't see the business growing as things are. I want to use my retail background to hand-sell my products to customers."

Alison looked over at Mr. Cavendish and he was nodding, listening to her attentively.

"I know that my business background isn't flawless," she said. "But I've put my heart and soul into this company and over the past year I've achieved some strong results. More new orders are coming in through the website, too."

Alison unclipped her sodden satchel and pulled out the ringbinder she'd assembled earlier; thankfully the sheets inside were still dry.

"Here, I brought the documents along, the ones you asked to see." She handed them to him over the large desk.

He smiled and opened the folder, starting to read. Alison had to stop herself from trying to gauge his expression. She looked out of the window instead, seeking distraction. The meeting room was up on the second floor and you could watch the goings-on in the high street. The rain was still falling. Some people had ducked into cafés and shops to stay out of it; old ladies and new mums were huddled together under the bus shelter. A single-decker rattled down the street and splashed a well-dressed woman holding a golf umbrella who shouted out in shock. Alison squinted—wasn't that Sally? Pete had mentioned she was back. She looked a lot more attractive. Her dark dyed-red hair was styled into waves, and even though her skirt was mud-spattered now, you could see that her clothes were trendy. She had on a wide belt that emphasized her still-thin waist and she wore high-heeled leather boots. Perhaps that was what happened after a stint in London.

"It looks like you're doing a roaring trade, Mrs. Lovell." Mr. Cavendish's voice broke into her thoughts. "I can understand why you feel ready to branch out at this point." Alison breathed a sigh of relief. She knew it wasn't over yet, but this was promising.

"But your income has fluctuated over the years—and I have to take into account what happened with your previous business. However, your husband's income is relatively high and steady, as I remember it. Is that right? And if so, would he be in a position to act as a guarantor?"

"Things have changed a bit on that front, to be honest," Alison said, her heart sinking. "Pete lost his job last year. But I'm sure he'll have a new one soon. And we have his redundancy payout in our joint account, which was really hefty."

"OK," Mr. Cavendish said, making a note. "I'll be honest with you, Mrs. Lovell. Although the amount you're asking for isn't particularly high, we are having to be very strict at the moment about who we lend money to. I'll need more information than I have here."

"I know," Alison said. "Of course—but look, why don't you check our account now, you'll see—"

"OK, let's do that then." He turned to his computer and tapped in her details.

Alison fidgeted in her chair and found her gaze returning to the window. Sally had vanished, and a tubby postman was there instead. He was opening up the post box and emptying the contents into his sack; the wind blew a few letters onto the street.

"Mrs. Lovell." The bank manager was frowning at the screen. "I'm afraid this isn't really tying up with what you've said. I don't understand."

Alison smiled at him, ready to help. "What seems to be the problem?" she asked.

"Are you sure your husband's payout is in the joint

account—the one you just gave me the details for—rather than in his personal one?"

"Yes, I'm a hundred percent sure," Alison said. "We decided it would go towards paying bills, and the everyday things."

"But Mrs. Lovell, this account is overdrawn. In fact you're very close to your overdraft limit."

Alison looked at the bank manager blankly. "There must be some mistake," she said.

"Perhaps your husband transferred an amount over to his own account?" the manager said. "Is that a possibility?"

"No," Alison said. "Pete wouldn't do that."

Would he?

"I'm sorry, Mrs. Lovell. You know I'd like to help you. But I just don't think I'd be doing that by lending you money at this point."

Alison walked back to the car in a daze. What possible reason could Pete have for transferring their joint funds? She wracked her brain. He didn't spend money on expensive hobbies, or clothes—it just didn't make any sense. The rain had eased off, but the wind slowed her progress and made the walk feel longer than usual. She shut the car door and put on the heating, waiting for the windscreen to clear. Business had been good this spring. The sunny days had brought shoppers out to browse the high street, and her clients were putting in reorders every couple of days.

The windows were starting to clear now, and as she thought back to the unopened envelopes on the hall dresser—Good Energy, Virgin Media, the water company—so too did her mind. Handling the bills had always been Pete's thing—he'd dealt with the finances and she'd done most of the cooking, it had been the way their domestic setup had functioned for years. But with Pete's redundancy, both of their roles had changed. What with everything that had been going on with the girls, and taking care of her mum, the truth of the matter was that she hadn't been keeping track of their spending, and if what the bank manager said was correct, neither had Pete. There might not have even been a transfer. The reality of the situation started to dawn on her. Their money could have, quite simply, slipped away.

She switched on the radio—it was playing the Commodores' "Easy." She switched it off again. She leaned the side of her head against the car window and rested there a moment. Her plans with Jamie suddenly seemed a world away.

Chapter 14

Jenny

"What about this?" Chloe asked, putting on a cream bird-cage veil, studded with pearls.

"It's gorgeous," I said, looking at the way her dark ringlets set it off. I reached out to touch the delicate netting. The lady running the stall, who had a distractingly generous, hoicked-up bosom, smiled in agreement. Chloe passed the veil over to me and I held it up against my own hair and looked in the little mirror hung up in front of us. "Pretty," I said. I looked like a proper bride with the net falling over my face. The detailing lifted it and it was clear it was the genuine article. "Original 1930s, that one," the lady confirmed, before turning to deal with a customer who was trying to force her large feet into some delicate T-bar shoes.

"I'm not sure if I want a veil though . . ." I said, hanging it back up on the hook a little reluctantly. "Is it really me?" Chloe tilted her head and narrowed her eyes at me a little. "Come on," I protested. "It's the first stall we've stopped at, Chloe," I said, defending myself. "Give me a chance."

"Would a glass of champagne help?" she asked.

"Yes," I replied. It would knock some of my retail hesitation on the head, that was for sure. "Wedding dress shopping while drunk," I said, laughing. "What could possibly go wrong?"

Champagne glasses in hand, we looked out over the vintage fair in the arches of the old Charlesworth railway station. It was just as Chloe had described it, stalls stacked with period wedding dresses, fascinators, handbags and jewelry. When Dan and I first got engaged, I'd dragged Chloe up to London and together we'd schlepped around the shops where patronizing shop assistants had shown us endless wedding dresses that were far too flouncy and not my kind of thing at all. I'd ended up a sweaty grumpy mess with nothing to show for our train fares and the day we'd spent looking. So I was grateful to Chloe for bringing me here to the vintage fair. I could already see that the clothes were much more my style, and the pressure was off, without fake-tanned saleswomen insisting that this diamanté bodice or that long net trail would look "to die for" on me.

"Have you and Dan thought about your first dance yet?" Chloe asked, taking a sip of the fizz. "Because if you haven't, I've had a few ideas," she said, breathlessly. "I think the—"

"Nope," I said, holding up my hand and laughing, knowing already what she was about to say. "Stop right there, Chlo." I shook my head. "Not the *Dirty Dancing* routine that couple did on YouTube. Don't even think it."

"But . . ." She gazed at me imploringly, not believing that she was already beaten on this one.

"No routines." I was resolute but still felt guilty for crushing her vision. "But we have got the playlist down to perfection," I said. Dan and I had been dancing around the living room the last few evenings, putting on our favorite tracks in turn and fighting our corner to have them added to the DJ set. We each got two chances to veto tunes—I'd said no to Slipknot already, and Dan had put the kibosh on Lady Gaga, despite my desperate pleas. "It's all pretty much sorted, apart from Chris finalizing the songs that he wants to play in his set."

"But it's never too late to change your mind," Chloe insisted. I raised an eyebrow questioningly. "About your first dance, I mean." Chloe stepped away from the bar and slipped an arm around my waist, whispering in my ear, "*I've had* . . ." She put her champagne flute down and put her other arm around me: ". . . *the time of my liiiiife*," she crooned in my ear. I felt her grip on me tighten.

"Not the lift! NOT the lift," I shouted, wheezing with laughter now as I felt my feet leave the ground and managed to wriggle free of her grasp.

*

By two in the afternoon, fortified by a mixture of fizz and Chloe's enthusiastic guidance, I had found the perfect dress. When I turned to look at myself in the makeshift changing room, I knew right away that it was a dress like no other.

It was a full-skirted fifties number, with a delicate sweetheart neckline cut from the lace top and tiny sleeves that brushed my shoulders, just covering them. As I swooshed from side to side the full thick petticoat followed me in a delayed response. I opened the curtain just a crack and peeped out at Chloe, who was biting into a handmade brownie. "Are you ready?" I asked her. "I actually think this might be the one, you know."

"Really?" she asked, her face lighting up, brownie crumbs on her chin. "Well get your bridey butt out here then and let me have a look." She took another bite in an attempt at damage-limitation as the brownie started to break into bits.

I stepped past the curtain and took a barefoot step towards her, trying to ensure the skirt didn't knock anything on the nearby table flying.

The moment I saw Chloe's eyes water and a flush spring to her cheeks, I knew I was right. "This is it, isn't it?" I said, looking for confirmation and wrinkling my nose a little.

"Mmm-hmm," she agreed, her mouth full of brownie. Even when she'd swallowed it, though, she didn't say a word. This dress was actually silencing Chloe. We both stood dumbly where we were for a moment.

"You know you have to buy it," she said, finally.

"I know."

She reached behind me and pulled out the price tag. She wolf-whistled and shook her head.

"We'll find a way," I said, with a shrug. Really, it was no longer a choice. I was in love.

Chapter 15

Alison

Alison and Pete were sitting at their kitchen table, with the financial paperwork for the past few months laid out between them. Their latest online bank statement was open on Pete's laptop screen.

"We're in a mess, aren't we?" Alison said, looking at the evidence surrounding them.

They'd spent the morning going through their bank statements, slowly, methodically, until they'd accounted for the whole of Pete's missing redundancy payment. Alison's suspicions had proven to be correct—the money had simply slipped through their fingers, unaccounted for. Pete admitted that when the lump sum first came through he'd decided to pay off their credit card bills, and he hadn't let Alison know. Neither of them had been keeping track.

"We'll sort it out," said Pete, quietly.

"But look at this," Alison said, holding up an old British Gas invoice. "We've buried our heads in the sand for too long already: replacing the boiler, servicing two cars, George's vet bills, covering Holly's stealing—money was disappearing all the time and we didn't even realize."

"And these?" She sifted through the papers and pulled out two red bill reminders. "This is really serious, Pete. It looks like we're going to be late on our mortgage payments this month— and we haven't even got enough cash left to cover all of the bills."

"It's not looking great, is it?" Pete conceded reluctantly.

"I don't get it, Pete," Alison said, frustration creeping into her voice. "You must have realized something was going wrong. I know it's a joint responsibility, but you've always handled the household stuff. I just wish you'd said something . . . not buried your head in the sand."

"Buried my head in the sand?" Pete said, a flicker of annoyance in his eyes. "I've had a lot on my mind, Ali. And anyway, since I do most of the cooking and cleaning now, I thought you might be keeping more of an eye on the bills. Or am I supposed to do all that, as well as find a new job?" Pete stopped himself and took a deep breath. "Look, we'll find a way to fix this . . . get a loan or—"

"Like I got a loan for the café, you mean? Oh yes, that'll be no problem," Alison said, only realizing once the words were out how bitter they sounded. Tears began to well up but she fought them back. "Do you understand what this could mean for us, Pete?"

Pete raised a hand to his forehead. "Yes," he said, but it was as if he was trying to block out her words.

"If we don't do something soon we could lose this house." Alison sat back in her chair.

Pete remained silent, wearily shaking his head. "That won't happen," he said finally.

"Really?" Alison said. "Pete, it's happening to people every day. Things were tough when my shop went bust, but it was never as bad as this. We could lose the place we worked so hard to buy, the only home the girls have known." Alison looked around their kitchen, the hub of their home, and then back at her husband, whose eyes were glazed. "Are you even listening to me, Pete? It's happening again, isn't it?"

Memories of their younger selves came back to Alison in sharp relief. "You said back then that I didn't need to finish my A-levels, that your band was going to be famous. And what happened? Nothing, Pete. We ended up living in that grotty caravan, with barely enough money for food. While my friends were at university, studying and having a great time, I was waitressing and scraping together the money for you to pursue your rock star dreams. Do you remember what it was like?"

Pete's eyes were cast down.

"We had nothing. You were rehearsing while I had to work all hours so that we didn't have to go crawling back to our parents with our tails between our legs." Alison remembered those days as vividly as if she'd just lived them.

"You promised me all those years ago that everything would be all right—and you know what, Pete? It wasn't."

Chapter 16

Maggie

Maggie had popped out to get muffins for herself and Anna. She was standing in line at the bakery looking at a picture message of Jenny's wedding dress when a text arrived:

> M. I can't stop thinking about you. I know there's still more to talk about, but come to dinner with me and we can start? Dx

In spite of herself, she felt a rush of excitement as she read it. She'd wait to answer, though. Her head wasn't clear. She'd give it a few hours, at least. Dylan wasn't forgiven yet, she reminded herself. Not for a single thing.

"One blueberry muffin and one chocolate, please," Maggie said to the girl behind the counter, realizing she had reached the front of the queue. She wanted to get Anna a little treat to thank her. When she'd got back to the shop on Tuesday after her day in London, she had found everything in perfect order; Anna had processed all the deliveries efficiently and the floor and display were spotless.

"Coffee with that?" the girl asked.

"No, just the muffins, thanks."

Maggie took the paper bag and went back to the shop where Anna was helping an older man pick out some flowers. Today, with the rain, customers had been few and far between. This man was in a green mac, gray hair back in a ponytail but balding on top.

"I had no idea it was our anniversary until I got the call just now," he said, flustered. "I mean, how do you women remember these things?"

Anna smiled reassuringly.

"Christine said before that it didn't matter—it's second time round for us both, you see—and she'd rather I surprised her on a different day. But then her friend Eve called to say that Christine was crushed. How can I possibly win?" He tapped his head with the palm of his hand in frustration. "Eve said I'd better put things right, and soon. Please say you can help me." There was a look of sheer desperation on his face.

"Of course we can," Anna said, motioning for him to come and take a closer look at the stock. "Let's go all out, I reckon, but stick with the classics. Some dark red roses, like these ones, a big bunch—if that's OK for your budget I mean?"

He nodded. It seemed unlikely he would turn anything down at this point.

"With some baby's breath in there too." She picked up a few stems to show him. "We'll wrap it up beautifully for you, Mr. . . . er?"

"Edmonds," he said.

"Mr. Edmonds. And how about we deliver them to your wife at work rather than you giving them to her at home? That way she's not waiting a moment longer than she has to."

The color was slowly returning to the man's cheeks. Maggie stood a little closer to Anna and the new customer, and the man looked startled. He had been so deep in thought he hadn't even seen her come in.

"Good idea, Anna," Maggie cut in. "I could call up your wife, sir, and say we're sorry for the late delivery." She tilted her head slightly. "What if our stockroom had been flooded this morning and all of our deliveries set back a few hours? That sounds about right."

The man was visibly relieved. "Oh yes," he said, "if you're sure you don't mind . . . what a very kind offer."

"No problem at all," Maggie said. "I'll leave you in Anna's capable hands, just give her your wife's contact details and we'll get onto it right away." Maggie could feel Anna's eyes on her, questioning, as she went into the back room.

The moment the door was closed, Maggie got her BlackBerry out again. She'd waited long enough, hadn't she? She texted Dylan.

OK, then. Where? I finish work at 6 p.m.

She pressed send and then immediately kicked herself for not waiting longer. What was she, fifteen years old? But Dylan's answer came in a flash, which helped.

Down in Brighton on a shoot. Come and meet me? Seafood and fizz at that little place in the lanes at 8?

Maggie took a deep breath.

Fine. See you there. M

She came back out into the shop. Anna was on her own by the till. She turned her head and asked, "Maggie, just to check, are you sure you want me to call that customer's wife? You're always saying our delivery times are what sets us apart, that it affects the brand if . . ."

Maggie paused. Hmm, that did sound familiar.

"You know what, one customer's not going to make a difference," Maggie said, as she rearranged plants on a shelf.

"Hang on, Maggie, you were nice to him because he

was trying to be *romantic*, weren't you?" Anna smiled like she'd just solved a puzzle.

"Maybe," Maggie said, not giving anything away. "I can't bear the thought of her being cross with that poor man, can you?"

When the shop bell jangled an hour after the lunchtime rush, Maggie looked up without thinking. She smiled when she saw Jenny, smart in a charcoal trouser suit and a crisp white shirt.

"Hello," Jenny said with a smile. She nodded at the clock. "My boss is away," she added by way of explanation for the late lunch hour. "Any chance you've got a minute to talk through the plans for my wedding flowers?"

"Yes, sure," Maggie said, pulling a couple of stools up to the counter. "It would be a pleasure." She turned towards her assistant. "Anna, would you mind putting a pot of tea on for us?" Anna nodded and walked towards the back room. Maggie went on, "And then do you want to join our meeting? I'd love to get your input." Anna turned around, her eyes lit up.

"She's a quick learner," Maggie said quietly to Jenny as they heard the kettle go on, "and weddings are her favorite."

Jenny smiled and went to get her notebook out of her bag. "Sure, it would be nice to hear what she thinks," she said.

"But first, while I have you to myself," Jenny said,

fixing her wide hazel eyes on Maggie's, and lowering her voice, "I'm going to need a full update. How did it go with Dylan?"

Maggie liked the sea-spray taste of oysters, and the ones here were the best. She prised one loose with her fork and swallowed it, before taking a sip of the champagne Dylan had ordered.

When she'd arrived at the restaurant just before eight he was already there waiting at a little table in the corner.

"Maggie, it's so good to see you. You look beautiful." He stood back, admiring her.

She'd put on a slate gray silk dress for dinner and tied her hair up loosely, so that strands framed her face and fell gently onto her shoulders. Her makeup brought out the green in her eyes and silver drop earrings hung down almost to her shoulders.

"Ah, the old Dylan Leonard charm," Maggie said, with a smile. "I bet the women you were photographing today heard the very same thing." She pulled out her chair and sat down.

"Not really, no," he laughed. "Actually I was doing a fashion shoot for *Attitude* magazine today, and the male models were pretty confident already."

They'd sat down and looked at the menu, ordering up oysters, crab and lobster and a few sides, talking about Maggie's day while they waited for the food to arrive.

"We'd planned to be out by the old pier today," Dylan said, as the waitress settled the plates on their table. "You know the one that burned down?"

"You mean the west pier," she said, "with the starlings."

"Yes, that's it. But with the weather today we had to change tack. We stuck with the outdoors—we had to, it's for the autumn edition so it's all coats and scarves—but we took the photos under the arches down by the sea instead."

"Sounds like fun," Maggie said, before swallowing another delicious oyster.

"You know what, once the rain had stopped it actually was. There were some great people. I'm remembering a lot of what I used to love about England."

He looked awkward for a moment, then took her hand. Maggie didn't know whether she should pull away or not, but the truth was it felt nice. She wanted to stay just like that.

"I still hate cracking these critters open, you know," Dylan said, taking his hand back and pointing to the lobster on the seafood platter.

"Here, let me," Maggie said. She took his plate and cracked the shell, scooping out the lobster meat for him and handing it back. "You always were a wimp with those."

He shrugged, smiling. "Are you still singing, Maggie?" he asked, picking up a forkful of lobster meat.

"Yes, sort of," she said. It wasn't, strictly speaking, a lie. "Every so often," she said. Like in the shower. To the orchids. Or to Maisy. But she hadn't sung a note to anyone older than her niece since signing her divorce papers. The moment she'd written her name on that line, reality had hit on all fronts; from then on she'd decided that singing was childish and indulgent, and belonged to a life she was saying goodbye to. She'd made a bit of money at it over the years, but with Dylan gone she needed to make enough to live on her own, and fast. She'd put away her music and put all her energy towards making her way in the flower business.

"I'm glad you haven't stopped," he said. "You've always had an amazing voice, Maggie. I still hear it sometimes, in my head I mean."

She fell quiet, embarrassed by the compliment, especially as she'd lied to earn it. Dylan's dark blue eyes fixed on hers. He reached over and touched her face, his hand lingering on her cheek. His touch was warm on her skin and made her long to be closer to him. The rush of emotion caught her unaware.

"Maggie, I wish I could take back how I hurt you." His eyes wandered over her face, taking it in. "But I know I can't. I made some really big mistakes, and I've learned from them. I'm hoping that we can find a way to start things anew."

Maggie looked into his eyes. He seemed sincere, and things did feel different; Dylan was calmer, she was stronger. The anger she'd felt during that first meeting was dissipating with every word he said. She didn't need Dylan, didn't need anyone; but as her eyes wandered to his mouth, and warmth spread through her body, she knew that she definitely wanted him.

"Anew," she said, the wave of longing taking over. "I suppose we could try that."

Dylan's face lit up. "To new beginnings," he said, raising his glass. She felt a rush of adrenaline as she clinked hers against it.

Maggie woke up the next morning wrapped in the crisp white sheets of Dylan's hotel bed. She was curled into his body and for a moment it felt like he'd never left. He was already awake and gently ruffled her hair. "Morning, sweetie," he said.

Maggie took in the unfamiliar surroundings and started slightly—sun was streaming in through the windows and she could hear the waves crashing outside.

"Hello," she replied, relaxing and snuggling in closer. Dylan tipped up her chin and kissed her gently on the mouth, reminding her of all the pleasure of last night—the shower, the blanket, the sofa . . . The physical connection was still there, and last night had proved it was stronger than ever.

Her phone alarm beeped, loud. "Ahhh. I've got to get . . ." she started saying, as reality began to kick in. What was she doing here? On the strength of a few words, she had gone back on all the other years of trying to erase Dylan from her life.

"Yep, me too," he said. He kissed her again, lingering this time.

It did feel good, and sort of right.

"OK, I'm going to jump in the shower," Maggie said. "And then we're both out of here."

Maggie opened the shop and flicked the lights to bring the place to life. Out in the back room she found the bag of clothes she'd brought in weeks ago, meaning to take them to the charity shop, and rifled through them. Black slacks and a pistachio V-neck top. The loose trousers were going to look a bit odd with the heels she was still wearing, but they would have to do. Putting the kettle on to boil, she got changed and poured herself a cup of Earl Grey. The motorway had been clear and even after stopping to get a pastry from the bakery, she'd arrived at the shop earlier than usual.

As she took her first sip of tea, and a bite of the Danish, she recalled how she and Dylan had left each other that morning. Her car had been parked on the seafront and he had kissed her goodbye there.

"Maggie, I don't want to jump the gun, but this feels like the start of something good, doesn't it?"

All the feelings she'd had when they were together had flooded back the moment they'd kissed. The chemistry, the buzz, the sensation that her other half—the man who knew her inside out—was back. Maybe, just maybe, she wouldn't have to deal with life alone, after all.

After a beat, she'd nodded and his face had lit up in response. It was difficult. She found it so hard to let go—to give in, and to trust that whatever was happening was happening for a reason. But if she didn't do that, was she really giving love a chance at all?

Dylan had looked gorgeous, with his hair still ruffled. Just thinking of him made her melt inside. When she had finally pulled away and got into her car he had stood there, watching from the pavement as she drove away down Marine Parade. She had caught sight of him in her rearview mirror, flagging a white and green taxi and getting in.

The jangling shop bell announced Anna's arrival. Maggie looked over and was met with a cheery wave.

"Morning, Boss," Anna called out. She looked smart in leather boots and a knee-length jersey dress.

"Hi, Anna," Maggie said, brushing pastry crumbs from her top. "You look nice."

"You sound surprised." Anna laughed, her big blue eyes shining. "But yes, I thought I'd try and make a bit more effort, stop being such a scruff all the time."

"I like it, it suits you."

The morning flew by, helped by a sudden influx of customers—a coachload of elderly French tourists who'd stopped off in Charlesworth on a tour of Sussex towns and villages. After they'd finally filtered out, arms full of plants and blooms, Maggie saw a familiar handsome face come to the shop door and went over to open it.

"Hello, Jack," she said, smiling and greeting him with a kiss. He was clean shaven today and smelled good, she couldn't help noticing. Out of the corner of her eye she could see Anna's face light up in interest.

"Come in, come in." She led Jack into the shop. He shook Anna's hand, introducing himself, and then looked around.

"Nice place," he said, admiring the displays.

"Thanks. We do our best," Maggie said, giving Anna a wink. "What can I help you with?" Maggie asked, her voice bright and cheerful. In contrast, Jack's brow was creased and it was obvious that there was something on his mind.

"It's Lucy," he said at last.

"Shall we pop out the back for a chat?" Maggie asked, and he nodded.

"Maggie, she's freaking out about the wedding," Jack said, as soon as they were alone.

Maggie had seen this a couple of times before. In fact, managing Bridezilla wobbles was one of her specialities. "What is it she's worried about?"

"The thing is," Jack said, "she's worried about you and Owen."

Maggie's heart sank. Lucy's wedding was by far the

biggest event in her autumn schedule, she didn't want any hitches.

"What about me and Owen?" Maggie asked, already guessing the answer. A memory of his taunting face flashed through her mind.

"She thinks you don't share the same vision," Jack said, shrugging his shoulders to show he wasn't taking sides. "She says it was obvious you didn't click the other day."

Maggie could have kicked herself. She knew she should have been the bigger person and just ignored Owen's arrogance, but she'd been so annoyed at the way he spoke to her she'd found it hard to hide.

"I mean," Jack continued, "I know Owen isn't the easiest person to get on with, and weddings aren't really his cup of tea, like he said—he has really strong opinions about environmental stuff. But underneath it all he's a good bloke."

How far underneath, Maggie thought to herself. She stayed silent and heard Jack out.

"Anyway," Jack stumbled on. "Lucy says if you can't work together she's going to have to lose one of you."

A wave a panic rushed through Maggie. With Jack and Owen's long-standing friendship she knew it had to be her that Lucy was considering giving the boot. She couldn't lose this. Lucy and Jack's wedding was her big chance—her shot at getting the publicity she needed, the kind of exposure that could bring her a serious investor.

"I see," Maggie said, swallowing her pride. "Thanks

for coming here and letting me know. And of course I'm keen to put things right. As it happens, I really don't have a problem working with Owen, I like his designs. I think perhaps the issue was that we were both just a little *too* excited about the wedding, that's all."

Well, that and his stuck-up, superior attitude, Maggie thought.

"Maybe the best way forward," Maggie said, "would be if you could set up a meeting with the two of us and Owen, so we can smooth out any misunderstandings?"

Jack nodded and looked relieved. Maggie might be gentle in some aspects of her life, but business wasn't one of them. She would try playing fair with Owen—but if that didn't work, well, there were other ways.

Chapter 17

Jenny

I dipped my paintbrush in water and painted in Charlie's ears and the darker parts of his face. He was the first chinchilla I'd ever painted, but he was turning out to be pretty cute.

My children's book was finally starting to take shape. I'd been coming around to Dad's a couple of evenings a week after work, when Dan was working late, and going up to my old room to work on it. I'd told Dad and Chris that I was working on a project, but hadn't told them what, and I hadn't said a word to Dan yet. The book was my little secret. When I was drawing, all the other things on my mind drifted away—Zoe's increasingly rude and unreasonable demands; how to make ends meet for the wedding . . .

Putting together the book also took me back to the

time after Mum left, when I was six and Dad was sometimes too tired to read to me. I'd get cozy in bed and look through my picture books before I fell asleep, Dad asleep next door and Chris downstairs. Those pictures and stories had made everything seem OK and helped me forget how much I was missing Mum. Now I liked the idea that maybe I could do that for another boy or girl somewhere—take them off to a different world for a while where they were safe and happy, whatever their real life was like.

I'd mostly been working on pictures of Jake so far, sketching out different poses for the little boy before trying the best ones in paint. He was chubby and sweet—keeping quiet at the dinner table, waiting for night to fall so he could go on another adventure with his chinchilla friend. I had my iPod on as I worked, and was listening to a summertime playlist Chloe had made. It was full of upbeat tunes, and shut out the sounds of Dad banging around in his workshop downstairs. I heard someone call out and removed my headphones.

"Jennnnnny," Chris's voice came. "Are you even still up there?"

"Sorry, Chris. Yes, I'm here!" I called back. I put the painting things to one side and went over to the banister to talk to him on the floor below.

"Ah, you *are* there," he said, without his usual smile.

"Headphones," I said, pointing to my ears, "couldn't hear a thing, sorry."

"Ah, cool, fine. Dinner's up, if you're hungry."

"Great, I'm starving actually. I'll be right down."

When I got down to the kitchen, Dad was dishing up chicken stir-fry onto three plates.

"You OK, love?" he said. "How's your project going?"

"Well, thanks," I said, taking a seat. As if it were something important, like research, rather than rodent-painting. "I've done quite a lot today."

Dad sat down and Chris wheeled up to the space at the end. Dad put our plates in front of us without saying a word. I glanced over at Chris, looking for some clue from him.

"Dad, come on." Chris looked serious. "Are you going to say something or am I?"

"What is it with the awkwardness?" I said.

"There's something I've been wanting to talk to you about, sweetheart," Dad said.

"Oh, is there?" So that's why he'd been acting so oddly lately. "What's up, Dad? Is it about the wedding? Look, I've told you before, I'm not expecting you to pay towards it. Dan and I have it just about covered. OK, not quite but we will soon."

"It's not that, Jen." Dad looked down. He looked tired right now, older than he should.

"What Dad's trying to tell you," Chris said, sitting up straighter, "is that Mum called him the other day."

"Mum?" I said, my voice hoarse. I put down the fork

that had been en route to my mouth. Mum wasn't in touch with us. She didn't call up, for a chat, just to see how we were doing. She hadn't even sent a birthday card for ten years.

"When? What did she want?" My chest and face were burning hot.

"About two weeks ago," Dad said. "I wasn't really expecting it." As ever, master of the understatement. "You know it's been twenty years since we last saw her? And ten since those last birthday cards."

Chris put his hand on mine and squeezed it, he didn't even have to look at me to know what I was thinking. Dad obviously felt the need to say all this out loud, maybe it was his way of making it more real. Chris and I didn't need reminding though, the dates were engraved on both of our minds.

When we were kids we'd tried to forget about Mum. Dad was so busy most of the time, keeping an eye on me and making sure Chris went along to his special play-group and doctor's appointments. He'd keep us enter-tained with games and activities so that we didn't have much time to sit around talking or thinking about it. But looking back now there was something missing. Dad had changed. It was as if he was stuck on tramlines, taking us to the places we needed to be but otherwise keeping to the house. If he had any time to himself he'd be out the back with his carpentry, sawing and nailing something together. Friends and family would call up, or come by, but he'd hardly say a word to them, just "yes" or "no" or "fine thanks." Even as a child I knew that he just wanted all those people to leave him alone. We were a unit and we muddled along together. We got along OK. Most of the time we were happy, in fact. In spite of the challenges he faced, Chris always wore a smile, and we used to play together a lot. We were just like other kids.

Then one day when I was seven, Emma, pretty and slim and the most popular girl in my class, came up to me in the playground. My heart had lifted, I was finally going to be asked to join in her game of French elastics. "Laura dared me to ask you something," she said, a laugh bubbling up in her voice. I could see her friends on the other side of the playground watching on. "Why's your mum never there to pick you up after school?" She tilted her face waiting for my response.

My headband was really digging into my head, and the plastic teeth were sharp. I tried to think of an answer. The stupid headband was too small, I thought as I moved the side bits. I'd told Dad the red one was better. Emma came closer to me. I could see all the freckles on her nose now. She smelled of strawberry Hubba Bubba. "Is it because you don't have a mum?" she asked, glancing back at Laura and the other girls, who were laughing.

I'd come home crying that night. I can still remember the raw feeling in my throat from sobbing, it had stung as I gulped my juice while Dad calmed me down. That was when he told me what had happened: that Mum had loved us all, but it hadn't been working living together, and one day Dad had come home and she wasn't there anymore. As teenagers Chris and I found out from Uncle Dave, Mum's brother, that soon after leaving us Mum had moved in with an ex-boyfriend of hers in Eastbourne. My guess is it was actually right after she left, but Uncle Dave didn't say that. I think he was probably trying to soften the blow.

"I'm sorry that your mum didn't stick it out with your dad, because he's a good bloke," he'd said. "But we all make our choices." Uncle Dave was a Hell's Angel. His choice was to spend his life on the road with other bikers, never tied down, so we didn't see him much, but Chris and I had always enjoyed it when he stopped by.

"I couldn't believe it when I heard her voice." Dad shook his head and looked away, recalling the recent memory. "But there she was." He looked back at me. "Our phone number's never changed, has it? I suppose she knew it by heart."

"Are you really telling me she called two weeks ago," I said, his words finally sinking in, "and you didn't think to mention it till now?"

"I know," Dad said. "I'm sorry. You just seem to have a lot on your plate at the moment. I should have said something sooner."

I felt sick to my stomach. I turned to face Chris.

"Look, Jen, I only heard about this yesterday. And it's weird for me too, believe me."

"It was you she really wanted to speak to, love," Dad

said, looking at me, his eyes weary and sad. "It was actually you she called about."

"Me?" My voice come out as a whisper. "Why?"

"Because . . . she'd been in touch with your cousin Angie. Found her on Facebook, she said. Angie told her to leave you be, that you had other things to think about, with the wedding and everything."

My heart was racing now. I waited for him to finish the story.

"The thing is," Dad started, "Sue—your mum—I don't think she really took it in, what Ange said. I guess she only heard the part about you getting married."

"Jen," Dad continued, cautiously. "She thinks she should be there."

"Be where?" I snapped back.

"At your wedding," Dad said. "Your mum wants to come."

Chris and I moved to the living room while Dad loaded the dishwasher. I'd told them both that there was no way I was going to return Mum's call. It really was as simple as that.

"You can take some time to think about it," Chris said. "Your wedding's not tomorrow."

"Time to think about what?" I said. "I don't see how you can be so understanding, Chris. How dare she do this? She's got two children, she can't just call up wanting to talk to me."

"I don't want to be in the middle of this, Jen," Chris said. "I've already got in the way of your relationship once, and I don't want to again. If you want her there at your wedding, you should let her come."

I shook my head. It was a mystery to me how Chris seemed to have let go of the resentment everyone expected him to have.

"I mean I'm not justifying what she did," Chris said. "Of course not. But I pity her, that's all. For whatever reason the fact she couldn't cope with me back then stopped her being your mum, too. Now we're all adults and things are different, we can make our own choices, and maybe you should give her a chance."

"Chris, I'm not having this conversation," I said. "You're my family, Dad is my family—and Mum, Sue, whoever she is, is just a woman who abandoned us."

"OK. I still think you should sleep on it," Chris said.

"I don't need to sleep on it." I felt something build up in me, anger, frustration, I don't know what, but it seemed like no one in my family could see that there was no discussion to be had here, and I knew I was in danger of taking it out on Chris. "I've talked enough tonight. I'm going home."

I got back to the flat just before nine, with a heavy heart and a head busy with thoughts. Bath and bed, that was what I needed. As I turned my key in the lock, though, I heard raised voices. I'd completely forgotten that Dan's best friend Russ was coming around tonight.

"Hi, Jen," Dan called out from the living room, where the two of them were playing MarioKart with the volume up high. Half-empty foil cartons lay strewn across the coffee table, curry dripping onto the glass top. Russ was swigging from a bottle of Becks. "*Woahhhhhhh*," Dan said, starting at the screen and moving the controller so that his kart went over to the left, "the lava nearly got me that time."

Russ called out "Hi, Jen," and flashed me a cheeky grin. I went into the kitchen to fix myself a cocoa. It was chaos in there, as if they'd raided it before settling in the living room. I put the kettle on and then started to tidy slowly and methodically, putting empty glasses and dirty plates in the dishwasher, trying to calm the annoyance welling up in me as I realized I was barely making a dent in the disarray. I took my cocoa into our bedroom, changed into my pajamas and got into bed. I looked at the clock and willed it to go faster, it was only nine-thirty. I got out a copy of the Marian Keyes I was halfway through and looked for my page, but the shouts from the front room were too loud for me to concentrate. Instead I just lay in bed, my mind racing. All I wanted to do was sleep, but the noise was getting louder—each time I closed my eyes and started to drift off I'd be woken up again. At around half one I heard Dan see Russ out. He creaked open the bedroom door and crept in, but noisily, in that drunk-person-being-quiet way.

"Dan," I said, looking up. "You don't need to tiptoe. I'm not asleep."

"Oh hi, babe, I thought you would be. It's late, isn't it?"

"Yes, pretty late." I rolled over, away from him, and tried to make myself drift off. Dan didn't seem to have a clue how wound up I was. Then I turned back around, unable to hold in my frustration any longer. "Did you really think I'd be able to sleep with all that noise you and Russ were making?"

Dan was taking off his T-shirt and had got it stuck over his head. His words muffled through the cotton, "Oh, sorry about that." He wrestled himself free. "But you know I haven't seen Russ for ages." He undid his jeans, pulled them off and climbed into bed beside me. "And you said you'd be at your dad's till late, didn't you?"

"I didn't feel like staying after all." He cuddled up to me in bed. Why couldn't he tell that things weren't OK?

I pushed him away and sat up. "Dan, this is my flat too, and I want to be able to get to sleep when I've had a long day." My voice was shrill, I didn't sound like me.

"Fair enough," he said. "I'll be quieter next time."

"But, Dan," I went on, not able to stop myself now, as the words came pouring out. "We're not students anymore, you know."

He looked at me, confused. "I know that, Jen," he said. He reached out an arm to touch me but I moved away.

"Don't touch me. Just don't." I carried on, my voice

louder now. "I get tired of being the grown-up, sometimes I need an adult to be with too. I'm spending all this time planning for our future and you—"

"Hang on, Jen. This isn't fair," Dan said, firmly, his brow furrowed. "I've been working all hours this past week, just to get money so that you can have the wedding day that you want, and—"

"So what are you saying?" I said, sitting up straighter. "That it's not the day *you* want? That you're not bothered what we do?" I felt a lump come to my throat. "Don't do me any favors, Dan, please."

"What?" Dan said, searching my face for something he'd missed. "Where's this all coming from? Of course I want our wedding to be great too. And it will be."

"But it won't." I was resolute. "It won't be."

I thought back to the vintage dress I'd splashed out on and which was now hidden away in my wardrobe. I hadn't even dared to tell Dan how much it cost. I knew that even with the extra hours he'd been putting in we were at risk of going over budget. Bigger than all of that, though, was the thought that my mum, after all this time, was trying to muscle in on our day. Where did I even start with that? How could I explain how that felt to Dan, or to anyone? My head spun; this was it, our dream wedding day was going to be ruined by debt and family drama.

Dan looked at me, his brow creased, and even in the heat of the moment I knew I wasn't thinking straight. I couldn't understand where all of this anger was coming from. The stress of the evening at Dad's, and the last few weeks, had reached fever pitch and I no longer felt in control.

"Jen, don't be silly—all that matters is you and me getting married," he said, staring straight at me. "I thought we'd talked this through?"

"Silly?" I said, shouting at him now, gathering up the spare blanket and wrapping it around me. "You think I'm being *silly* now?" My cheeks were burning with fury. "Can't you see it's all going to be ruined?" I turned my back on him and marched out of the room, but as soon as I'd closed the door my eyes blurred with tears.

I took the blanket and dragged myself into the living room. It still smelt of curry, but Dan wasn't there, and that was a good thing. I curled up on the sofa with a cushion under my head and stared up at the white wall. A shaft of moonlight was cutting across it. I could hear the distant hum of motorway traffic.

Our argument echoed in my head. Was this what married life was going to be like? Cross words and compromises? As I thought of how dismissive Dan had been, my dress and my mum's reappearance slipped right down my list of worries. It felt like he didn't understand me at all. I pulled the blanket closer around me, and closed my eyes.

Chapter 18

Jenny

"Going once . . ."

Alison gripped the sleeve of my rose-patterned cardigan tightly, and I held my breath.

"Going twice . . ."

Maggie, on my left, had my other arm in a viselike grip.

"And . . ."

"*Ouch*," I yelped, as Maggie's hold got even tighter, pinching my skin.

"Oops, sorry," she whispered to me, as an old lady in the row in front of us gave us a disapproving glance over her shoulder. "Nerves."

"Sold, to the lady at the back." The elderly auctioneer squinted to see, and Alison let go of my cardigan and stood up to give him a better look. "In the fetching red dress."

We cheered as Alison sat back down and turned to us.

"Well done us," Ali said, with a smile. "What a complete bargain."

We'd come along to the local antiques auction with modest expectations. There'd been a lot of tat for sale, admittedly; cat statuettes and a giant serving plate shaped like a carp. But among it we'd spotted and snapped up a prize 1930s tea set. And Maggie had bought some art deco glass-fronted wooden cabinets for Bluebelle.

Going to the auction wasn't exactly what I'd felt like doing when I'd woken up that morning. I'd been stiff from a night on the sofa, and it felt weird that Dan had already gone out. He plays football every Saturday morning, but normally we find time for a lie-in together with the papers before he heads to the park. This morning I'd slept late though, until just after eleven. I'd dashed to get myself washed and dressed in time for Maggie, who was picking me up in her car.

"Shall we call it a day, go out on a high?" I asked the others. I didn't want to be a killjoy, but I was finding it hard to rustle up my usual enthusiasm for the teacup hunt this morning.

"Leave before we bankrupt ourselves, you mean?" Maggie said. "Yes, that's probably a sensible idea."

"Tea?" Alison said. We both nodded.

There was a makeshift stand in the adjoining room, which sold polystyrene cups of tea and coffee, and paper plates of cakes and raisin scones. We sat on plastic chairs at a wooden table and Maggie got her sketchbook out. With everyone else still at the auction, we practically had the place to ourselves. Our voices echoed off the walls.

"The Mad Hatter's tea party was always my favorite part," Alison said, as Maggie showed her some of her sketches for the wedding. "When he gets the measuring tape out to measure people's heads for hats? I loved that. Anyway, I think filling the teacups with flowers is going to look great."

Maggie spread our treasures out on the wide wooden table—so that we could all take a second look. The lady running the stand had raised her eyebrows a fraction as she brought over our teas and struggled to find a space to put our drinks down. Maggie moved the teacups aside to make room. She looked serene and elegant today, dressed in an emerald green shirtdress with simple gold bangles that jangled to announce her every move. Her hair was held back at the sides with vintage bronze hairclips. But it wasn't any of that which made her look so different today—it was the sparkle in her eyes; she seemed softer, magnetic.

I felt the opposite—tired, brittle and hurt after the row. Alison's dark hair looked sleek, pulled back into a ponytail with a quiff styled forward, but my guess was that in spite of the makeup and her scarlet dress, she wasn't at her best either.

"Thanks for lending me the books, Jenny," Maggie

said warmly, handing them back to me. "I think getting the details right will help give me the edge on Owen."

"I thought you said that the bride wanted to see you work better *together*?" Alison said.

"Yes, that's right." Maggie laughed, her hair glossy under the strip lights. "As long as I'm *better* when we're working together."

"Maggie." I narrowed my eyes at her. "You're all . . . *radiant*." I pointed at her cheeks. "You've got this *glowy* thing going on." She also seemed to have an irrepressible smile on her face. "Is there something you should be telling us?"

"Ha ha. Sort of," she said, coyly. Alison and I exchanged a look.

"Yeesss?" Alison and I prompted in unison. By the looks of things Alison needed cheering up with some gossip as badly as I did.

"Is it Dylan?" I guessed. Maggie had mentioned that their meet had gone well, but she hadn't given many details.

"Yes, it's Dylan," Maggie said, looking as if she might spill over with the news. "It's a long story, and it's early days, but I'm beginning to think this one might just have a happy ending."

By the time Maggie had finished filling us in we'd drained a tea each and munched our way through flapjacks, a slice of carrot cake and a slab of millionaire's shortbread. Alison and I had listened, rapt, as Maggie talked.

"Like I told you, back when I met Dylan I thought him being The One would make it all go smoothly, but of course it didn't. At all."

Alison nodded in that knowing way she had.

"But now I feel we're meeting as two different people, people who know better what it takes to make a relationship work."

"Four years is a long time," I said, thinking back to the early days of my relationship with Dan.

"It is," Maggie continued. "And I think we've both grown up, realized what it is we want and need. I've always been a bit of a romantic, I suppose. I'm not sure that real love ever goes away."

"But doesn't he live in New York?" Alison said. "I mean, I don't want to put a damper on things, but what does that mean, in terms of the two of you?"

"New York is still his base, but he might be able to get a few jobs here in England over the summer. He'll be in Charlesworth tomorrow, as it happens. He wants to see the shop, my house, my life here. I've said he can keep his stuff at mine while he's traveling around," Maggie said, smiling. "So he's not such a hobo, I mean."

"Wow, things are moving along pretty quickly," Alison was still smiling but she had a questioning look in her eye.

"Life is short," Maggie replied, without any hesitation.

"And we already know each other through and through. I don't really see the point in waiting around any longer."

"Well he certainly sounds gorgeous," I said. New York, his photography, the passionate reunion Maggie had told us about . . . he did. Living in Charlesworth most of my life I hadn't really met any men like that. "Before I forget," I said. "Sorry to change the subject, but I've got a date for your diaries—my hen night. Saturday July the eighteenth."

I glanced at my phone as I spoke and the high I felt about my upcoming hen mixed with a sinking feeling when I saw the time. It was two o'clock. Dan hadn't texted me after his football game. He always texted me.

"Ooh," Alison said. "Your hen. Excellent. It's been a *very* long time since I went on one of those." Maggie got her diary out and wrote it in.

"Hey, isn't that . . . ?" Maggie caught sight of someone out of the hall's grand windows. I turned in time to see Pete walk by. Alison immediately put a hand up to her face and turned her head so that he wouldn't be able to see her through the glass.

"Alison!" Maggie said, teasing. "Are you *hiding* from your husband? What's going on?"

Alison wasn't laughing though. The color had drained from her face. "Don't. I just want a break from everything today." Alison's strength and confidence seemed to dissolve away in an instant.

"But I thought things were going well," Maggie pressed

her. "The offer from Jamie, the new café. You sounded really excited."

I nodded. "It sounded great, Ali. Was Pete not keen?" I asked.

"You know what, it's just not happening," Alison said, her voice flat. "I've told Jamie I can't do it."

I looked out the window and watched Pete's back disappear from view. He was laughing, I realized then. And he was with a woman whose dark-red hair fell in waves.

Chapter 19

Maggie

"But we can't have people actually falling down a rabbit hole." Maggie shook her head. "That doesn't make any sense."

She was at Joey's café with Jack and Owen. Jack had gone to order sandwiches for their lunch, leaving the other two to discuss their ideas.

"They won't really be falling down it, Maggie," Owen said, speaking slowly like he was talking to a child. "It'll be like a tunnel that they walk through. We'll build sculpted archways and grow plants over them." Maggie listened, trying to picture it. She was struggling. As Owen talked, dark curls of hair fell across his eyes and he pushed them back.

"A tunnel. And the wedding guests will be like moles

in holes?" Maggie challenged him, a childish urge to put down his ideas proving impossible to resist.

Owen closed his eyes briefly and breathed out slowly through his mouth before his eyes came to rest on her again. "Rather than grown adults hula-hooping, you mean?"

Maggie opened her mouth ready to let the insults fly. Just then Jack arrived back at the table, putting plates of sandwiches between them.

"Was it the lychee and passion smoothie you wanted, Maggie?" She nodded. "And apple juice for you, Owen?" Owen nodded too, unable to hide his irritation with Maggie. Jack looked puzzled and turned back towards the counter.

Owen started to explain again, leaning towards her, his tanned forearms resting on the table. Maggie bristled. She hated having to keep quiet, but it was the only sensible thing to do. This boy must have been at least six years her junior, couldn't have worked on nearly as many weddings . . . in fact, come to think of it, had he even worked on *any*? And yet *he* was patronizing *her*? She felt the annoyance start to build up again. She bit her tongue, so that Jack wouldn't see them at odds again—the whole point of the meeting was to show that they could get on.

"The point of the tunnel is really only visible on the inside," Owen explained. "As guests walk through, they'll see that the walls are covered in flowers, as well as the books and jam jars, the things that Alice notices when she falls. There will be spaces in the structure, so that shafts

of sunlight are coming through to light up the inside."
Owen indicated with his hand how the tunnel would work.

"It'll be angled downhill, so guests will have the experience of downward movement, and it means that when they land at the bottom—on the chessboard floor—they'll be through and into Alice's world, with croquet, mushrooms and everything else."

Maggie had to admit that she was starting to warm to the idea. But she still wasn't completely convinced it would work. "What about elderly guests? Lucy's grandparents? Will they be whizzing down the rabbit hole too?"

"It's a slope, Maggie, not a fairground ride," Owen said, his voice softening a little. "And if anyone has mobility issues they can just go down the ramp to reach the Alice garden instead."

"Hmm," Maggie said, finding nothing else to object to. "It does sound like quite a good idea, I suppose," she conceded. Owen raised an eyebrow. He sat back in his chair, but he looked tired, not smug like Maggie had expected.

"I hope orange juice will do," Jack said, returning to the table, putting the drinks down and pulling up a chair to join them. "I honestly don't know why Joey's even write a menu when they never seem to have anything on it."

Maggie heard her phone ring in her bag—when she got it Dylan's name flashed up on the screen. "Excuse me a minute, would you? It's a work call I have to answer." Moving away from the table she pressed the green button. "Hello?"

Outside, a couple of people were smoking in front of the café, so she moved to the side of them, stopping outside the window right in front of Owen and Jack.

"Hi, M." Dylan's voice sent a tingle over her skin. "How's your day going?"

"Good, thanks, I'm at a meeting about the Darlington Hall wedding I told you about. The big one, with that intolerable guy? But otherwise it's all going well."

A little girl dropped her lollipop on the pavement by Maggie's feet while her mother's back was turned. As she picked it up, dirt and a leaf clinging to it, Maggie reached down to stop the girl putting it back in her mouth. The mother spun round, threw Maggie a dirty look, and pulled her child away. The little girl was sucking on her lolly, and looked pretty content. As Maggie stood to her full height again she caught Owen looking at her through the glass, and quickly turned her back to the window.

"Ah the challenges of working life," Dylan said, "I wish you luck with it, sweetheart."

"And how's your day?" Maggie inquired. "Are you still in Brick Lane?"

"Yes," Dylan said, animated. "It's a great shoot actually, it's good to be back in the East End. There's so much to photograph here, and there's nothing quite like it in the States. But listen, Maggie, are you still on for tonight? Maybe we could have a romantic dinner at yours?"

"Yes, sure," Maggie said, "I'll pick up some food for us on the way home."

"Perfect. There's something I want to talk to you about, actually," Dylan said.

"OK," Maggie said, checking her watch and realizing she should bring the conversation to a close, even though she could have talked for hours. "Just come over whenever you're ready. I'll be back by seven or so."

"See you then," Dylan said.

When she stepped back inside, Owen and Jack had started on the food and Owen was talking, waving a hand at his friend to emphasize the point he was making.

"But seriously, last season we didn't take home any silverware and it drives me crazy."

Maggie settled into her seat and reached for a duck wrap.

"Honestly, we deserve more than this and if we had a decent manager . . ."

"But it's not just that," Jack said, "morale's been low for a while and I think it's to do with—"

Jack finally noticed Maggie and raised a hand very slightly to signal the end of the football conversation. Owen shook his head and looked down, clearly wanting to finish their chat, but deferred to his friend and, at this point, boss, on the matter.

"Sorry, Maggie. Everything OK with your work call?" Jack asked.

"Oh yes, fine, thanks," she said, taking a delicate bite of the wrap. A bit too much soy sauce, but still pretty good. Joey must have employed a new chef. They never seemed to last long, though.

"I wish all my clients made me smile that much," Owen said, half under his breath.

Maggie narrowed her eyes at him. "And just how many clients do you have, Owen? I'm dying to know. Got many weddings of this size under your belt, have you?"

"Maggie, I'm thirty-one, not thirteen," Owen said, not rising to her bait, "so do me a favor and st—"

It was Jack's look of panic that made Maggie step in. "Sorry, Jack." She said, putting a hand on his arm. "We're friends really, aren't we, Owen?"

"Oh yes," he said, a weary look in his eye. Was he really in his thirties? Maggie thought. He looked younger.

"So." She got out her notebook and wiped off a tiny smudge of soy that had fallen on it. "We've agreed on the following ideas, and I'll get some costings. Look, here's the list. She turned it so that Jack and Owen could see and they read carefully through it.

"OK, yes—looks good to me," Owen said. "Jack, what do you think?"

"Great, yes. Email it to me and I'll run it by Luce tonight," Jack said, smiling and relaxing for the first time.

"Owen—once we have Lucy's OK, we can work out quantities and finalize the orders."

"Sounds good," Owen said. "Although with the tunnel, I'm not sure which flowers are going to work best. I've got a structure at my workshop, a mini version. You might want to look at that for ideas?"

"Oh yes, Maggie," Jack said. "You should definitely go and see it, it's really cool. Owen's workshop's only about twenty minutes' drive from here."

"I see, yes," Maggie said. She'd hoped to wind up the rest of the planning without too much face-to-face with Owen, but it would be useful to see his model to work out which colors would be best to weave in. "I can't today, though," she said, motioning for the bill. "And to be honest the whole of this week's pretty manic. I have a wedding in Hove. How about two weeks' time? Shall we put something in the diary?" She got hers out.

"You *are* a busy lady," Owen said, "but sure, there's no hurry. How about Friday, the tenth of July?"

The waitress brought the bill over on a saucer and Maggie passed her the cash, hushing Jack's protests. "Sure. Friday the tenth it is."

Maggie gathered her things. "OK, I've got to shoot. I don't like to leave Anna alone for too long. The truth is she's getting so good at her job I'm worried she might take over." Maggie smiled and reached out to shake Jack's hand, then Owen's, but this time his eyes didn't meet hers. "Do give my best to Lucy, Jack. I look forward to hearing what she thinks of the ideas."

*

"The scallops look good," Maggie said. She'd popped into the fishmonger after shutting up the shop that afternoon. "Yes, fresh in this morning, as always," the man replied.

"Could I have a dozen, please," she said, and scanned the display to see whether there was anything else she could add.

The fishmonger handed the scallops to her in a bag. She'd get some fresh asparagus and prosciutto from the supermarket on the drive home, and pick up some samphire. For dessert there was butterscotch ice cream in the freezer and some raspberries, and there was plenty of white in the wine rack.

She stepped back outside. The high street was buzzing, the pavements lively with people enjoying the warm summer evening. She put her shopping and handbag on the passenger seat of her Beetle. She didn't know exactly where she and Dylan were headed, no, but there were butterflies in her stomach and she was looking forward to seeing him as much as she had when they'd first met.

Maggie was sitting in the living room with a glass of sparkling water when she saw Dylan pull up into the drive in a green convertible MG. She leapt up and went to the door, where he met her with a bouquet of stargazer lilies and a kiss.

"Hello, gorgeous," he said, handing her the flowers.

"Hello," she said, taking the flowers from him with a

smile. "And thank you, these are beautiful." Lilies weren't her favorite—she'd looked after too many funerals for that—but these ones were very pretty.

"Phew," Dylan said, pretending to wipe the sweat from his brow. "It's never been easy buying flowers for you, you know."

Maggie laughed. "And the car?" she said, craning her neck to see it.

"I rented it today. Seemed worth it as I'll be traveling around England a bit—what do you think?"

"Very nice," she said.

"Fancy a quick spin?" Dylan asked.

"I'd really like to, maybe another evening though," Maggie said, looking back into the house where she had been preparing their dinner.

"Sure," he said, stepping inside.

Maggie led Dylan through to the kitchen and he slipped a hand around her waist as she walked.

"Glass of Prosecco?" she asked, picking up a bottle from the counter.

"Yes, please," he replied.

She popped the cork and as she turned to fill two slim glasses he kissed the nape of her neck. He'd always liked it when she wore her hair swept up like it was tonight. The back of her flowery dress was low, and with his kisses the spaghetti strap slipped off her shoulder. He held her, but his kisses stopped suddenly as he took a step back.

"Your tattoo, Maggie," he said, running a finger over

her shoulder blade and following his touch with another kiss. "Your songbird. I've missed it."

She turned around to pass Dylan his glass, and there was sadness in his eyes.

"It's so good to have you back, Maggie. I don't know how I let you go."

"So I'd forgotten how spectacular the colors in Brick Lane are," Dylan said later, as they sat in the dining room during the meal. "The Bangladeshi sweet shops, you know, the ones filled with pinks and oranges, all those delicious-looking treats . . . and then the sari shops? Incredible. I sent some of the first pictures over to the American client and they went crazy for the concept."

"Oh really, yes I—" Maggie started.

"Said they wanted *all* the photos taken there," Dylan said.

"That's nice," Maggie said.

Over dinner they talked through old times, the years when they were first together, the paths it was safe to retread, the days before they were married. They reminisced about the cramped but cozy one-bedroom flat they'd lived in back then. Maggie had been training up in flower arrangement and brought in a bit of cash from her jazz singing; Dylan was learning the ropes as assistant to a notoriously demanding photographer. Slowly though, the conversation had shifted back to the here and now, and Dylan told her about his work plans for the summer.

"I have a new client who wants something completely different. They're a Boston-based fashion brand, classic, far less edgy, targeted at a middle-aged, more conservative market. They're putting together their autumn catalog now."

"Is that a bigger job?" Maggie said, passing him a bowl as she opened the ice cream tub.

"In a way, but it's pretty straightforward. They always pay on time, but to be honest it's not my favorite type of work—it's very tame. Have a look for yourself," Dylan said, getting a spring catalog out of his bag to show her. She flicked through the pages, taking in the glossy shots of flawless models in floral blouses and pressed chinos.

"See what I mean?" he said.

"Sort of," Maggie replied.

"But this project does come with an advantage—or rather the potential for advantage."

"Oh yes, and what's that?" she asked, tilting her head slightly.

"This is what I wanted to talk to you about." A smile spread over Dylan's face. "The look they're going for this time is quintessentially English," he said. "You know, pretty twee," he laughed. "Not a style I'm nuts about, but the upside is that Charlesworth is the perfect location."

Maggie flinched inwardly at his comment. Charlesworth was her home now, after all, and she was really fond of its quaint cottages, lilting pace of life, and the rolling hills that surrounded it.

"I'm thinking of doing a shoot up in the cornfields,"

Dylan said, and Maggie warmed to the idea. The expanse of warm yellow she could see from her bedroom was one of her favorite things about the house, and she was glad he could appreciate the beauty there.

"But I think what they'll probably like best," Dylan continued, "are photos taken on the green, with the high street in the background. You know what I mean, a few old ladies doddering around in the background, outside the post office maybe."

"OK," Maggie said, trying to imagine how an outsider would see the place where she worked and lived.

"The thing is," Dylan started, "it would mean I'd be able to stay here in Sussex for most of the summer. Luca has offered to keep an eye on the U.S. side of the business for me."

Maggie was listening, but she wasn't sure she was really keeping up with what he was saying.

"What do you think?" he asked, his face expectant.

"About which part?" Maggie said, trying to piece together what he'd been saying. Dylan had been talking so quickly she'd lost track.

"I love your house, it's beautiful. But more importantly, and I hope you know this by now—I'm still in love with you." He took her hands in his, over the table. Her heart was beating hard now. "Would you have room for me here?" His dark blue eyes were wide, waiting for her answer. "Let's live together, just the two of us again."

Chapter 20

Alison

"OK, girls, it's half eight—you should be out of the door by now," Alison shouted upstairs, holding a hot mug of tea in her hands. Holly came running down first, her rucksack and PE kit bag in one hand, school shoes in the other. She sat at the bottom of the stairs doing up her laces, dodging enthusiastic licks from George and getting the giggles.

Sophie came down next, at a more leisurely pace, tying her black hair back in a hairband. "There's no hurry," Sophie said, her voice cool. "I'm not going with Dad. Matt's driving me into school today."

"Oh he is, is he?" Alison said, caught off-guard. She adjusted her posture to compensate, put her shoulders back and ensured her face gave away none of her worry. She was really starting to long for the Sophie who'd been her friend, rather than her constant adversary. "Well I hope he's got time to come in and meet us first."

Holly looked up eagerly. Sophie rolled her eyes. "Of course not. Don't be silly, Mum, we'd be late." Holly's face fell, and Alison's heart did too, as she felt her last shred of power slip out of her hands. "And I don't want you guys peering out of the front window at us either."

"He better be a safe driver," Alison said, trying to claw some control back. "When did he pass his test? Come to think of it, how old is he?"

"Eighteen. He passed his test ages ago." Sophie shrugged off her mother's concern. Eighteen? So he'd really only just passed. And he was three years older than her—wasn't three years a pretty big age gap? Alison's patience was wearing thin. She hadn't been sleeping well for days, kept up by worries about money. She couldn't face starting today with another argument with Sophie. She looked at her watch.

"OK, fine, Sophie. Have it your way this time. Hol— seeing as it's just you, could you nip over to Amy's house and see if her mum can fit you in their car? It'd give Dad a bit more time this morning."

"Sure, Mum," Holly said, getting up. Alison gave her a kiss on the head goodbye.

"And, Soph, don't worry," she said, turning to her elder daughter and trying to lighten the atmosphere, "we won't be staring out the window. Believe it or not, we have better things to do." Sophie's face was blank and she didn't respond. "Just make sure Matt drives slowly. And bring him in next time, will you?"

Once Holly had left, Alison walked through to the living room, where Pete was sitting reading the paper.

"You're off the hook this morning, darling. Holly's getting a lift with the Boltons and Sophie's new boyfriend's giving her a lift to school. He's eighteen, Pete. What do you think about that?"

Pete didn't look up. "Hmm," he replied, turning a page.

"Did you hear what I said, Pete?"

"Yep," he said, glancing up from a feature about house prices, his eyes wide and innocent. "No school run this morning. Great."

"Pete," Alison started, but he'd started reading again, sinking deeper into the Chesterfield sofa. I will not ask him what he's going to do this morning instead, Alison thought. I will definitely not ask him that.

But God—was he really just going to sit there?

By midday, Pete had interrupted Alison's work six times. Where was the fabric softener? Was Holly's costume for the school play sorted? When he came in asking where the rubber gloves were she finally cracked.

"Pete—look," she told him, turning away from the sewing machine where she'd been making some patchwork cushion covers to sell on the website. "I know I'm at home," she said, "but I can't be available all the time."

Pete's eyes widened and he looked hurt. Alison went on, "I mean, imagine if I'd walked into your old office, found you at your computer and asked you where you'd put the Fairy Liquid."

Alison's words hung between them. Then Pete's face changed, his expression hardened.

"I do understand." Pete paused for a moment. "I'm not stupid. I'm trying to keep the house in order and make sure the girls have what they need." Color was starting to rise in his face now. "And back when you used to do it, I'm pretty sure you always said that was a proper job." Alison searched for the words to defend herself, but Pete carried on. "I'm sick of you having a go at me, Ali. I know things are not easy financially, but . . ."

"But—but what, Pete?" Alison sat forward in her wicker chair, her frustration rising further. "You know what, 'not easy' doesn't even cover it anymore."

Pete nodded. "I know," he said, avoiding eye contact with her.

"We could lose our home, Pete." Pete was listening and looking up now, but his expression gave nothing away. Alison wondered if the words were even going in. "And now here I am trying to make us some money so that we can keep a roof over our heads, so that I can start to think about getting my mum the help she needs, and you're, you're . . ." She felt like she was holding on to her temper by the tiniest thread.

"I'm what, Ali?" Pete said, reacting at last.

Despair took hold as Alison answered him. "Pete, you say you're doing the housework but the last time I came out you were watching *Cash in the Attic* and eating Hobnobs. Have you even looked at the job sites today? When was the last time you even glanced at that section in the paper, rather than reading the sports?" Pete shuffled uncomfortably and cast his eyes down.

Alison's heart sank. She couldn't believe how much pain she was causing him. And the nagging tone of her own voice—who was this harridan she was becoming?

"I don't know how we got here, but it can't go on like this." Alison pulled on her red wool cardigan and started doing up the buttons. She had to get away from Pete, away from the house. "I'm going out."

"So that's the solution, is it?" Pete said, running a hand through his hair. "You just walk out when things get difficult?"

Alison glared at him. "Oh, if only, Pete," she said, growing numb now to the hurt they were causing one another. "You know how untrue that is. For months now I've been patient, trying to earn us all a living."

Pete sat down on a wooden chair by the doorway, and his head fell into his hands. "Alison," came the quiet response. "I know you think I am, but I'm not lazy."

Alison could hear the desperation and sadness in his voice. "I was looking, and looking—but you know how it is, the NHS. Some of the jobs that used to be there just don't exist anymore."

"I know that, Pete," Alison said, but her patience was gone now, "and I understand it's hard—but what are you going to do, just give up?"

Pete stared at her blankly. She pushed past him in the doorway, went down the hall and slammed the front door.

Chapter 21

Jenny

Nothing took my mind off my own problems quite like handling one of Chloe's emergencies. We were tucked away in an empty office that afternoon, with warm cups of tea and some Bourbon biscuits I'd sneaked out of the office supplies cupboard.

"It's my dad's sixtieth—that is clearly a big deal, Jen," Chloe said, holding back tears.

"Yep, I'd say so," I said, putting my arm around her. I hated seeing her upset like this.

"It just made me realize that Jon's never going to understand what I need from him, Jen. I mean he'd known about Dad's party for months—and then he tells me he's going to Ravi's stag instead. It's over. Completely over."

Chloe was working the mascara-streaked look better

than most. It wasn't elegant, but if you squinted it looked more sixties chic than office heartbreak.

I passed her a Bourbon.

"Why are you squinting at me?" Chloe asked, puzzled. "Anyway, I know I'm still young." She furrowed her brow. "I mean, twenty-five is still young, isn't it?"

I nodded. "Of course it is, you fool."

"And I want to focus on my career, for a while anyway," she went on. "But I don't want to be on my own forever, Jen. The thing is, I've been with Jon for so long now I don't think I'd know how to be with anyone else—or even find someone else." Chloe was yoga-toned, warm and naturally pretty. I'd give her five minutes on the singles' market, if that. So long as she could stay away from Jon for good this time, that was.

Through the frosted glass I saw a group of journalists approaching the door. "Ah, Chloe," I said, slapping a hand to my forehead. "I forgot I switched the rooms for the editorial meeting. They'll be in here in a minute or two, we're going to have to duck out." I reached over and used my sleeve to wipe away the most obvious mascara drips from under her eyes, before standing and helping her to her feet.

When we stepped outside the journalists were chatting to one another and didn't even seem to notice us walk by. But Ben, a cocky young reporter who'd just started and had been hovering around Chloe's desk since day one, spotted us—well, Chloe—right away. Sensing his chance he called out, "Cheer up, Chlo, it may—" but shut up when I gave him a glare.

Work was full-on and Zoe was still being a nightmare, but it was proving to be a welcome distraction. Back at my desk I got on with updating a document of articles, images and advertising required as we neared the print deadline—it was our busiest time and this month I was grateful for it. Things between me and Dan had been pretty strained since our row, and we'd reacted to the tension as we always did—by staying out of the house more than usual. As for my children's book . . . Whenever I picked up my pen or a paintbrush I'd go blank. Nothing came. My ideas for the story had dried up, and when I worked over existing outlines the results were clumsy—I'd end up leafing through old copies of *Smash Hits*, or staring out of the window. The conversation with Dad and Chris ran through my mind again and again. I'd started to question why I was spending all this time planning our wedding when Mum was there now, looming over it.

I sent the finished document on, then checked my emails. Stationery orders, meeting rooms to be booked. All fine. And one personal one. From Susan Haybridge. Subject line: Hello. *Haybridge.* My mum's maiden name. A chill ran through me. I clicked out of the inbox and looked over at Chloe, sitting at her desk with a sorrowful look on her face. "Tea?" I mouthed. She shook her head, nodding in Gary's direction to show she was snowed under with work.

I'd emptied my in tray, processed all the invoices, visited the water cooler twice, tidied my desk, sorted out Zoe's files, ordered Chloe those cat-shaped paperclips she liked—and it was still only quarter past eleven. Finally I opened the email from my mum. I felt dizzy. I could just delete it. I could just ignore her email, like she'd ignored us for the last however many years. What did I owe her? Nothing. *Nada. Niente.* But my eyes drifted back to the screen. *Dear Jenny*, I read.

Hello there. When your cousin Angie told me you were getting married all I could think was—my baby is all grown up. That's amazing, it really is.

I'd love to be there to see you tie the knot, Jenny. You know how proud I'd be.

Me and Nigel are down in Eastbourne. Maybe you know that. Anyway, it wouldn't take long to get to you, on the day.

Hope you are well, sweetheart. Angie said you've found yourself a good man.

Please write back.

Love, Mum xx

I closed the email before I was tempted to reread it. "Love, Mum." "You know how proud I'd be." The words were hollow and empty. How could she pretend to love me? How could she think she had a right to be proud of me? I was furious. Had she ever even known what it meant to love someone? She'd rejected Chris because he wasn't perfect—Chris, who we all adored, who everyone cared about, who looked after other people far more than they'd ever had to look after him. Now this stranger, Mum, *Susan*, with her nice little life by the sea, with Nigel (whoever he was), had decided it was time to love me again? It wasn't the right time. It would never be the right time.

I opened up a new blank email message—then closed it. How could she do this? What gave her the right?

Taking a deep breath, I opened a new message window again and began to type:

Hi Chloe,

   Some cat paperclips are on their way to you—in blue, pink and yellow. I'm sure they'll help you become a super-journo in no time. Or at least take your mind off things with Jon this week.

   Jen x

I clicked send. Mum couldn't touch me, unless I let her. All I had to do was put her back in a box and shut the lid. Easy as that.

"This is great," Dan said, eating a big forkful of chili con carne at our kitchen table that evening. He broke the pervading silence for a second; I'd never realized how loudly the kitchen wall clock ticked until tonight.

"There's loads, so dig in," I said. There really was a

lot of food, particularly as I'd hardly put any on my plate. The shock of Mum's email was still fresh and I couldn't summon up any appetite.

"OK, Jen," Dan said, "as much as I'm crazy about chili—and you know that's a lot," he looked over at me, his gaze wavering and uncertain, "I'd much rather know what's going on with you."

I looked down at the table.

"So are you going to tell me?" he said, taking a sip of beer. "It's been over a week now with you hardly talking, and I'd really like to have my girlfriend back." He covered my hand with his and for a moment I felt calm, and safe.

I didn't want to talk, to analyze. I just wanted everything to go back to normal. I'd closed the box, hadn't I? So nothing should be spilling out here.

"I'm fine, Dan. It's just the wedding stuff. You know how it is—there's still a lot to sort out."

Dan shook his head. "I don't believe you, Jen. You love organizing things, and anyway you were fine earlier last week, really excited in fact. But the night Russ was over, you were like a different person."

"It's nothing." I shrugged it off. "Just, you know, the pressure," I said, pouring myself some beer out from his can.

"Jen," Dan said, his voice more insistent now, and with a slight edge to it, "don't lie to me, please. Look, I know what's going on. Don't shut me out."

"What do you mean?" I said, my hackles rising.

"Chris told me," Dan said slowly. "About your mum getting in touch."

The defenses I'd built up so carefully, to protect the precious bubble that was me and Dan, came tumbling down in that moment.

"Why didn't you say something, Jen? Chris has been really worried about you, said you just walked out of your dad's last Friday without even saying goodbye. He wanted to check that you were OK, so he told me what happened."

"So you've been talking about me behind my back?" I snapped, my cheeks flushing. "And why all the questions now if you knew all along?"

Dan stayed silent, then said, "I wanted you to talk to me, Jen. I wanted you to tell me yourself."

"This is absolutely nothing to do with you," I said, getting to my feet, my chair screeching back. Dan's jaw clenched at my sharpness. "Nothing at all," I repeated, but quietly now, my eyes filling with tears.

My questions slipped away, unanswered. Dan reached out to touch my arm. Looking into his warm brown eyes, I realized there weren't any replies he could give that would fix the way I felt. I couldn't let my mum do this to us, I wouldn't let her. I closed the box again and locked it this time. Tears started to spill onto my cheeks.

Dan got up and took me by the hand, leading me slowly towards our sofa. He held me then, not saying anything, just stroking my hair, gently. I touched his chest, turned to kiss him, felt his lips against mine, familiar, comforting. I knew now I would find a way to tell him about my mum—how I felt about her, what she'd said—and that somehow he'd help me decide what to do. But now, this evening, I just wanted to feel like myself again, to lose myself in Dan's warmth, to feel his stubble against my face, to be close to the man who I wanted to spend my whole life with. He kissed me again.

Chapter 22

Alison

As soon as she had slammed the door on her row with Pete, Alison realized she'd locked herself out. That afternoon she'd walked for miles, far too proud to go back to the house and face him again. She and Pete had always bickered, what couple didn't? But this had felt different, more serious. This time she had allowed that thought into her head, the one she usually tried to ignore—*Would it be easier?* The question was relentless: *Would it be easier being apart?*

The fresh air helped clear her head a little, although the edges remained frayed. Ali had walked up the hill to the left of their house and over into the cornfields, following a sprinkling of poppies that marked a loose path. She'd clambered over stiles, the wind gently ruffling her hair, grateful she'd at least grabbed her cardigan before she left.

As she climbed over a low stone wall to walk down by a stream, she thought about marriage.

How were you supposed to stay in love with each other for decades and decades, when you were both changing all the while? Then there was money, kids, aging parents, the multitude of things life threw at you every day. Alison pulled her cardigan tighter around her. Even her parents hadn't made it, and everyone had assumed they were the perfect couple. She'd seen her friends hit the hurdles during married life, and quite a few had fallen. Why did there seem to be a rule book for everything apart from marriage?

When Alison had got home later that afternoon, Pete had let her in without question or acknowledgment, clearly no readier to talk than she was. She'd said hello and gone straight through to her workshop. As she walked through the door an idea came to her. It was silly, really, but all the same she couldn't shift it—she'd always believed that things happened, and people came into your life, for a reason.

She switched on her laptop and typed the name, Mrs. Derek Spencer, into the search engine. The name on the box the tea set had come in. She added the place: Charlesworth. Her mind buzzing with possibilities, she pressed the return button and waited to see what fate had in store.

Willow Tree Close. It was a part of town that Alison knew well, a place as calm and quiet as the high street was bustling. She looked around at the houses and thought back to her own. She and Pete were like strangers to each other still and their bedroom felt hollow. Was she really deluded enough to think she'd find the answers she was looking for here?

Being in these hidden-away streets again brought back memories. It felt like she was discovering a secret tin of photos and cinema tickets that she'd buried as a child. As a little girl the shaded communal gardens here had been her escape—on the way home from school she and her friends used to push the loose railings aside and sneak in to make daisy chains; as teenagers they'd given each other leg-ups and landed the other side, heady with the same spirit of adventure. In the longer cool grass, under the weeping willow, there had been furtive cigarettes, stolen kisses and dozens of whispered secrets. The residents of the surrounding houses must have had keys to the gate, but they didn't seem to use them, preferring to chat on their front steps, or while they hung up their washing in their backyards. Every time Alison had gone there the gardens had been empty, ready to be discovered all over again.

Today Alison's eyes were trained on the 1930s houses. Eighteen, twenty, she carried on along the row until she reached number thirty-two. From the online records it had looked like Mr. and Mrs. Derek Spencer could still be living there. It wasn't very different than any other house on the close. The flowers around the door were a little neater, perhaps, the hedge more carefully tended. She stepped up to the door and pressed the bell.

The woman who opened the door had a warm smile. "Hello," she said, almost as if she knew Alison. She was smartly dressed, in a yellow twinset and a sky-blue skirt that matched her bright eyes. It took a moment for Alison to register the hunch of her back, the deep lines in her face, her hands liver spotted and gripping a wooden walking stick.

"Hello, Mrs. Spencer," Alison said, glad she'd made the effort and put on a smart skirt and blouse for the visit. "You don't know me," she said, searching for the right words to explain what had brought her there. "But I bought a tea set," she said, shuffling her feet. "And I think once it might have belonged to you."

Mrs. Spencer's eyes drifted downwards, as if she was trying to remember. *How silly of me*, Alison thought, *to have come here. She must be at least eighty. Of course she doesn't remember*. Alison gave it one more go. "It had forget-me-nots on the cups," she said, "and a sugar bowl, with little silver tongs." She remembered the photo. She pulled the Polaroid of the tea set out of her jacket pocket and held it up so that the old lady could see it. "Here—this is it."

A flicker of recognition passed across Mrs. Spencer's face right away. "Ah, of course! Oh yes. Forgive me, dear, my memory's not what it was. We gave that to our neighbor Gareth just last month. They are ancient old things really but we were always fond of them. We were going to throw it out actually, but Gareth thought he might be able to make a bob or two so we gave it to him for the stall."

"I'm glad you did," Alison said. "I bought it with two friends and we think it's beautiful."

"How nice," she said, genuinely.

"I'm Alison," Alison said, holding out her hand for the older lady to shake.

"Ruby," she replied with a wide smile, her handshake firmer than Alison had expected. "Would you like to come in for a cup of tea?"

"That would be lovely," Alison replied.

Mrs. Spencer—Ruby—walked Alison through into a tidy little living room that smelt faintly of biscuits, with framed photos of children on the mantelpiece and crochet coverings on every other surface. In the armchair facing out to the window with a book in his hand was a gray haired man in smart trousers and a white shirt, wearing thick, dark-rimmed glasses.

"Derek," Ruby said to him, gently. "We've got a visitor. This lady is Alison."

Derek got up from the armchair and stood to greet her.

"Hello, my dear," Derek said, with a smile. "Welcome. How nice to have a young guest. Shall I put the kettle on?"

"Yes, do," Ruby said warmly. "And there's some Battenberg in the cupboard, could you pop that on a plate too?"

Before she'd arrived, Alison had worried she'd be

intruding, but right now she felt like the Queen on a state visit. Ruby plumped the cushions on another armchair nearer the sofa, then motioned for Alison to sit down.

"So, dear, the tea things," Ruby said, as Alison took a seat. "Yes, I do remember them." She paused, and looked a little more misty-eyed than she had by the front door. "Derek," she called out, louder, "you remember our old tea set, don't you?"

Derek peeped through the strands of the bead curtain by the kitchen. "What was that, dear? Tea's nearly ready, yes."

"No, darling. Not that. This young lady and her friends bought our tea set. You remember the one we gave to Gareth along with the books?"

"Oh yes, the one with the flowers. I do." Derek ducked back into the kitchen. Alison could hear him pouring the boiling water into a teapot. A moment later he reappeared carrying a tray with sliced Battenberg, plates and three cups and saucers and put it down on the table between them. Alison looked at the cups, admiring them—each one had a tiny picture of a thatched cottage with a country garden on it and the saucers matched. Derek sat close to Ruby on the sofa and Alison took in the picture—Ruby's hair was styled into perfect white curls and a delicate gold locket hung around her neck.

"Help yourself to some cake," Ruby said, motioning to it.

"Yes," Derek said, as if continuing something he'd already been saying. "We needed to clear some space. The problem is we can't get up the stairs like we used to. So last year our son and his wife helped us bring the bedroom downstairs, did a conversion. It works for us, doesn't it, Rube?"

Ruby nodded, and gave Alison a little wink, clearly used to her husband's long stories.

"We didn't want one of those stairlifts." Derek shook his head, dismissing the idea.

"Andrew and Julie asked us recently if we'd let them convert the top part of the house into a flat for our granddaughter, Suzie. She's a student, you see, and it'll mean she can move out of her parents' house without it costing a fortune."

Alison nodded, smiling.

"We liked the idea," Derek continued, "Suzie is a gem. Anyway—long story short, sorry, dear, I do go on sometimes—we realized there was far too much clutter up there. Still is, we've only just started really. We were fond of lots of the things, but time passes, doesn't it? Some things start to matter less." He leaned forwards and poured the tea, then milk, and passed Alison a full cup.

"But that tea set saw us through many years," Derek said, a faraway look in his eyes.

"Oh yes," Ruby chipped in. "We used to get it out when friends were round, and every Sunday after church."

Alison bit into a slice of cake as she listened. "Lots of happy times here," Ruby said, with a smile.

"I can imagine," Alison said. There was something welcoming and easy about the atmosphere in the Spencers' modest, cozy home, as if the walls themselves carried memories of music and laughter. "How long have you lived here?"

"We moved in just after the war," Ruby said. "Derek had been away in Germany and I was here, working at the factory. At the time, in the first flush of love as we were, the wait seemed to go on forever."

Looking at the two of them Alison wondered how they could ever have been apart—they were even holding hands as they talked.

"It wasn't easy," Ruby continued, "but during that time apart we both made a lot of friends—friends for life." Ruby pointed to a color photo on the wall of a group of ladies as old as she was, her in the center, all smiling for the camera. "And when Derek came back . . ." Ruby looked at her husband and Alison noticed her squeeze his hand gently. "Well, we didn't want to wait around any longer, did we?" she laughed. "After all those romantic letters back and forth, we could finally get married and make a home together. We got that set as a wedding present, didn't we, dear?"

Derek nodded, "That's right. My aunt Brenda gave us that."

"A wedding present?" Alison said, the words tumbling out. "Then you should have it—I'll get it back to you."

Ruby laughed kindly, her cup rocking a little in her hand.

"Oh no, dear. Don't you worry. It was the 1940s. We didn't have wedding lists like now, and everyone would end up buying you the same thing. Four china teasets we got for our wedding! Who needs that many? Not us. I'm happy that your one has gone to a good home. It's funny though, isn't it? Four teasets for little old us and then you three ladies having to share."

Alison noticed then that above the couple, on the little bookshelf over their heads, there was a black-and-white wedding photo.

"Is that photo of you?" she asked, curious, before she could stop herself.

"Yes," Derek said. "Pass it over to Alison, Ruby."

Ruby reached behind her and gave Alison the silver-framed picture to look at. Ruby and Derek, younger but still recognizable, stood on the steps of Charlesworth church.

"Lovely," said Alison. She took in the slender, dark-haired bride in a long-sleeved white lace gown, the man next to her handsome in a dark suit and horn-rimmed glasses. They were standing as close then as they were sitting now, two halves of a whole. It was so different from the pictures Alison had collected and pinned around her dressing table mirror—there was no awkwardness to them at all; here was a couple who, now as then, were meant to be together. In the photo Ruby's slim hand was enveloped by Derek's. They were looking directly at the camera, but it seemed as if all they really wanted to do was look at each other.

"You look very happy," Alison said.

"Yes," Derek said. "We still are." He used the tongs to put two cubes of sugar into his tea and stirred it, then took his first sip. "I always leave it for a bit. I don't like it too hot, you see."

"Derek's right, we are happy. But even in that photo, well the smile's only ever half the story, isn't it?" Ruby said. She hesitated for a moment, then carried on.

"While Derek came home from the war, my brother David never did. He was killed over in Germany, you see." There was a distance in Ruby's eyes as she spoke. "When we got the telegram just before the war ended, I thought it would be the end of my mother and father too. Losing David was a reminder of how important it was not to wait about, but I missed him terribly. In those first few months of our marriage I wasn't really all there, was I, Derek?"

"No, you weren't yourself back then," Derek said. "The girl I'd left when I set out in uniform loved dancing and good times, but the life went out of you for a while, didn't it?" He rested a hand on Ruby's knee.

"War is cruel," Derek continued, "we all know that. It was strange for me too, coming back to Charlesworth, the peaceful town I'd lived in all my life, but having seen things that other people hadn't."

"But then our Jimmy came along," Ruby said. "And things got better. He reminded me of David from the day he was born, and I still feel like I got a piece of my brother back that day. Anyway, things change when you become parents, and we just got on with it. So we've had bad times and good," Ruby said, "like any couple. But we've always tried to be there for one another. Work through things as a team. Not give up."

"Sometimes she drives me round the bend," Derek said, earning himself a playful jab in the ribs from his wife. "But I wouldn't be without her. Not for a minute," he smiled. "She's my—what was it that Spanish fella at work used to say?—my half orange. That's right. That's my Ruby."

Alison finished the cake on her plate and took another sip of tea before putting the cup back on the tray. She saw Ruby's eyes rest on her wedding ring as she did so.

"It looks as if you're married too, Alison. You'll know what it's like then, the ups and the downs."

Alison nodded, smiled.

"Any children?" Derek asked.

"Yes, two lovely girls, twelve and fifteen," Alison said, then corrected herself with a wry smile, "I mean, I say lovely . . ."

Ruby laughed. "I know what you mean. Our sons were pretty boisterous at that age. But you don't love them any less, do you?"

"Not for a second," Alison said, realizing how true it was. "Anyway, Ruby, Derek," she went on, "I should be off. But it's been so wonderful to meet you." Alison sat forward in her chair and smiled.

"OK then, dear," Ruby said. "I'm sure you've got lots to do today. But it's been a pleasure."

Alison got to her feet and said goodbye, Derek held her hand affectionately between the two of his for a moment. When he let go, Ruby led her to the door.

"You're welcome any time, you know, if you're ever passing," Ruby said, seeing her out.

"Thank you, Ruby." Alison turned to go, then stopped and turned back as she remembered something. "Did you say you had more things to clear out of your attic?" she asked.

"Oh yes," Ruby said. "Lots of old furniture and things. None of it is any use to us anymore, and Gareth said the things are too big for the stall. It's just all quite heavy, you see."

"I think I know just the person to help you," Alison said, a smile coming to her face. She took a piece of paper out of her bag and scribbled down a note. "Here's my phone number, perhaps you could give me a call to fix a time?" Ruby accepted the paper with a grateful smile.

Alison turned and took her first steps back towards home.

Chapter 23

Maggie

Maggie sat back on the sofa and surveyed her living room. On the coffee table a copy of *Dazed and Confused* sat alongside her *Elle House and Garden* magazine, a leather jacket was slung across her piano stool, and scribbled notes cluttered the surface of the breakfast bar.

One of the biggest changes since Dylan had moved in was the way that his music came back with him. She was still adjusting to coming home to the sound of raw guitar riffs when he had an afternoon off. This Sunday he'd given in, though, and it was her Nina Simone album they were listening to as they sat together reading the papers. As planned, they had the day all to themselves; they'd even switched off their phones and computers and resolved to let work wait till Monday for once. Dylan had made eggs Benedict and they'd eaten out on the terrace, sipping fresh orange juice and freshly brewed coffee, the sun creeping over the lawn and warming the patio. After breakfast Dylan had gone out for the papers and they had spent most of the morning on the sofa together reading them. Maggie surveyed the cozy disorder of the living room and caught Dylan's eye. He squeezed her foot and put down the culture section he was reading, a broad smile on his face.

"Maggie, I've got a surprise for you."

As he got up, she pulled her cream satin dressing gown tighter around her and sat up.

"A surprise?" she asked. "How come?"

"It's a housewarming present, of sorts. Hang on a minute." Dylan left the room and went outside. A couple of minutes later Maggie heard his car door slam shut. He returned with two very big flat packages, wrapped in brown paper.

"Here you go," he said, propping them gently against the cushions of the sofa she was sitting on, and grinning. "Go on, open them."

Maggie opened the smaller of the two first, ripping the paper carefully. She saw a hint of the silver frame, then ripped more to see the picture inside: a photo of a New York street scene. It was a doorstep sale outside a tall brownstone house, a young family selling lamps, pictures and other bric-a-brac on a makeshift stall, their little boy playing on the front step and his sister playing hopscotch on the street in front. The colors were vivid and the kids looked as if they might leap right out of the frame.

"This is one of yours, isn't it?" Maggie said, turning to Dylan.

"Yes," he said. "I took it last year and thought you might like it. No teacups there I know, but it still looked like the kind of place you might enjoy looking for bargains during a weekend in the Big Apple." Maggie reached over and gave him a kiss.

"I love it," she said.

Dylan beamed. "Good. Open the other one now," he said, impatient.

Maggie opened the second package, which was slightly larger. It took her a moment to work out that it was a photo of the view through a large, warehouse-style window. Through the glass was a leafy park, and at the sides of the photograph she could make out the interior of the room, a laptop, and some books on a desk, large photos and a street map pinned to the wall. The green foliage outside was so bright that the room itself seemed faded by comparison. Maggie cast her eye over the detail, the pictures within the picture, prints of models in swirling fabrics, ads, a curled photo of a beautiful blonde in a seventies floppy hat.

"Is this your studio?" Maggie said, the picture coming together as a whole now.

Dylan smiled. "Yes. What do you think of the view?"

Maggie nodded, rearranging her position and looking at it again. "Nice," she said. It was interesting, in a way. But it was his world, she thought, the one that didn't include her.

"I thought we could put that up in the bedroom," Dylan said. "So that we both have our views to look at in the morning."

"OK," Maggie said, "sure. Yes, if you'd like that."

Dylan picked up the two pictures. "Have you got a hammer?"

By the middle of their first week living back together, Dylan had woven himself into the very fabric of Maggie's home. Her bedroom and ensuite were colorful with traces of him—discarded T-shirts, boxers, aftershave, a shower gel in black packaging that made the bathroom smell of man, and a razor. Sometimes, in the middle of the night, Maggie would feel unsettled, the change had come so quickly and she was struggling to adjust. But then she'd feel Dylan's warm skin next to hers, move closer and put her arms around him, and the doubts would disappear.

On Wednesday evening, with Dylan over in Amsterdam on a work trip, Maggie got her wedding ring out of its box on a shelf and looked at it again. The first time she'd put it on, during their small wedding ceremony at Islington town hall, she'd felt like the luckiest woman alive. She closed the box gently and put it back down on her dressing table.

As she drove around a corner Maggie glanced in her rear-view mirror to see steam billowing out from her Beetle's engine. She'd put her foot down on the brake and had just started to slow down when the car spluttered to a complete stop.

After closing the shop on Thursday, Maggie had taken a trip out to a church over in Easton. A young couple, Hannah and Ian, had contacted her about doing the flowers for the christening of their baby girl Anya, so they'd decided to meet and walk through the venue together and talk about what displays might work. The village church was beautiful; the evening light threw diamonds in stained-glass colors across the tiled floor and wooden pews. In front of the seats were hand-embroidered prayer cushions.

The couple had been full of enthusiasm, full of pride for Anya, and excited about sharing the day with their family and friends. After the demands of bridezillas like Lucy, and the complicated wedding she was working on in Hove, this was a welcome relief to Maggie. Wandering up and down the aisle with them, suggesting yellows and reds to match the jewel shades in the windows, she had been reminded of why she'd got into the flower business in the first place. When Anya, cozy in Hannah's sling, finally began to get restless, they had said their goodbyes and agreed to talk again soon.

It was dusk by the time Maggie had got onto the A-road back to Charlesworth and her engine had begun to protest. When it cut out completely, she had managed to pull over onto the shoulder and out of the way of the tractor behind her. She went around to the back of the car, opened it up and steam poured out—it was too hot to get close enough to see what was wrong.

Typical. She hadn't had a problem with the Beetle since she bought it new, so yes, it was probably about time—but why here, where she had no phone reception and couldn't call the AA? She got her mobile out of her pocket just to check—yep, not a bar. She put it away in her bag.

She imagined Dylan sinking a cold Amstel by the Dutch canals, sun sparkling on the water, and recalled how he'd urged her to close the shop and join him. If only she had. She held back the urge to kick the car in frustration and tried to think practically. She looked up at the sky, which was darkening quickly now. There were no streetlights for miles, and she knew from experience that soon she wouldn't be able to see her own hands in front of her face. This route was a familiar one—it was a long walk back to Easton, at least an hour and a half, and an even longer one to Charlesworth. Nothing but fields for a good distance, but she could see a couple of farmhouses, on the route back to Easton, where she might be able to use the phone. At least she was wearing flats, she thought. She grabbed a cream jumper from the back seat and locked up the car.

She'd been walking for about half an hour on the near-empty road when a car behind her tooted its horn. She was already at the very edge of the road, with the bramble scratches to prove it, so presumably the driver was simply showing his appreciation of her rear—and she wasn't about to give him the satisfaction of turning around. As the car neared her it slowed right down, pulling level with her. She kept her eyes focused on the road ahead. The sky was a little darker now though, and her irritation was tinged with an edge of anxiety. Here she was, walking on her own without even a functioning mobile. She was strong, yes, but not invincible. The vehicle continued to crawl along beside her. Her heart and mind were racing. Looking up, after what felt like an eternity but must only have been a second or two, she saw it was a truck, rather than a car, and that the broad-shouldered driver was leaning across the cab to wind down the window.

"Maggie?" the driver shouted. She recognized his voice right away. Owen. Of all people, it would be Owen. Of course. Maggie loathed to admit it, but at that very moment she was glad to see him. He slowed the pickup to a complete stop.

"I didn't mean to startle you," he said, his tone softening. "What on earth are you doing out here?"

"I broke down," she said, pointing back along the road

towards her Beetle, realizing she'd walked so far now it was no longer visible. "Down that way, I mean," she said, looking at her ballet pumps, once cream but now scruffy with mud.

"Ah, I must have passed it. Jump in then," Owen said, matter-of-factly, unlocking the door and motioning for her to get in.

"OK. Thank you," Maggie said, relieved, stepping up and getting into the cab.

"Where did you leave the car?" he asked, starting up the engine again before she'd even closed the side door.

"About two miles back the way you came. But look, Owen, if I could just use your phone, I . . ."

Owen took a hand off the steering wheel, got his phone out of his pocket and passed it to her while keeping his eye on the road—"Check it," he said, not unkindly, "but I'm pretty sure I can never get reception on the way to Easton."

"Oh, yours too," she confirmed, after a look at the screen.

"Look, why don't I drive you back to the car?" he said, turning to look at her. There was a gentleness in his eyes Maggie hadn't seen before. "I used to have a Beetle as it happens, so I know my way around the engines pretty well. I'll take a look, see if I can't fix it."

"You don't need to . . ." Maggie said, then thought of how much sooner she might be able to get home. Dylan might even be trying to call her and she didn't want to miss him. "You know what, that would be great." She would only be hurting herself by refusing. "I'd appreciate that, Owen."

"No worries," he said, with the hint of a smile.

As Owen sped along the country lane, she noticed the bits of twig and flower attached to their seats. She looked up at his face as he concentrated on the road, it must have been at least a few days since he'd last had a shave. When he caught her looking he said, "Radio?" flicking it on before she answered.

Maggie reached forward to put his phone down, into the little well by the gearstick. Then she saw it, bundled into that space. Jewelry, a thin silver chain, with an emerald pendant. Her breath caught in her throat.

Lucy's necklace.

It was just after ten when Maggie finally got home. She'd asked Owen not to worry about fixing the car, that she'd changed her mind and would call the AA after all. He had seemed nonplussed, and had dropped her at the Fox and Hound, the first pub they found, as she asked. They'd let her use the landline. Owen had offered to wait, but she had told him to go. She'd ordered a glass of red while she waited, thoughts whirring. With dozens of weddings on her CV, Maggie really thought she'd seen it all. But after what she'd seen in Owen's car, she wasn't so sure.

Lucy Mackintosh, she thought to herself, *what on earth are you up to?*

Chapter 24

Jenny

"Honestly, I can't tell you how sweet they were with each other. Holding hands the whole time—imagine that, in your eighties." Alison was sitting on the squidgy armchair in my living room, a big mug of tea in hand. "I mean sometimes I consider it a good day if I haven't throttled Pete by the end of it."

Maggie and I laughed. It was obvious that, despite what she said, Alison and Pete were pretty unshakeable. "They sound wonderful," Maggie said, and I nodded my agreement. "I suppose when you've lived through the things they have," she continued, "you're far less likely to take each other for granted." Maggie was curled up on my checkered sofa, while I was sitting on the wicker chair next to it.

"They didn't waste any time starting a family when

Derek came home," Alison said. "And they really have been through thick and thin since. Some of the things they said were a good reminder about waiting out the bad times as a team."

"It's funny how easy it is to forget that, isn't it?" I said. That morning I'd filled Maggie and Alison in on my mum's reappearance, given them the short version of her leaving and told them what a relief it was to finally let all those feelings spill out talking to Dan. "I think it's great that we know a bit of our teaset's happy history," I said. "It makes me even more fond of it. If that were possible."

Dan popped his head around the door. "Right, ladies, I'm going to leave you to it. I'm off out to the pub with Russ. I'll see you later, Jen." He came closer to give me a kiss goodbye, his warm mouth on mine, and the women gave dramatic sighs.

"Ahh, young love," said Alison. Dan gave her a little wink.

"He really is a *dish*," Maggie said, as soon as he'd gone back out the door. "Hang on to him, Jen."

"Why, thank you," I said, laughing. "I do quite like him, if I'm honest."

"Talking of tying the knot . . ." I continued. "My errant mum aside, there are two women who I definitely want to see there on my big day. And I hope they don't mind me scrimping on postage."

I stood up and pulled out two card invites from the

drawer of our wooden bureau. "Ta-da!" I said as I passed one each to Alison and Maggie.

They'd turned out pretty nicely in the end; the paper was high-quality stock—Chloe had used her feminine wiles on the magazine printers and had got a discount—and I'd added a line drawing of a 1940s tea party, with a table piled high with cake and pork pies, and me and Dan behind it all, peeking over. Chris had chosen an elegant wartime font and it fit the look perfectly, making the whole thing look like an illustration plate from one of my favorite old children's books.

"I hope you can come and witness the teaset's debut performance," I said, excitedly. Handing out the invites really made the wedding feel real.

"These are perfect," said Alison, looking at the card in her hand. "Original and totally *you*."

"They really are gorgeous," Maggie added. "Just right. Who did the illustration for you?"

"I did it, actually," I said, sounding more confident than I felt. This was the first time I'd shown my drawings to anyone since secondary school. "I've always liked those black-and-white line drawings so I thought I'd have a go myself."

"They're wonderful," Alison said, nodding her approval. "And you and Dan there too, just a few simple lines but, yes, without a doubt it's you."

"Aw," I said, waving the compliment away, feeling a

blush rise to my cheeks. "Thank you. But more importantly, do you think you can make it?"

"August the second—yes, definitely," Alison said. "Pete and I are doing without a holiday this year—long story . . . but the upside is we'll definitely be free."

"Great," I said, leaning round to look at her invite. "It should say Pete's name on there too, does it? I put Dan in charge of writing them out, and while I'm a hundred percent sure of his abilities . . ."

"Yes, it's here. He'll be pleased. It's been a while since we had a wedding to go to. All our friends married ages ago, or decided not to, and God help us, we've even started getting invited to divorce parties." Alison laughed, but looked round at Maggie, realizing her faux pas. "Sorry, Maggie, that was a stupid thing to say, I didn't mean . . ."

"No, no, it's fine, don't worry," Maggie said, laughing it off. "Unconventional setup it might be—kicking off a new romance with a divorce, there's no hiding that—but actually things are going pretty well with Dylan."

"You can give me that back, then," I said, taking the invite out of her hands.

"Whaaat?" she protested.

I got out my fountain pen and wrote Dylan's name carefully next to hers, with a little wobbly "&" before it.

"There you go." I passed it back and when she saw it she smiled.

"It's nice to have another name attached."

She reached for one of the pistachio cupcakes I'd put out on a commemorative jubilee plate and began to peel off the paper, absentmindedly.

"How's it going with finding time to see each other?" I asked. "I mean, you with Bluebelle, and him and his photography—you must both be pretty busy."

"I know, it's true, but the way things are going I don't think that's going to be too much of a problem."

"Oh yes?" I said, curious. "Why's that?"

"He's just moved in."

Alison looked up from her diary, where she'd been doodling around the wedding date she'd penned into a fairly empty-looking month.

"Really?" she gawped.

"Yes," Maggie said, giving nothing away.

"But it's only been a couple of weeks!" Alison said.

Maggie shrugged, "We already know each other, and neither of us could see the point of waiting around. A bit like your friends Ruby and Derek, I suppose."

"He really must be a great lay," Alison said, giving Maggie a smile.

"And you do look happy," I said, taking in the brightness of her eyes, the way they lit up when she talked about Dylan. "Have you told your mum and sister yet?"

"I told Mum, yes, and she's thrilled. It's strange really, she saw me through all of the heartbreak of the divorce, the teary days, the restless nights, the endless dramas— and yet she never really ruled Dylan out. For some reason she couldn't be angry with him, even when I was. She'd liked him from the start and she wanted more than anything for us to find a way to patch things up. I guess my mum was right all along."

Half an hour later, Maggie had left to go back to the shop and I was flicking through my iPod for a new album to put on.

"You don't mind me hanging around, do you, Jen?" Alison asked, from her spot lounging on the sofa.

"Of course not," I said, "it's a pleasure to have your company." As it happened, it was also a nice excuse to put off doing the pile of laundry that was threatening to take over our bedroom.

Alison picked up her wedding invite again and idly ran a finger over the raised text.

"I can't wait to have a boogie with you at the wedding, Jen," she said. "Although let's pray Pete doesn't make an exception and get up on the dance floor too."

"Really?" I said. Dan had two left feet, but I'd always assumed Pete was a good dancer, I suppose because I knew he was musical.

"Oh yes," Alison said. "Total catastrophe on the dance floor. I didn't cultivate a gay best friend for nothing—it was pretty much my only chance of swing-dance survival." Alison's finger strayed onto the image. "I really do like your drawing," she said. "Have you done anything else I could see?"

I looked over from where I was standing, "Well," I said, feeling a little self-conscious, "what sort of thing do you mean?"

"It's this new café Jamie is setting up—he's going to have room for some pictures on the walls too, a space for mini exhibitions, and he wants local artists to be a part of it. Well that, and I'm just nosy, too."

A picture from my children's book popped into my head. I hadn't shown my little project to anyone yet. "I do have something I could show you," I said after a pause, feeling more excited about the idea now. "I mean, it's not suitable for the café, but if you really are interested?"

Alison sat up in her seat, a smile on her face. "Of course I am, go on, get to it," she said, clapping her hands twice, sending me on my way.

I went to my room and came back a minute or two later with the card box that contained *Charlie, Carlitos and Me*. After talking things through with Dan the other day, my head had felt clearer and I'd restarted work on the book, finishing some of the pictures and deciding on an ending I was happy with. When I'd brought the box home from Dad's, Dan had been curious, but I'd told him it was a wedding-related surprise and he shouldn't start nosing about, and I think it had stopped him snooping. I brought it over to the coffee table and, sitting down on the carpet, opened it and took out the pages to show Alison.

"I've been working on this for a little while now. It's a children's book." Alison's eyes lit up and she held the first page in her hands as if it were something precious. "I started it a few years ago," I said, "then put it away for a while. When I found it at my dad's a few weeks ago I decided to work up the illustrations properly. It's almost finished now."

Alison went through the pages one by one, taking in the story, and occasionally letting out a hearty laugh. "Holly would have adored this when she was little," she said, looking up and smiling. It was strange to be sharing something that I'd kept to myself for so long, and my stomach felt tight. As she reached the final page she put the pages back with a satisfied sigh. "I *knew* Carlitos would manage to bring all of the Peludo family over in the end," she said, as if she still had one foot in the Andes herself. "Jen, it's terrific," she said, without hesitation. "I love the story—and the illustrations are beautiful. First the invite, now this—why've you been hiding your talent all this time?"

I breathed a sigh of relief. It felt like all the work had been worth it.

"I hope I'm not the only person you're planning on showing this to," Alison said. I hadn't really thought any further than just getting it finished.

"I guess," I said, mulling it over. "I could show it to Dan when he gets back. And maybe Dad, he's always liked my drawings."

Alison was shaking her head, "I don't mean like that, Jenny. I mean, if you want to show it to them you definitely should, but you should let some children's publishers take a look at this too."

"Are you serious?" I said.

"Yes, Jen. Never more so." Alison's eyes lit up as she remembered something. "An old friend of mine, JoJo, works for a small press in London, actually. I haven't seen her for years, but last time we spoke she said they were looking out for new writers and illustrators for their list. I've been meaning to catch up with her anyway, so why don't I set up a lunch and take this along with me?"

"Ali, that's really generous of you," I said, putting the lid back on the box. "But I'm not sure I'm ready to share it with anyone else yet." The knock of my mum reappearing from nowhere, shaking things up, had thrown my confidence somehow. Anyway, I'd really only done this for fun.

"I'm not being generous," Alison said, with a warm laugh. "And the thing is, I'm not sure I'm going to take no for an answer."

Chapter 25

Alison

"Ninety-five pounds!" Holly said proudly, holding up her pink notepad. "Plus the three weeks' pocket money I've given you back. Am I nearly there?"

Holly was saving hard to pay her parents back after they'd bailed her out of the spree on Chrissy's mum's credit card. It had only been a few days since Alison had gathered her family together and discussed how they could rein in their spending, but, surprisingly, both girls had really taken up the challenge.

At Jenny's flat the other day, after they'd looked at her children's book, Alison and Jenny had cracked open the wine, and after a glass or two Jenny had finally got the truth out of her about the financial mess she was in. "I just don't know where to start," Alison had confessed, putting her Malbec on the coffee table. "I'm blaming Pete for this, but the truth is I don't know where to begin fixing it myself."

Jenny hadn't wasted any time thinking of practical tips to help her get back on top of things, and that evening had emailed over some budget outlines Jenny had used in the past to help her dad keep his finances in check. Alison's panic had settled into a more comfortable acceptance of the fact things were going to have to change. "Little things can really make a difference," Jenny had reassured her.

"That's fantastic, Holly," Alison said, looking at her daughter over the kitchen table. "How did you manage to make that?"

"I sent a Facebook message around my friends asking if any of them wanted to buy the clothes I'd bought with Chrissy at half the price. Loads of people responded—I mean it was all brand-new stuff, nice things."

Pete widened his eyes at his wife, impressed.

Alison couldn't put her finger on when it had happened, but at some point over the last few days, the distance between her and Pete had begun to close. Meeting the Spencers had reminded her of something—marriage worked, when you worked at it. She and Pete had taken tentative steps towards one another again and with a touch here, the offer of a cup of tea there, the lines of communication had started to open up again. Both of them had accepted that their difficulties couldn't be glossed over. They'd reluctantly agreed that, in the short term, they would need to ask Alison's brother Clive for some help. He'd been happy to offer them a loan.

"Well done, sweetheart," Alison said to her youngest daughter. "That will really help—Pete, look, that's our phone bill covered now, and a bit towards the gas."

Pete nodded. "Nice work, squirt," he said to Holly, smiling proudly.

"So am I nearly there? Towards paying you off?" Holly asked.

"We said we'd pay half, so you have fifty-five pounds to go. That'll have to come out of your pocket money for a little while still."

"Or you could wash some cars, Hol," Sophie chipped in. "I did that last summer, just ask the neighbors round here—I charged seven quid a go."

"Good idea, Soph," Alison said, making a note in her new red notebook.

"Sally has just moved back in around the corner," Pete chipped in. "You could ask her."

"Really?" Alison said, pleased to hear the news about their old neighbor. "She found a place?"

"Yes," Pete said, "a smaller—"

"You really should sell the Clio and get a bike," Sophie interrupted them. Alison nodded and noted it down, knowing that this time at least, her daughter was right.

Sophie put down the slice of carrot cake she was eating and said, "I've switched to another tariff on my mobile, so my calls are all included. I don't use the landline at all anymore." She hesitated, trying to remember something else. "Oh, and Matt says if we got a different printer for your studio, Mum, you'd spend loads less on print cartridges."

OK, Alison thought. So Matt didn't sound all bad. "Right, sure, I'll look into that," she said.

"Pete, what about you?" she asked her husband.

"I tried a different supermarket last week, and bought from the cheapo range. I didn't even notice the difference, taste-wise, did you?" The girls shook their heads no. "And—get this—our vegetable patch has had its first crop!" Pete's brown eyes were shiny with excitement that transformed his face. "We'll be eating arugula and zucchinis and whatever else it was I planted there," he said, furrowing his brow. "It was looking very green when I last looked anyway."

Alison smiled at her husband. A zucchini off the grocery bill might not make the world of difference, but the big change was the light that was starting to come back into Pete's eyes.

"OK, guys, nice work," Alison said. "Right, any other business?"

"Yes," Holly said proudly. "I have something." Alison and Pete exchanged looks. This was news to them both. "I'm going to be an artist. And a writer. Like Jenny. She's helping me with my drawings."

Alison and Pete smiled—Alison had wondered what those two had been talking about when Jenny had popped around.

"Nice one, Hol," Sophie said. "You can look after Mum and Dad in their old age then."

"Hey, we're not there yet," Alison protested. "And in the meantime I have something to add," Alison said. In a rare moment all the eyes in the room were fixed on her. "It's not to do with money, but while I've got all three of you tearaways in one place I wanted to tell you something."

"What is it, Mum?" Sophie asked, her eyes wide.

"Remember when Janet from next door had a fit about George going in their garden?"

"Oh God, yes," Pete said, putting his head in his hands. "I can't believe you left me to calm her down, that woman's a nightmare." Holly sniggered.

"The thing is," Alison continued. "She may have, sort of, had a point." Alison nodded over at George, and Holly furrowed her brow, confused. "Their spaniel Cassie is pregnant," Alison said. "And as they never let her out when she's in heat, Janet's pretty sure there are some little Wolfaniels on the way."

"Woah!" Holly leapt up from her chair. "Puppies! Cool. Can we keep them?"

"Oh, sweetheart, I'm sorry. I know it would be fun, but we really can't keep any of the pups ourselves—dogs are expensive and it just wouldn't make sense right now. Jamie wants one though, and Janet is going to keep one to give Cassie some company. Jenny and Dan are thinking about it too—Jenny thinks her dad would be happy to care for one until they get a place with a garden," Alison said. "So they'd be close by and we could see them grow up."

"Imagine the cuteness," Sophie said, and Alison saw a flash of the little girl her teenage daughter used to be. "As tall as George but with floppy spaniel ears." She smiled, giving George's fur a stroke.

"OK," Alison said. "I think that is everything. So you can scoot, but we'll have another house meeting in a couple of weeks to see how everyone is getting on."

"Right, cool," Holly said. Her and Sophie's chairs scraped as they pulled away from the table and darted upstairs again.

"Alison," Pete said, touching his wife's shoulder gently once the girls had left the room. "Can we chat for a minute?"

"Of course," she replied, picking up a few of the mugs they'd been drinking from and taking them over to the sink. "There's a bit of washing up to do, but why don't you come and talk to me while I do it?"

"Actually, I was hoping we could talk properly. In private, I mean."

"Oh, sure. Yes. Right," Alison undid the apron she was still wearing and hung it over the back of one of the chairs. "Shall we go into the den?"

Pete nodded and they walked over there together. Once inside Alison shut the door after them and they sat down on the well-loved red sofa.

"What is it, Pete?"

"I know we're doing all this as a family," Pete started, running a hand through his hair. "And the girls are doing a good job, aren't they?" Alison nodded and saw Pete take a deep breath before he spoke. "But I know that what we need, really, so that our home is secure long-term and you can expand your business, is for me to be back in work."

"Oh Pete . . ." Alison said, moving towards him and putting her hand on his leg. "I don't want you to feel under pressure—you know I'm sorry about everything I said the other day. The changes we're making are meant to make things easier."

"It's not you, Ali," Pete said. "I can see for myself what we need." He reached out and touched her hair, smoothing a loose strand back behind her ear. "I love you. And the girls. Our family is what matters. But we both know we need money too. I want to work, but the truth is, I feel stuck," Pete said. "You know how it's been, most of the jobs advertised aren't at my level of experience," Pete explained, "and the interviews I have had haven't gone brilliantly. But Harry—you know we got laid off at the same time—he got a job this week, and it's a top role. He'd been having trouble too and in the end he went to see someone, a careers consultant."

Pete looked at Alison, trying to gauge her response.

"She helped him with his CV, interview technique, that kind of thing. I never thought I'd say this, but if I'm honest I am a bit rusty with all that too, and I wonder if

235

it's holding me back. It's not cheap, but I wonder if it would be worth going to do the same."

"Why not," Alison said, mulling the idea over, "give it a try." Pete looked relieved. "The money Clive's lent us will cover the mortgage and bills for two months, and I have some payments due in next week that would give us a bit extra. When that money comes through, I think this would be a good use of some of it."

"OK," Pete said. "I'll set up an appointment."

Pete hesitated for a moment.

"Ali." She looked at him and he took her hand in his. She remembered that misty December night long ago when they'd curled up under blankets in their tiny flat with a bottle of wine and a stash of mince pies, and he'd asked her to marry him. She thought back on all the adventures and laughter they'd shared since then.

"Ali," Pete said again, "I'm going to make this work. I want our family to be strong, like it used to be."

Alison felt a lump in her throat. She wanted more than anything to see the man she'd married, energetic, confident and fiercely funny, come back.

"It will be, Pete," Alison said, touching his cheek, and starting to believe it. "It will be."

Chapter 26

Maggie

"Do you want a coffee, Dylan?" Maggie asked, doing up her lace bra. When he sleepily stirred he tried to haul her back into bed.

"I can't," she laughed, slapping his hands away, "the shop won't open itself." She'd missed him when he was away in Amsterdam, but it had been a lot easier to get to work on time. "And haven't you got a shoot today in any case?" She was sitting down on the edge of the bed now, stroking his hair gently.

"I have, yes." There was a gruffness to his voice, he'd stayed out late after the shoot last night. The art director, Sam, was a good friend from the U.S., Dylan had called to say, and they'd been catching up over a whisky or three. "We decided last night to shift it back to a ten o'clock start." Maggie raised her eyebrows. "It's in everybody's best interests," he said with a smile.

He raised himself up slightly, so that he could see out the window, the glimpse of his bare chest tempting Maggie back under the covers. "And look, Maggie, it's a horrible murky gray start to the day anyway."

He'd hung the framed photograph of his studio just next to her own window; the sun in Brooklyn shone as brightly as ever.

"OK, darling," Maggie said, doing up her slate gray-and-lilac-flowered shirt. "I'll see you this evening, but a little later than usual. I'll have to pop out after closing, it's to do with the Darlington Hall wedding again. Where are you filming today anyway?"

"Out in the cornfields," Dylan said. He didn't sound exactly perky yet, but was getting a bit closer to it. "So we definitely need the sun out. English weather, Christ . . . sometimes you spend half the day waiting for just an hour or two when you can take some decent shots."

He buried his face back into the pillow, but was still alert enough to tap her on the bum when she bent over to pick up her shoes. "Hey!" she protested, then gave him a last kiss goodbye before slipping downstairs and out of the front door.

Trade at the shop was brisk. Anna had been busy organizing deliveries while Maggie was attending to the customers who came into the shop. The day was still gray, and splashes of sulky drizzle had started up when her mobile rang: LUCY M flashed up on the screen. Maggie caught Anna's eye, pointed to the phone and ducked into the back room to answer the call.

"Hi, Lucy," Maggie said, her tone calm and serious. She'd already decided to forget all about the necklace she'd seen in the cab of Owen's car. She had a job she was being paid to do, and what Owen and Lucy got up to was really none of her business.

"Maggie!" Lucy gushed. "I absolutely adore the designs for the garden. Jack showed me what you and Owen have come up with and the concepts are fantastic."

This was better than she could have hoped for. When she'd seen Lucy's name on the display she'd automatically assumed she'd done something wrong, fallen short of Lucy's sky-high expectations, so her enthusiasm was a welcome surprise.

"Daddy likes the ideas too and we both want you to get going on them right away."

"Lucy, that's great," Maggie said. "I'm so pleased."

Maggie popped her head out of the door to check Anna wasn't overwhelmed with customers. She was currently dealing with one of Charlesworth's more attractive young men, a guy who worked in the boutique next door, and she looked happy enough to be left to it.

"Hi, Lucy—sorry, yes, you were saying."

"Yes, Daddy's chuffed, thinks his friends are going to find it all a real hoot. But here's the big thing, Maggie."

Maggie waited.

"I called *It Girl* magazine with the plans and they adore the idea, they're after an exclusive in fact! They adore the whole rabbit-hole thingamajig. Maggie this is *just* what I've been hoping for. It could really help to move things forward with my modeling. And, it could mean great things for Bluebelle du Jour, too."

Maggie's heart leapt. This really did sound like good news. At the moment it felt like everything in her life was finally starting to slot into place.

"Lucy, that's terrific. Thanks for letting me know. I'll call Owen now and see about getting the plans finalized and the quotes done as soon as possible, so that we can give *It Girl* a heads-up on the details in plenty of time."

"Brilliant, Maggie," Lucy said. "That's just what I hoped you'd say. I knew I could count on you."

The rest of the morning passed in a blur of telephone orders, flower arranging and payments and even with Anna's help it was midday before Maggie had a quiet five minutes to call Owen.

She went out the back and scrolled to his number.

"Hi, Owen," she said, as he picked up.

"Maggie, hi. What's up, stranded again?"

"Not this time. Car needed a new fan belt, but it's as good as new now. I'm actually calling because I've just had some excellent news from Lucy. I'm coming around to your workshop later today anyway, like we'd planned—but it means we'll have a bit more to cover while I'm there."

"What is it? You sound like you've won the lottery or something." Owen was as cool as ever. But that's because he doesn't know yet, Maggie thought. Once he realized what this coverage could do for his landscaping business he'd be every bit as excited as she was; and hopefully it would smooth the way for better relations.

"I'll explain when I get to yours," Maggie said, glancing at her diary, "but I think we'll need a bit longer than we first thought. Is it OK if I come around a bit earlier, say two o'clock?"

"I'm out on a job in Grayville today, and I get back at half past. That OK?"

"Great. See you then." When they'd said goodbye Maggie hung up and with a spring in her step returned to the shop floor.

"You look happy," Anna said. "What's going on?" Maggie was dying to tell her, to tell someone, but she didn't want to tempt fate. She'd have the opportunity to talk it through with Owen, and then, when they had proper confirmation from the magazine, she'd be able to share the good news.

"Anna, are you still OK to mind the shop this afternoon? I know it's a bit hectic, but you seem to have everything under control."

"That's fine, Maggie, no problem at all," Anna said,

her usual upbeat self. "You know what, it's getting easier—with the practice I mean."

"Good," Maggie replied. "I've been hearing great things about you from the customers. In fact I reckon you deserve a bonus for everything you've done this past month. A contribution to your car fund, maybe?"

"Yay!" Anna said, glowing. She had been saving for a secondhand car since she'd passed her test at the start of the year. Then she narrowed her eyes. "Unless you've got ulterior motives—are you planning on making me Bluebelle's newest delivery girl?"

"Aha! I wasn't, but there's an idea . . ." Maggie said, laughing.

The drive to Owen's workshop took Maggie out of town, through trees thick with leaves that met at the top and formed a tunnel of green. She was driving with the top down, a spotted blue and white headscarf keeping her hair more or less in place. The sun had finally come out, shafts of light forcing their way through the foliage, and Maggie wondered how Dylan's shoot was turning out—the conditions should be just right for taking photos now.

She reached Owen's address after twenty minutes on the road, a group of converted stables around a big cobbled courtyard. Maggie parked next to his truck, and gathering her things, walked towards number three, in the far corner. As she approached the door she peeked in through the windows of the surrounding workshops—a carpenter was hard at work in one and the others looked like artists' studios. Next door to Owen's was a room filled with pieces of metal that glinted in the sunlight—as Maggie got closer she saw hand-crafted jewelry laid out inside.

A couple of yards away, Owen's wooden front door was half open. When she got there she pushed against it and stepped inside.

"Hello?" she called out.

Owen was next to the sink, stacking some tools. Hearing her voice, he turned around, "Hi, Maggie," he said, almost as if they were friends.

He looked different in his own setting. His clothes fit the scene, rather than looking out of place and scruffy like they had at the hall. He seemed more relaxed. Half of the workshop space was filled with garden implements and plants; the other half was a makeshift office, with a computer and a pinboard covered with plans and images. Owen came over to greet her, shaking her hand hello. It was formal, and awkward, but it would have to do.

"Sorry—" he said, looking down and seeming to notice his muddy hands for the first time as he pulled them back. "I haven't had a chance to wash them yet. Why don't you go through out the back and I'll bring us both a cuppa."

He walked ahead of her and opened the glass-paned wooden door on the opposite side of the room. Maggie looked out into a beautiful walled garden—wisteria lined the back wall and jasmine and honeysuckle climbed to their left. Birds flocked to a little bird table by the door.

There was a bench made from driftwood and Owen motioned for her to sit there.

"Take a seat," he said.

She sat down and took in the sights and smells of his garden; the jasmine climbing up the pale brick gave out a scent that brought back childhood summers. There was a sculpture in the corner on a plinth too; simple, but pleasing, smooth and white with a hole through the middle. Maggie took her satchel off and put it down beside her, getting the folder out, ready to take the notes. She heard the taps running inside as Owen washed his hands and put the kettle on to boil.

He reappeared a couple of minutes later with a tray of tea and a couple of biscuits. He put them down on the driftwood table.

"This is a little oasis, isn't it?" Maggie said.

"Thank you. I like it out here. It's calm and quiet."

Maggie nodded, smiling. Since she'd decided to forget about the Lucy thing, being civil had started coming more easily.

"Where is your sculpture from? It looks like a Barbara Hepworth," Maggie said; the bold Cornish sculptor had always been one of her favorites. She turned to Owen and saw that his gaze was on her, not the sculpture.

"It's a copy," he said, with a smile. "My grandfather used to live down in Carbis Bay in Cornwall near her during the war. He admired her sculptures and modeled some of his own on hers. When he died he left this one to me."

"Copy or not, it's beautiful," Maggie responded. "All I got when my granddad died was a stuffed squirrel and a carriage clock," she laughed. His eyes were still on hers, steady, and she realized her laugh had come out sounding nervous.

"So what's with the hurry today?" Owen asked. "I mean, I know you wanted to see the tunnel model, and we can look at that in a minute—but on the phone it sounded like there was something else you wanted to talk about?" Owen pulled up a wooden chair to sit opposite her.

"Yes. It's good news," Maggie said, sitting up straight. "Lucy called me this morning and told me that *It Girl* magazine really like the concepts—particularly the rabbit hole—and they want an exclusive." Maggie smiled. "You know it's just what Lucy's been hoping for, and obviously it's going to be great publicity for both our businesses."

Owen looked completely unmoved. In fact if anything Maggie thought maybe she saw his face fall a little. "Great publicity?" he said, raising an eyebrow as he spoke.

"Yes," Maggie said. "I mean I've been waiting for something like this for ages, some high-profile exposure. And the same would be the case for you. I mean I don't want to jump the gun, but if this all goes smoothly it could be life changing."

"Well, that's great for you, Maggie," Owen said dully.

"But not all of us want life changing." His expression was cold.

"I like my life," he went on, the arrogance Maggie had first seen coming back in an instant. "And my business, just as they are. You know weddings aren't my thing. I don't need an exclusive photo deal with a glossy magazine to promote my business, especially when I'm doing something I would never usually do—I normally get landscaping work by word of mouth and that's how I like it." He shook his head as if he were struggling to comprehend where she was coming from.

"We might be creating floral croquet hoops for this event, but my day-to-day work is no frills, environmentally conscious gardening. Hard, honest work; not just frilly self-promotion. I doubt a bunch of *It Girl*-reading wannabes are going to be interested in what I do. And even if they are, I can't imagine they'll be the kind of people I want to be generating new business with."

Maggie realized she'd been holding her breath as he talked. She slowly let it go and took a moment before responding.

"Owen, look, I see your point," she said, trying hard to be diplomatic, "but I still think this could be an ideal opportunity for both of us. How can you just dismiss all of the readers of a magazine like that, especially when they're likely to have money to spend?"

"Maggie. In my view it's about how a business grows,

not just how big. I've always intended to build things slowly, stay true to the values I started this out with."

"And that's how I work too," Maggie countered, feeling suddenly defensive.

He raised an eyebrow. "Really?" he said. "Maggie. Are your flowers even fair trade?"

"Yes," Maggie replied, hesitantly. "I mean, I think so. Or if not, they will be . . ." she stumbled. Anna had been talking about it lately and she was sure she'd put it on a list of things to look into.

Owen continued, "Jack told me you're flying in roses from South America. Have you thought about the carbon footprint this wedding is going to have?"

"No . . . to be honest . . . I mean Lucy gave me her outline and this is how I—" Maggie said, then stopped for a moment to compose herself, taking a deep breath. "Owen, I know how to plan wedding flowers, I've been doing it for years, and I've had no complaints at all from Lucy or Jack about my ideas."

"I'm not disputing that," Owen said, staring down at the ground now, "but the more I think about it, the more I wonder if this wedding is the right project for me. It just seems like ethical considerations aren't even coming into the decisions. Our priorities aren't the same."

Maggie felt a rush of indignation, and her cheeks flamed.

"How can you just assume that?" she said, furious. "I

understand that you're focused on your own work, but shouldn't you at least get to know other people properly before you make judgments?"

"The way I see it, we all have a responsibility, Maggie . . . but if it's your dream to be in a magazine . . ." Owen said, shrugging his shoulders.

"What do you know about my dreams?" Maggie got to her feet and picked her satchel back up again. "Nothing, Owen." She fixed him with a glare. "You're self-righteous and snobby and—"

The words she'd wanted to say disappeared as Lucy's emerald pendant flashed across her mind. She tried to push the image away and remain professional.

"And what, Maggie?" Owen taunted her. "What else am I, seeing as you know me so well?"

"It's just . . . How *dare* you take the moral high ground with me," Maggie hissed. "You may want to pull out of the wedding, but I'm pretty sure your reasons have nothing to do with any of this."

"Oh, really?" Owen said, both eyebrows going up this time.

"Yes, really," Maggie said. "I saw Lucy's necklace in your car, Owen."

He was silent for a while, looking down at the ground, and then shook his head.

"Look, Maggie, I'm not keeping you here," he said, getting to his feet. "You're the one who came dashing around, worried that if you didn't you'd miss catching a few accounts from WAGs and *Big Brother* rejects." The vitriol was really flowing now. "Do what you like. But obviously there is no way you're using any of my ideas without me."

Maggie turned her back on him and walked back into the workshop, the hopes she'd had for the Darlington Hall wedding in tatters. As she left, she looked over her shoulder and shouted, "You can be the one to tell Lucy then, that her fairy-tale wedding—or whatever it really is—is *off.*"

Maggie put her foot down hard on the accelerator on the way back to her house. From what Lucy had told her, it was the rabbit hole idea that had interested *It Girl* most and without it the deal might well fall through. She imagined Owen would be calling Lucy right now, telling her he'd changed his mind, or that Maggie was impossible, and they'd have to find another highly skilled landscape gardener to replace him at short notice. She saw her dream of a shop in London slipping out of her grasp. She didn't want to think about it anymore, what she needed was a gin and tonic in the comfort of her home, and for Dylan to tell her that everything was going to be OK.

She parked in the drive and let herself into the house. There was music playing; Dylan must have left the setting on timer by accident this morning. The automatic lights and sound were supposed to deter burglars when the two of them were out of the house. As she set her bag down in the living room though, her heart stopped. There was soil in the pale carpet, and following the trail she saw that her delicate gold birdcage had fallen to the floor and the pink orchid inside it was lying on the carpet, the stem broken. Most of the earth in the pot had spilled out and the petals were broken and bent.

Her first instinct was to call the police, but something stopped her. What could she even say to them, other than there was a broken plant on her living room floor? She'd had an upsetting day, and she needed to be rational. Accidents happened, and perhaps the hook she'd put up on the wall hadn't been strong enough to hold the birdcage after all.

She put the damaged flower in its pot up on the counter by the sink. It was then she heard a noise upstairs, as if someone had dropped something. Tiptoeing, she walked over to the stairs and tentatively crept up them. Was that noise coming from her study? That was where most of the things of value were kept, including the jewelry she'd inherited from her grandmother.

As she reached the landing, a woman's laugh rang out. Her bedroom door was open and as she stepped forward, Maggie took in the scene. Dylan lay in bed, naked, his hair ruffled, just as she'd left him this morning. In a cruel parody of the moment she'd left, a blonde woman was standing by the side of the bed, wrapped in a pale blue towel that Dylan was trying to wrestle off her.

"Maggie—oh, crap, Maggie," Dylan said, hurriedly

getting back into his boxers. The woman with him looked awkward, and pulled the towel—one of Maggie's from the en suite—more tightly around her.

Maggie stood still. "So it's you . . ." she said. It suddenly clicked. She addressed the woman. "You must be Sam."

The blonde nodded, "Yes," she said, with the trace of an American accent. Maggie's eyes flicked for a split second to the print on her bedroom wall, the one Dylan had taken of his own studio, to confirm her suspicions. There in the foreground was the same woman, glossy blonde hair and her face half hidden under a floppy seventies hat; a picture within a picture, her photo pinned to Dylan's studio wall. This woman had been in Maggie's bedroom all along.

"I'll get my things," Sam said, lowering her head and hurriedly gathering up her clothes from around the room before ducking out into the landing to put them on. Maggie ignored her completely, her eyes firmly fixed on Dylan's. They were both silent until Maggie finally heard the front door slam.

"Maggie," he started, his head in his hands. "I'm so sorry," he said, looking up at her imploringly, his brow furrowed. "It was . . ."

"Oh please don't," Maggie said, her voice ice-cool in spite of the adrenaline that was coursing through her veins. "Don't patronize me, Dylan."

"I didn't know she was going to turn up, I swear."

Dylan started, getting up and taking a pace towards Maggie.

"And so, what?" Maggie said, stepping back, the anger bringing a tremble into her voice now. "You would have had to wait till you next went back to the States to bed her? Or wait until someone else came along?"

"It's not like that," Dylan said, taking another step towards her, puppy-dog eyes wide.

"You make me sick," Maggie said, shaking her head, her cheeks burning now. "After everything you said? You *made* me forgive you, you convinced me you'd changed, Dylan, just so that you could make an even bigger fool out of me this time."

She went over to the window, pushing past him, and opened it wide. On her dressing table in a little box was the wedding ring she'd once thought she might put on again. She thought about picking it up, then stopped herself; gold was in demand at the moment, she'd be able to sell it. Instead she unhooked Dylan's print from the wall. Panic flickered across his face as she took it down. He reached out but before he could stop her, she lobbed the frame out of her window, throwing it with all her strength, and they both watched on as it shattered on the tarmac of the pavement in front of her house.

"I think you'd better grab what you can and go, Dylan," Maggie said, calm returning to her voice. "Don't you?"

Blitz Spirit

(July–August)

Chapter 27

Alison

Alison stroked Pete's arm. "It's seven o'clock, darling," she whispered to him gently. He stirred and then jumped a little.

"What?" he said, confused.

"It's seven o'clock, darling," Alison repeated.

"Oh, thanks, Ali."

Pete got up, still clumsy with sleep, and went over to the shower. It was only his third day at work, and his morning routine wasn't automatic yet, but Alison didn't mind waking up a bit early to nudge him and make them both coffee. The girls would be downstairs breakfasting, but these past couple of days Ali had left them to it and sneaked back upstairs so that she and Pete could enjoy another few minutes in bed together.

She'd then pile up the pillows and lie back to talk to

him as he got dressed in his suit for work. His stubble was gone now but his untidy curls were still there; she could tell he still wanted to retain the look of someone who had been in a band, once. It had only been a fortnight since Pete saw the careers counselor who had kick-started his job search. He'd come home afterwards, buzzing with an energy she hadn't seen in him in months.

"We went right back to the beginning," he'd said, "and looked at the skills and experience I have and what I could do. It's made me realize I was limiting myself to finding almost exactly the same role, in the same sector."

Things had then moved so quickly it had surprised them both. Pete had seen a job in communications for a drug addiction charity, interviewed and been offered the job that same week.

"You look sexy in that suit, you know," Ali said, and Pete bent down to kiss her.

She had on her silk kimono and her hair was loose.

"You look pretty gorgeous right now too."

"I have to see my husband off to work with a smile on his face," she said, pulling him in closer for a passionate kiss.

"Apart from that, what are you up to today?" Pete asked, taking a reluctant step back and doing up his tie.

"I'm meeting up with Jamie to look at the new shop space," Alison said, trying to keep the regret from her voice. "He signed the lease last week."

A sadness fell across Pete's face then, as they both

thought of the café dreams Alison had given up. "Ali, I'm so sorry you couldn't—"

"Shh," Alison said, silencing him with another kiss. "It's fine, Pete. Really, it is."

When Alison and Pete got downstairs their two daughters were sitting at the breakfast table. Toast was going cold on plates they'd shoved to one side and George was up on the bench tilting his head against the table, trying to reach for a piece. Sophie was leaning forward and applying eye-liner to her little sister's eyelids. Both girls looked up, startled, as their parents entered the room.

"Holly, upstairs now," Pete said, "makeup off. Come on, I'm sure Mrs. Brannigan is getting pretty tired of calling us by now."

Holly sheepishly dashed under his raised arm and up the stairs with her head down.

"Sophie. You know better." Alison shook her head. "Holly could have got sent home for that."

Sophie sighed, put the lid back on her eyeliner and tucked it away in her bag. "You've got to admit it made her look cooler." A smile played at the corners of her mouth. "Who wants a geeky younger sister?"

"Better that than a suspended little sister, if you ask me," Pete said, sending her upstairs to get ready. Alison looked over at him, and as his eyes met hers she saw the partner she loved.

*

Alison swept a finger along the mantelpiece in Jamie's new café premises, sending a layer of dust loose into the air.

"This old fireplace is going to look great once we get it cleaned up," she said, inspecting the original tiles, and then glancing around the rest of the room.

The space Jamie was renting was located opposite the flower shop and next to the gift shops and boutiques that Charlesworth's residents were so fond of browsing. The windows were large enough for the café to attract passing trade and natural light was flooding in, casting wide rectangles of sunshine onto the wooden floorboards.

"And the backyard," Alison said, "I reckon you could spruce that up easily, get some garden chairs out there, make the most of the second half of the summer?"

Jamie smiled, and nodded. "Couldn't agree more, in fact I was hoping to take advantage of your good nature a bit there." Alison laughed.

"And as for the walls," Jamie said, pointing at the whitewashed brick, "there are a couple of local artists who are interested in exhibiting their work here. One does canvases with graphics of 1940s tins, packaging; and another, a student, puts together these gorgeous patchworks. You'd like them." Alison looked over at the wall, picturing how they'd look.

"And then there's Adam, he's Brighton-based," Jamie continued. "He takes photographs of burlesque dancers, close-ups of nipple tassels, stockings . . ." Alison's eye-brows shot up and Jamie gave her a wink. They both knew Charlesworth wasn't quite ready for that.

"Come over here, into my office, Ali." He grabbed a couple of deck chairs and placed them against the far wall so that they could survey the whole shop from where they were sitting. "It looks good, doesn't it?"

"It's going to be fantastic," she replied. "And guess what—I've found just the place for you to get some authentic period furnishings."

"Really?" Jamie said. "I've been trawling auctions but so far all the stuff I like has been way out of my price range."

"How does free sound?" Alison said.

"Are you serious?" Jamie said, a grin spreading across his face.

"Absolutely. And you don't have to go far for it, either. I've met a terrific old couple in Willow Tree Close who are clearing out their attic—they have tons of original fur-niture up there by the sound of things. I had a chat on the phone with them yesterday and they say that if you agree to take the lot and arrange the removal, they'd be happy for you to have it."

Jamie's eyes lit up. "That sounds ideal. It's all going to be a bit rough around the edges in here, mismatched chairs and so on, so I'm sure we'll be able to make use of most things. You're a gem, Ali, thank you."

"Anytime," she said.

"But listen," Jamie said. "I actually wanted to talk to you about something else." His tone was more serious now. "I've been thinking about how to launch the café with a bang. We'll have a party here when the place is finished, and I want to follow that up by starting the early evening events: stitch-and-bitch sessions, crochet workshops, bunting classes—maybe even some rebel cross-stitch, you know . . . skulls and crossbones, that kind of thing. Sophie will probably be able to fill you in," Jamie said, moving his hands animatedly as he spoke.

"Anyway," he continued. "I thought I might know just the woman to run them." He gave Ali's arm a squeeze. "Imagine it—no overheads to think about, income as soon as you have a few attendees. I bet word of mouth will bring you big groups in no time. I mean, what else is there to do around here?" Jamie said, with a smile. Yes, the quiet was part of Charlesworth's charm, Alison thought, but it was true that it meant there were plenty of residents with spare time on their hands.

"Anyway, Ali," he said. "What do you think? Tell me you're in?"

Alison smiled, then took his hand firmly and shook it. "You've got a deal. And even the bank manager's not going to be able to stop me this time," she smiled.

Jamie beamed. Alison thought over some potential attendees; her sister-in-law was struggling to teach herself to knit, and Anna from Maggie's shop would enjoy the rebel cross-stitch. Hadn't Megan in her pilates class asked about bunting too? Hopefully she'd have a full house in no time.

"I can't wait to get started," she said, full of excitement.

"And, Jamie," Alison said, after a pause, looking around the shop's interior, "I still hope that maybe a few months down the line, you know, when Pete's earned us a bit of money and we've paid off our debts. Maybe we could talk again, about renting this place together?"

Jamie smiled. "Of course, hon. That door is always open."

"Good, I'm pleased," she said.

Alison watched her friend as he gazed out over the room. "You know what, Jamie? You look really happy," she said, gently.

"I do?" he said.

"Yes, you definitely do," she replied, with a nod.

"I suppose I am," Jamie said, leaning back on the blue-and-white striped fabric. "Remembering how to be, at least. And it's not just the shop," he said coyly.

"No?"

"Nope," he replied, a smile at the corners of his mouth. "You know Adam, the burlesque photographer I told you about? He takes the occasional break, takes a few pictures of people in clothes too." Alison raised her eyebrows and smiled. "Ali, do you remember the day I took George with me down to the beach for a run? Adam spotted us."

"Oh right, so he's a wolfhound enthusiast?" Alison said. "George, that old rogue. Does this guy want a cross-breed puppy? The litter's nearly due."

"Adam does like George," Jamie said, taking his time over saying it, "but, well, he seems to like me quite a bit too."

Alison put her hand on Jamie's. She could have whooped with excitement, but she held it in—it was still early days.

"He's got good taste," Alison said. "And I'm glad to hear it, Jamie."

They both looked out of the window then, at the people walking past. Women and men were peering in through the windows, although the glass panes were still grimy with plaster dust, trying to make out what the empty shop might soon become. One little girl pressed her face up against the glass but the steam from her breath meant she could see even less. Teenagers on their lunch hour scurried by, swinging their bags and chattering. If they'd lingered long enough they would have seen a middle-aged couple on deck chairs, slightly weathered by time but impeccably styled, and with a little more knowledge of how to be in love than they'd thought they had.

Chapter 28

Jenny

"Right, what's going on here?" I asked, putting the hot mugs of tea down on the table and looking at the men in my life. "You may as well say. You three are in cahoots about something, and don't think it's getting past me."

Dad, Chris and Dan were watching a DVD of *Fawlty Towers*, but when I came back into the living room, it was clear that I'd interrupted something more important than one of Manuel's cock-ups. Dan shuffled up on the sofa to make room for me, and I handed him one of the teas I'd just made. Dan and Chris exchanged glances and Dad tried to look very busy reading his copy of the *Mirror*.

"Stag night planning," I said, "I can smell it a mile off." After a steely look from me, Chris finally raised his hands in surrender.

"OK, OK," he said. Chris was in charge of organizing

Dan's last night as a single man. "We may have been lining up a few things."

"I wish you'd tell me a bit more about what you're doing to my poor husband-to-be."

"It's nothing too bad, Jen, I promise," Chris said, wholly unconvincing.

"Anyway," I said, "I thought the stag wasn't meant to be in on any of this?"

Dan took a swig of tea and shifted uncomfortably in his seat.

"Just hints, Jen," Chris said. "So he's got an idea of what to look forward to."

"Hmmm," I said, eyeing my brother and dad with suspicion. "As long as I'm not peeling him off the bathroom floor in the early hours of the morning, that's all I ask."

"Nah," Chris reassured me. "You can trust us. And come on, Jen, knowing your friends it's far more likely to be the other way around."

I pictured Chloe, the other girls from work, my school friends; actually, yes, that was probably true. My hen was only a week away now and, despite being nervous about what they might do to me, I was really looking forward to spending time with the girls. Chloe hadn't given much away, but I knew she was inviting some old friends of mine I hadn't seen in ages and I couldn't wait to catch up with everyone over cocktails. Cocktails were obligatory, weren't they?

My phone rang in my pocket and I saw Maggie's name

flash up. I pointed to the phone and excused myself. As I got up and walked out of the room into our hallway, I could hear the men resuming their chat in stage whispers.

"Maggie!" I answered, grateful for some female interaction. "How're things?"

"Jen?" came a small voice. It hardly sounded like Maggie at all.

"Yes, it's me. What's up?"

"I've been an idiot," she said.

"Are you OK?" I asked. Maggie usually sounded so confident and calm on the phone.

"I'm fine," she said, "but also I'm not. I just don't really know what to do with myself, Jenny. I'm at work but I can't focus on anything. Everything's gone a bit wrong. Any chance you could come by the shop?" she asked.

"Of course," I said, "I'm at my dad's but I'll drop by Bluebelle now. Give me ten minutes."

"Thanks, Jen," Maggie said. "I really appreciate it."

I poked my head around the door to the living room. Dan was looking pretty settled on the sofa and Chris was cracking open a beer for Dad. The volume was up, and pre-match football commentary was booming out.

"Dan," I started, and his eyes flicked up to meet mine. "You're OK here, aren't you? I'm just going to swing by the flower shop to see Maggie."

He smiled and nodded. I went over and gave him a kiss, before picking up my bag. "Right, you lot, enjoy." I waved at Chris and Dad, then turned back to Dan. "See you at ours this evening."

It was only a short bike ride over to Maggie's shop. I cycled past kids playing out and pavements littered with hula-hoops and skateboards, mums keeping watch from the doorsteps. A vision of my own mum's face flashed before me for a moment, her voice calling for me to come back in for tea. But just as quickly as it arrived, it was gone.

When I got to the high street I chained my bike to the lamppost outside Bluebelle du Jour and pushed open the glass front door, entering the shop to a jangle of bells. Anna, Maggie's assistant, was at the counter bundling up a bouquet of cornflowers and fragrant sweet peas.

"Hi, Jenny," she called out. "What do you think?" she asked, holding up the flowers to give me a better look at the arrangement.

"Wow," I said, "stunning." Anna had a good eye, and every time I dropped into the shop I'd noticed how she gave even simple bunches a distinctive twist.

"Cool," Anna said, with a grin. "So how's it all going with the wedding planning?" she asked.

"It's the hen night I've got to contend with first," I said, raising my hands to my head, feigning despair. "What are they going to do to me, Anna?"

She laughed, placing the bouquet on the counter to wrap and wiping her wet hands off on her apron. "I'm sure they'll be gentle." She tore off a big sheet of white paper to wrap the stems in. "Maggie's out the back, by the way," she motioned with a nod of the head, "doing the accounts. She's expecting you, so just go on through." And then, in a whisper, she said, "Try and cheer her up, will you?"

Maggie was tucked away in the far corner of the dimly lit back room, a spreadsheet open on the computer and a red ringbinder open in front of her. She jumped slightly as I walked in, and put a hand to her heart.

"Ah, Jenny. Hi." She smiled, but her voice was flat. "Sorry, you startled me."

"Maggie, what's up?" I asked. "What's happened?"

She pointed behind me. "Close the door for a sec, could you?"

I shut the door and walked over to her desk, where she'd pulled out a little stool for me to sit on.

"Oh, only something I really should have been smart enough to see coming," she said.

Her eyes were red and her blotchy skin was visible, even under her carefully applied foundation.

"What do you mean?" I asked.

"It's Dylan," Maggie said. "Argh. I'm so furious I could spit. With him. With myself. This is such a cliche I can't bear it, Jen." She ruffled the back of her hair, looking away for a second. "I caught him with another woman. In my bed."

"Oh, Maggie, no," I said, my hand going to my mouth, at a loss for a more helpful response.

"I know. She was American, horribly attractive," Maggie went on. "I could have killed them both."

"But he's only just moved in," I said, still in shock. "He gave up New York for you, didn't he? And all of those things he said," I began, with an uncomfortable feeling that I was making things worse.

"Exactly. Can you believe it?" she said, shaking her head. "He couldn't even keep it in his pants long enough to give us a chance."

"But how could he be so stupid?" I said. "I mean bad enough to do it . . . but in your house? What was he thinking?"

"Part of him wanted to be found out, I reckon," Maggie said. "To make it easier. He's always been a bit of a coward like that."

"Unbelievable, that he would—" I started, but stopped myself and touched her arm gently. "God, I'm really sorry, Maggie."

"Well, so am I," she said, creases in her brow starting to show, "but then I'm not. It's better that I found out now and not years down the line. However, as much as I tried to hold back my hopes, the truth is they were sky-high." She shook her head as she spoke. "It's hard, Jen."

Maggie's eyes were wet with tears now, but I could see she wasn't going to let them fall. She saw me notice. "I can't cry!" she said, blinking them away. "I will not let him make me cry." I put my arm around her, and her slim frame felt more fragile than before.

"It's his—"

"Loss?" Maggie finished, sitting up straighter and forcing a smile. "I know, Jen. And I'm better on my own. I know that."

That seemed a bit drastic, but something told me now wasn't the time to challenge it.

"Anyway, to top it off, the Darlington Hall wedding is going pear-shaped too. It was all brilliant and then, well, the landscape gardener is impossible to work with, and God, it's all turned into a bit of a mess, Jenny." She rested her head on my shoulder and began to cry.

Here was Maggie; serene, quick-thinking Maggie, with her own business and ten years more life experience than me. What could I possibly say to make her feel better?

"You know you're stronger than him, don't you?" I said, finally. "Strong enough to cope with all of this." She was taking deep, slow breaths, trying to control her sobs.

"You may be right, Jen," she said, unconvinced. Then she lifted her head and looked me in the eye, her green eyes bloodshot but determined. "In fact, you know what, you are definitely right."

"What you need is," I said, smiling, "and don't laugh, I know it's wildly inadequate but hey, it's all I've got to offer right now . . ."

"Go on, tell me," she said.

"A night out with the girls." Maggie took one look at me, then rolled her eyes and slumped back onto my shoulder.

I shrugged her off and shook my head. "Nope, I'm afraid it's not that easy," I continued, smiling, "because, in case you've forgotten, it's my hen next Saturday night, and there's absolutely no get-out clause, misery-guts or not."

Maggie groaned, then I saw the first hint of a smile creep onto her face.

"Look," I said, giving her a nudge, "I know you're excited about it really. And I promise that for one night at least we can make you forget that Dylan ever existed."

Maggie's smile was slowly growing. "And Lucy Mackintosh's stupid wedding—can you make that disappear too?" she asked, hopeful.

"What wedding?" I said.

"Promise?" she asked.

"I promise," I said, pulling her to me for a proper hug.

Chapter 29

Maggie

Maggie couldn't get comfortable. It was half-one in the morning, but sleep wasn't coming.

Her bed didn't feel like her own anymore, and even after she'd taken Dylan's things to the town dump, he still haunted the place; the one part of the world that she was used to having control over. Two days after she'd left, Sam's perfume lingered too, or at least it seemed that way to Maggie.

Whether or not Sam and Dylan's taunting spirits were still there, the fact was that Maggie was cold and her bed felt empty. She reached down and pulled a soft green blanket over her sheets. Her phone, on the bedside table, beeped with another message from Dylan. She pressed the button to read it:

Maggie, just let me explain? I know I messed up,
but there are reasons. I miss you so much. Call
me. Dxx.

Reasons? Really? She deleted it. She flicked through
her inbox to check she'd erased every other text from him,
then saw an older message she'd somehow missed and
never opened. It was from Owen.

Maggie—you left your folder with the sketches
here. I'm at the workshop all weekend if you need
them back. Owen.

Oh great, she thought. That's just what I need.

On the drive over to Owen's workshop Maggie put some
Ella Fitzgerald on to soothe her nerves. Over a breakfast
of muesli and fruit she'd texted him back saying she'd
come over at one, and he'd sent a minimal response to let
her know that was fine. She resented having to go back
to his place, but if she was going to continue with Lucy's
wedding plans, she would need her sketches; it was as
simple as that. She was a professional, and she could separate her emotions from her work. She'd simply swallow
her pride, and be in and out of his workshop as soon as
possible.

The scenery on the quiet A-road was wasted on Maggie today, and her thoughts drifted back to the previous

night. She'd finally got off to sleep about two, but when she awoke, after a blissful few minutes of amnesia, the memories and anxiety had flooded back. How could Dylan—why *would* Dylan—put so much effort into winning her back only to throw it all away in an instant? To think she had been on the cusp of introducing him to her friends—that she'd already told her mum and sister that they were an item again. It was all so, so . . . *embarrassing.* Rather than the pain of heartbreak, what she felt was humiliated.

She arrived at Owen's at ten to one, and realized she must have unwittingly been over the speed limit for most of the journey. She walked towards the old stables and saw that Owen's door was closed this time, but after her sharp knock it took less than a minute for him to appear.

He looked different today, his dark curls even more dishevelled, his khaki T-shirt so crumpled it looked as if he'd pulled it off the dirty laundry pile. There was a tiredness around his eyes that she hadn't seen before—but Maggie realized that the dark circles under her own eyes would probably be just as bad. Touche Eclat could only do so much.

"Come in," Owen said coolly, taking a step back and motioning inside. "I've been repotting some of the plants so it's a bit of a mess, but . . ."

For another lecture about robbing from the poor to furnish the rich with floral arrangements? No thanks, she thought to herself.

"I won't, if it's all the same to you," Maggie said, standing firm. "Thanks for letting me know about the folder. I'll need it for the wedding as you know." Her feet stayed rooted to the doormat.

"Sure." Owen stepped back inside and disappeared for a couple of moments, returning with the folder and passing it to her. "Are you sure you won't stop for a minute?"

Maggie shook her head and concentrated on putting the folder back in her satchel.

"Look, Maggie," Owen said, in a no-nonsense way. "I'd like for us to be on better terms than this. We left things badly the other day."

"What, do you feel guilty?" she said, clicking the clasp on her bag shut again and looking up at him. "You should," she continued. "You were way out of line. But if you want to pull out of the wedding, then that's your decision." Maggie stood up straighter. "How did Lucy react when you told her? Or did you two have more important things to do than discuss that?"

"Actually I haven't spoken to her yet," Owen said, his voice calm. "And for God's sake, Maggie, please can you stop it with this stupid conspiracy theory? There's nothing going on between Lucy and me, and it's pretty ridiculous that you'd think there was, to be honest."

Maggie recoiled. Oh, she thought, a blush creeping up her neck. Oh dear.

"Jack's my best friend, Lucy's his fiancée, end of story." Owen looked unruffled.

"But, but . . . the necklace?" Maggie said, her mind racing, losing whatever cool she might have had left.

"Ah, the necklace," Owen said. "Or, as you clearly see it, the evidence. Yes, it's Lucy's. She gave it to me because she wanted the stone reset and my neighbor here is a jeweler. If you go next door I'm sure he'd be happy to show you the new setting now."

Maggie felt her cheeks burning hot. She knew she was in the wrong, but she didn't want to back down.

"Maggie, look," he said. "Come inside? The kettle's just boiled."

At least Owen hadn't broken the news to Lucy, yet, and if there was still a way to salvage the wedding she had a duty to Lucy—and to her business—to find it. She stepped inside and sat down on a worn corduroy-covered sofa that was placed against the wall. From it she could see the garden through the wide windows, with its jasmine and honeysuckle and a group of birds crowding onto the little bird table. Owen handed her a chipped mug of milky tea heaped with sugar she hadn't asked for, and she cradled the mug in her hands while he took a seat next to her.

"I'm sorry," Maggie finally managed to say. "I shouldn't have jumped to conclusions."

"It's OK," Owen said. "It was an honest mistake, even

if the case for the prosecution was pretty flimsy. Anyway, you don't know me, and if you did I hope you'd realize I'd never do something like that."

Maggie's face relaxed a little.

"By the way," he continued. "I meant almost everything I said to you the other day." She raised an eyebrow at that and her instinct was to leave. "But still, I'm sorry." He looked down and ran a hand over his hair. "For the way that I said it. I never meant to offend you, I know I was harsh. It's a bad habit of mine. You're not the first person I've upset like this, just ask Jack. But listen," Owen went on, "I was wondering if we might be able to meet in the middle somehow."

Maggie looked at him in disbelief.

"Are you sure about that? You made it pretty clear when we spoke that you've got nothing but distaste for the way that I run my company."

"That's not what I meant at all," Owen countered. "I respect your business, and the way you manage it."

"Really?" she said.

"Yes."

He looked away from her as he said it. That T-shirt really could do with a good wash, she thought, and the denim of his jeans was wearing pretty thin in places. But sitting beside him, she couldn't help noticing that he smelled good; his arms and neck had a sheen of fresh sweat that she took in, alongside the soil and leaf smells of outdoors.

"I know I must have sounded self-righteous," he said, turning back to look at her.

"Too right," Maggie said, quietly.

He ignored her and continued. "And judgmental. And I handled the situation all wrong. But I know you're more experienced than me with this sort of event, and maybe that made me feel a bit small."

OK, Maggie thought, surprised. Perhaps I can work with this.

Owen carried on. "I should be better at understanding people whose values are different to mine."

"But there you go again," Maggie said, all the feelings that had made her walk out the other day flooding back. "That's not it at all. My values aren't that different. I'm not celebrity-obsessed, and believe it or not I don't hate polar bears."

Maggie stopped herself as she realized she was starting to lose her thread.

"Anyway, I don't know why you insist on pigeonholing me like that." Maggie's head hurt from all the confrontations of the past few days. She just wanted it all to stop. "I hadn't thought all of the ethical choices through, no," she said, close to giving in now through sheer exhaustion, "but that's not because I don't care. It's just that most of the time I've been slogging my guts out to meet deadlines and make ends meet."

"But can't you see that while you've been meeting your

deadlines, your environmental choices will have already made an impact," Owen said, forcefully.

"Enough," Maggie retorted, getting to her feet. "I didn't come here to be preached to, Owen. I really, really can't handle any more arguments now."

Owen looked up at her, surprised.

"Your life is so simple, isn't it?" she went on. "So I don't always live mine perfectly, but do you have any idea what the last few weeks have been like for me?" Maggie's voice strained as she struggled to keep control of her emotions.

"No," Owen said. "I don't. But it always seems pretty rosy over there with your flower business, and you've got your own house, haven't you? I just assumed—"

"Rosy? Ha!" Maggie gave a wry laugh. "No, Owen. It has not all been rosy."

"Sit down," Owen said. Reluctantly, Maggie took a seat next to him again.

"What's been going on?" he asked, gently.

"Nothing," she said. "I mean nothing and everything. My life got turned upside down for a while, but it'll be fine."

"Really?" he said. The look in his eyes seemed to change, soften a little. "I'm sorry to hear that. Are you sure you're OK?"

"No," Maggie said, tears springing to her eyes. "Actually I'm not that sure at all."

Owen's hand reached over to touch Maggie's where it

lay on the sofa, and they both rested on the floral fabric of her tea dress, next to her thigh. She didn't pull her hand away.

"I want you to be OK," he said, hesitating. "You deserve to be happy. And for what it's worth, I know you're not really as bad as I made out. You don't seem like a polar bear hater to me." He smiled. "Perhaps, if I'm honest, I wanted you to be."

They locked eyes. Maggie's heart was beating hard in her chest.

"It would all be easier that way," he said. "If there were some concrete reason why I could stop caring about you."

He was close to her right now. Really quite close. Had his mouth always looked that tempting? He reached a hand up to touch her hair, and her chest constricted. She put her hand up to block his.

"Owen, stop," she said, her voice soft, hushing the rush of adrenaline she felt under the surface.

He dropped his hand and looked down. She saw that the man who had made her so angry was now fragile in her presence. She sat up straight and looked over at her bag and jacket. She was going to get up and go. She'd pick up her things and go. Five minutes and she'd be out of here and on the road. But she should really say something first. She turned back to him.

"Owen, I'm sorry, I'd better . . ."

He nodded, silently. She raised her hand to touch the side of his face. His skin was warm, and in an instant his hand covered hers. It felt familiar, his touch. Her mouth met his full lips and she felt the warmth of his kiss, tasted part of that scent of outdoors that had drawn her to him earlier. Owen brought her closer and his hands ran through her thick red hair as if this was the only chance they'd get. Then he pulled back for a minute to look over her face, to take everything in. He didn't say a word.

Maggie kissed him again and let the rush of feeling block out every other troubled thought.

Chapter 30

Jenny

Alison was sketching out a thigh in charcoal, Maggie was focusing a little higher up, and I was sipping champagne from my glass and fighting the urge to giggle. I suspected it had been Ali's idea to build in a creative element to my hen party—and here we all were in one of Charlesworth's artists' studios, with a pretty gorgeous naked male model in the middle of the room.

"I tell you what," Chloe whispered to me, picking up a piece of chalk to add the highlights on the model's body—she was really launching into the drawing with gusto. "He is nearly enough to make me backtrack on swearing off men."

Maggie, overhearing, caught her eye and winked. Chloe seemed to have turned her back on Jon for good this time, and she seemed more confident with every passing day. It was good to see how Maggie was starting to bounce back after Dylan's betrayal too.

"I know what you mean about temptation." I glanced over at the model again and smiled. "And there I was, thinking I was ready to sign up for a lifetime of monogamy."

When I finally got over the awkwardness of not knowing quite where to look, I sketched in the outline of the man's body, the muscles, and then began to fill in the dark and light patches and the detail. The fizz of the champagne was making me feel light—as I was drawing I could hear voices around me, the girls laughing and having fun together, pouring more bubbles, and every so often I'd hear a snatch of conversation and join in. When we finally looked up at the clock it was nearly six, time for us to step back from the easels and move on to the next venue.

"Hey, Jen, move back, let's see yours," Chloe said, pushing a rogue curl out of her eye and shuffling round to get a better look at what I'd drawn.

"It's good, isn't it?" she said. "Hey, Alison, you're arty, aren't you?" Chloe shouted over. "What do you think of what Jen has drawn? I think it's good."

Alison came over, and cast an eye over my picture and took her time responding.

"Not bad at all, Jenny," she said.

I blushed, uncomfortable with all the attention. But then I thought of the package I'd given Alison to pass on to her friend—the book I'd finally finished working on. I knew publishers received tons of submissions, but perhaps it wasn't mad to think I might stand a chance?

"OK, ladies." The woman running the session came around to where we were standing. "Ooh that's nice," she said, looking at what I'd drawn. "I'm afraid we're going to have to let Marcus put his clothes on again now."

The girls reacted with a chorus of dismay.

Alison jumped in. "OK, so we're done with the hors d'oeuvres, let's go on to the main course. May the eating and drinking commence!"

"So, we asked Dan," Chloe said, "'What is your favorite part of Jenny's body?' What do you think he said?"

"Er, hmm . . . I don't know. Bum?" I replied.

"Nope!" Chloe said jubilantly, handing me another shot glass. "Eyes. What a charmer. Drink!"

I downed my sambuca. Two hours ago things had all still been fairly civilized—we'd left the studio and come here to Jasmine's, a Chinese restaurant on the high street, for dinner and drinks. We had a corner table and a half dozen more of my friends had come to join us; girls from uni and school I hadn't seen for ages and who I was touched had made the effort to come—as soon as we hugged hello, the years apart had seemed to dissolve; they all seemed just the same. Annie, the girl I'd once played with out in our street, showed me photos on her iPhone of her baby girl. "She's gorgeous," I told her; it was clear that she was brimming over with pride about the new arrival.

"I love her to bits," she said, "but you know what, I haven't been out for months, and I really can't wait to get a bit wasted with you tonight." She gave me a squeeze.

Dan's sister Emma was there too, laughing and covering her ears at the more explicit Mr. and Mrs. questions. There were a few, and I had been sort of relieved to get them over and done with, but embarrassment aside, I was loving having all of my closest girlfriends here. Women from different times and places in my life but who had all formed some of my favorite memories, and were throwing themselves wholeheartedly into making sure I'd have new happy memories of tonight.

Maggie and Chloe were huddled together talking about something away from the rest of the crowd when I interrupted them.

"What's going on over here?" I asked. They'd only met that morning but had really hit it off.

"Nothing," Maggie said. Chloe looked sheepish.

"Nothing?" I said, unconvinced.

"OK, there is something," Maggie said, and Chloe nudged her sharply in the ribs. "Chloe's got her eye on someone and we were just working out a little plan of action."

"Really?" I said, feeling excited but also a little left out. "And who's the new man?"

Chloe was blushing fiercely now, something she didn't often do.

"Oh no . . ." I said. "It's not . . ."

Maggie was trying to stifle her laughter.

"Marcus?" I guessed, remembering the buff model we'd all been drawing earlier. Chloe looked relieved, exchanging looks with Maggie and nodding.

"Yes, him," she said, giggling. But there was something in her eyes that hinted it wasn't him at all.

I couldn't remember the last time I'd laughed like I did that night. Sometimes when I went out, Dan would be on my mind, or I'd be thinking about work—but now all I felt was the warmth of these friendships. I looked over at Alison and Maggie opposite me, squabbling over the prawn crackers, and felt sure that we were going to be in one another's lives for good.

"You don't know what's up next, do you, Jen?" Alison said.

"What? There's more?" I'd genuinely thought that after the naked man I was off the hook.

"Did you really think Chloe was going to let you off this easily?" she replied.

"You have to tell me," I said, leaning closer, taking advantage of the fact that Chloe was deep in conversation with one of our work friends at the other end of the table. "I mean it. You know I hate surprises."

"Ooh I couldn't," Alison teased. Then Annie, leaning over, a little worse for wear by now, mouthed at me "KAR-A-O-KE."

"Yes!" I whispered back at them both. "*Brilliant.*"

Chloe had come up trumps. I'd always had a thing for karaoke, and there was a private room above the Fox and Pheasant where we'd go after work sometimes. Chloe doing her Tina Turner to "Nutbush City Limits" tended to be a highlight. I have a godawful voice but it's never mattered, we always end up in stitches.

I was biting into a prawn wonton when I heard the door to the restaurant open behind me, and felt a breeze on the back of my neck.

"You wait until—" Alison started. But then she stopped mid-sentence and her face took on a more serious expression.

"What is it?" I said, following her gaze over my shoulder.

There, beside all the women who I knew I could count on, stood the woman who had walked out on me.

Nothing can prepare you for meeting a mirror image of yourself. I'd never realized my mum and I looked so alike until she was there, in the Chinese restaurant, hovering by the table and waiting for me to say hello. It was clear from Alison's reaction that she had noticed it too. It's odd. I'd seen pictures of my mum, of course, but the similarities hadn't come across in those. They were Dad's faded old seventies prints and none of them had really been sharp enough for me to make out the features that were my own. But I could see it now.

I'd had quite a bit to drink which made it harder to

take everything in. I found myself focusing on just one point, on her mouth which looked just like mine, the same full lips, but with lipstick. The room began to spin.

"Jenny," she said, holding her arms out, only a slight tremble in her voice betraying her calm manner. "Look at you."

I turned from my mum back to Alison, whose concerned expression prompted me to say, "Yes, it's her." My voice sounded croaky. "I think I'd better do this on my own."

As I turned back to face my mum, I heard Alison pass on the message and gently herd my friends away. I had a vague awareness of the women I'd come with leaving, saw them out of the corner of my eye, whispering and gathering up their things. I kissed goodbye to one familiar face, then another, felt gentle, reassuring touches on my arm as the hens trooped out. I heard Maggie say I could call her later, whatever time it was, but I don't think I even answered. My mother was still there, looking me over.

"What a beautiful woman you've turned into," she said, smiling. Her expression seemed relaxed, but there was an awkwardness to her stance that reminded me we should probably be sitting down.

When I turned back to the table, it was nearly empty. My mother squeezed onto the padded seat opposite me, got herself settled and took my hands in hers. Her eyes were watery. "Wow. You really are all grown up."

"Mum." I sort of squeaked it, in a voice that didn't

sound like mine. I knew instinctively that this was my mother; but I didn't really know this woman at all. Her hair was bright with white-blonde highlights, her lips were painted a deep red, and she was wearing leather trousers, heeled boots and an electric blue ruffled blouse. I felt invisible in my slate gray wrap dress, even with my chunky green necklace and Jimmy Choos.

"Congratulations, Jenny." She reached under the table and squeezed my knee. She smelled of caked foundation and perfume. The scent didn't bring back any memory of my childhood, like I'd sometimes idly imagined it would. "Have you been having a good night?" she asked.

"Mum." Some of my strength was returning at last. "What are you doing here?"

Her face fell a little. "Oh, love." She glanced around, dodging my stare, "I know you didn't respond to my email, but email's not always the best way, is it? So impersonal, not right for catching up at all." She rearranged some strands of hair in her fringe as she spoke. "So when I found out about your little shindig tonight, well Ange didn't want to tell me, but when she said Chinese I guessed it must be here—I thought if we could just meet face-to-face we'd be able to work things out properly." She motioned to the waiter, beckoning him over. "A bottle of rosé, my good sir, for me and the bride-to-be!"

I'll be honest, I was struggling. The waiter came back with the wine and two glasses and began to pour. "You see, darling," Mum continued, "when you get to my age you realize life's too short to hold grudges. The thing is to forgive and forget, move on."

She lifted her glass and I, robotically, lifted mine to clink against hers. "Your dad's not bitter, about Nigel and me, you know," she said, looking me in the eye now. I gawped at her in disbelief. "He told me that on the phone. It's all just water under the bridge." She gave a gentle shrug.

"You and I were always very close," Mum continued, her confidence slipping to let in a shaft of something that surprised me: neediness. I'd taken a sip of the sweet wine but when I heard what she said I nearly choked on it.

"That was over *twenty years* ago, Mum," I said. "And we may have had a bond then, but I'm a different person now." My mind was awash. "And anyway, what about Chris, or have you forgotten all about him?"

"Oh, darling," she said, pulling at the ruffles on her blouse to straighten out the front. "You know it's not the same, with boys. Girls and their mums have a special relationship, no matter what. It's what makes having a daughter special."

"Oh really? Dad seems to think we're both pretty special. And he'd know, of course—given that he brought us both up." Gathering confidence now, I kept my eyes on hers, even though I could see she was longing to look away.

"Do we really have to dredge up the past, Jennifer?" she said, shifting in her seat.

"Chris is here in the present, not the past, Mum. And the two of us are a package. You leaving made that happen, brought us together more than anything else. If you want to be a mum again, or whatever it is you really want, then you have to deal with both of us. Or neither."

"But, love, I was thinking we could look to the future, like you are doing with—David, is it?"

"Dan," I corrected her.

"Yes, look to the future and all that you have ahead of you. I told Nige, I said, 'It's now or never, Nige—my little girl is becoming a woman.'"

I got to my feet. "You know what, you're right, Mum. I don't want to dredge up the past—not at all. Which is why I didn't reply to your messages. And it's why I definitely don't want you at my wedding."

I stood there, looking down at the woman whose absence had colored so much of my life.

"Maybe I should also have said that I didn't want you ruining my hen night, but I thought you might just work that one out for yourself."

The woman I knew as my mum but who felt like a stranger to me was finally lost for words. I picked up my coat and bag and walked out.

I'd called Dan from the cab—it was only a ten-minute walk home, but it was raining hard, plus my feet hurt. Friday night Dan had been out for his stag, so he was at home recovering. As I got out of the taxi he was standing by our open front door with a concerned expression on his face.

"Jen, are you OK?"

God, sometimes I hate it when people say that. As he took me into his arms I began to sob—in a blubbery, spluttering way, not a gentle, sweet way. He led me upstairs and sat me down on our sofa, bringing over one of his zip-up hoodies to warm me up. He held me for a minute while I cried and then tipped my chin up to look at me. He saw right away that cocoa wasn't going to cut it.

"She didn't ask a thing about me, or Chris," I said, when the sobs finally slowed. "She just spoke as if we should be carrying on where we left off. But that was two decades ago, Dan. Twenty years. What was she thinking?"

Dan stroked my hair and held me close. "God," he said. "I really can't believe she came to your hen night."

"I know," I said, starting to find a smile. "I was having a really bloody nice time too. The girls from school had come all the way from London and Bournemouth, and best of all there wasn't a willy-shaped straw in sight. We were going to go to karaoke . . . but then she turns up and ruins everything. I don't think I even like her, Dan. She's just a stranger. I had nothing to say to her at all."

"Why tonight?" Dan said, shaking his head. "I mean, sorry, babe, I don't want to make it worse, but I feel annoyed with her even though I don't know her. I hate seeing you so upset." He wiped away a tear from my cheek. "How could she think it was a good idea to just turn up?"

"That's just her way, Dan," I said. "Dad has given the odd hint that back when she was still living with us, life was a bit unpredictable. He said she tended to do things when it suited her, rather than when they needed doing. I know he tries not to say anything negative about her, but I'm pretty sure it was a bit of a whirlwind at the time. Maybe back then, when Mum's ex got back in touch she got swept up in the drama of that romance. I don't know . . . and perhaps she came to the hen night because she liked the idea of a big reunion with me, in front of an audience."

"She doesn't sound anything like you or Chris," Dan said. "Or your dad for that matter. It's difficult to imagine."

"Yes, thankfully. Although I do think she and Dad loved each other. He says she used to bring him out of his shell, that they were chalk and cheese but he wouldn't have wanted a wife just like him."

"I can see his point. I can't think of anything worse than being married to a woman like me," Dan said, pausing to picture it. "No, I'm definitely happier with the wife I'm going to have."

Dan kissed me, then led me by the hand to our bedroom and got out my favorite Gruffalo pajamas. He talked to me about his evening, the DVD he'd been watching, while I changed into them. He climbed under the duvet, lifted it for me to get in and held me while I fell asleep. I knew Mum must still be in Charlesworth somewhere, but here in Dan's arms I was out of her reach.

Chapter 31

Alison

"Pastry delivery," Alison said, popping her head around Jenny's doorway brandishing a white paper bag.

Jenny was sitting up in bed in her pajamas, bundled in the duvet with a magazine propped up on her knees. The blinds were down, letting only a chink of natural light into the room, and a low murmur was coming from the radio. Jenny's eyes were panda-like with smudged mascara and her blonde hair was tied back in a tufty ponytail.

"Ali, hi," she said, looking a bit startled. "Come in, sit down." She flattened out a bit of duvet. "Sorry it's such a mess in here."

Alison sat down on the bed, tucking her legs up under her. "I hope you don't mind me popping in. Dan let me in on his way out to the shops."

"No, no, it's good to see you, let me get a plate . . ." Jenny said, looking at the paper bag and starting to get up.

"Stop right there," Alison said, holding her hand up playfully. "You stay put, I'll grab one."

Alison returned a moment later with a plate and put the pastries on it. She passed Jenny an almond croissant and took a plain one for herself.

"It felt wrong leaving you last night," Alison said. "But it seemed like you needed some time alone with your mum."

"Oh, don't worry. You were right." Jenny took the tiniest of nibbles from her pastry. "We do have a lot to talk about." Jenny's voice caught and Alison could see she was on the brink of tears. "But we didn't. Talk, I mean. I don't want to until I know that she's sorry for what she did. She doesn't seem to regret a thing, Ali—she just went on about looking forward not back. And I don't think Chris is part of this vision she has for her new life at all."

"Really?" said Alison. "It's hard to fathom, isn't it?" Alison gently shook her head. "He's the kind of son any mother should be proud to have."

"You're preaching to the converted here, Ali," Jenny said, with just a hint of her usual smile. "Chris is all that and more. While from the outside it may look like Dad and I are supporting him, it's almost always been the other way round."

"So what did you say to her?" Alison asked.

"What I just said to you, about not being ready to talk,

and that I don't want her there at our wedding. I was pretty clear. After that I just walked out," Jenny said.

"Fair enough," Alison said. "If I'd left the girls, walked out when they were so young . . . It's pretty surprising that she expects to be welcomed back into your life, no questions asked. The love, or like even, is something she forfeited, isn't it? Doesn't she realize it needs to be earned back?"

"She says that Dad has forgiven her," I said, "so I guess she thought I would too. But Dad's only done that because he's never stopped loving her. I bet he's still holding out hope—even after all these years—that they'll find a way to patch things up."

"His decision is his decision," said Alison. "And yours is yours. You've let her know how you feel, and that's important."

"I know," Jenny said. "And it's over now." There was an emptiness in her eyes.

"You've got a wedding to a wonderful man to look forward to, in just over two weeks' time," Alison said, with a bright smile. "What do you say we focus on that instead?"

Jenny nodded without a word, then covered her eyes with her hands, as if trying to stop herself from crying. Alison moved in closer and put an arm around her.

"Is there something else going on, Jen?" Alison asked. Jenny wiped her eyes.

"I'm just not feeling excited, Ali. About getting married. All I feel is flat." Alison stroked her friend's hair.

"What I can't get out of my mind," Jenny said, taking a deep breath, "is what if Dan and I have children and I do the same thing?" Her words were slow and considered. "What if I can't settle either? What if, however much I'm in love with him now, I stop loving Dan one day, the same way she stopped loving Dad?"

Jenny turned to look Alison in the eye. "She left us, and half of me is made up of her, Ali."

"Wherever your genes came from, you're your own person, Jenny," Alison said, "and you know yourself better than most. Having doubts before you make this kind of commitment is totally natural." She gave Jenny's arm a squeeze.

A moment later Alison got up and went over to the window, opening the blinds with a snap and letting the light stream in. Jenny winced as the sun hit her.

"Come on, you're not a vampire, Jenny. It's past midday—even Sophie and Holly will be out of their PJs by now." Jenny looked down at her pajama shirt. To top things off it now had a bit of marzipan from the croissant stuck to it.

"Get in the shower." Alison pointed to the door, ignoring Jenny's pleading look. "I'm going to tidy up a bit in here and then there are some people I want you to meet."

"So this was how the schoolhouse looked back then," Ruby said, showing Jenny a black-and-white photo of a classroom.

Jenny cast her eye over the picture of the place that was going to be her wedding reception venue, and Alison peeked over her shoulder. Little boys in shorts and girls in pigtails were lined up in front of the large blackboard for their school photo.

"There's our Jimmy," Ruby said, pushing her reading glasses up her nose and pointing to a boy with freckles in the front row. "He'd only just started then and you can tell, can't you? He was a bit nervous, poor lamb."

Jenny, Alison, Jamie and the Spencers were sitting at a table in Jamie's café—or rather the building site that was going to be Jamie's café. It was still very much a work in progress, with crates, ladders and piles of plaster dust on the floor, but the place was slowly beginning to take shape, with tables and colorful mismatched chairs by the window now, a specials board lying on the counter, and a till ready to be plugged in. On the walk over, Alison had told Jenny about her morning's work—helping Jamie clear out Ruby and Derek's attic and bringing the furniture over in the back of her car.

Jamie had insisted that Ruby and Derek come over and take a look at where their bits and pieces were going to go. Ruby had been delighted at the idea and had gathered up some old photo albums to take with them. "There's all sorts in here," she'd said. "They might give you some ideas for the décor." While Alison was out seeing Jenny, Jamie had sat down to look through the albums with them.

"You're having your wedding party at the schoolhouse, aren't you?" Derek asked, looking up at Jenny and pointing at the photo of little Jimmy's school days. "I am, yes," Jenny replied. Alison could tell from her voice that tears still weren't far from the surface, but she was looking a whole lot better than she had been that morning. She'd put on gray skinny jeans with a white T-shirt and a purple cardigan and blow-dried her hair until Alison had given her the nod that she was looking respectable enough to be seen in public.

"Ooh, and look at this one of the town hall," Ruby said, passing the other women a photo of the place where Jenny and Dan were set to say their vows. The photo was taken from quite far away and the building looked more or less the same as it did now.

Ruby smiled. "Look at it closely," she said. Alison and Jenny squinted to make out the figures on the steps; they were children, but this wasn't a formal school photo. They were carrying satchels and something else that neither of them could quite make out.

"See their gas masks?" Ruby said. "That's where the evacuees arrived, this lot were straight off the train."

"I wasn't around then of course," Derek chimed in, "but Charlesworth had quite a few, didn't it, Ruby?"

"Yes," Ruby said, casting her mind back. "They came in from London and the local families around here put them up. It was a bit of a change for our little old town, I'll tell you. But a lot of the families enjoyed it. I heard there was even a romance, a girl from London who grew up and married a boy from here," she said.

"How sweet," Alison said, before picking up one of the photo albums and turning the page. "Those ads on the wall are great," she said, pulling out a photo of children playing near the high street. Bold signs for cleaning products and Brillo pads were painted onto the brick. "Maybe we could do something similar in here." Her eyes drifted out to the empty backyard.

Derek and Jamie had started talking about the café's electrics, and they got up, leaving the women at the table. They walked over to the light sockets where wires were still loose, and as Derek leaned in closer to inspect one, Alison could hear him offering Jamie some words of advice.

Ruby turned to Jenny then. "Are you looking forward to it, dear? Getting married?"

Jenny's eyes started to water again as she nodded.

"There's nothing wrong with being nervous, you know," she said, with a kind look. "It's a very big step. Alison knows that too, don't you?"

Alison smiled, adding, "Yep, I do, and on the good days it'll seem like the best decision you ever made."

"I know Dan's the right person," Jenny said, "but how can I be sure that I'm up to it? That I'm strong enough to stick with marriage?"

She looked over at Ruby. Between them were the photos that marked out the decades Ruby and her husband

Derek had spent together, smiling children's faces, candles on birthday cakes, sandcastles by the sea.

"Well, dear, I was excited about marrying Derek, but gosh, I had those doubts too," Ruby said. "You know what the trick has always been for us?" she went on. Jenny and Alison's full attention was on her. "Shepherd's Pie on Tuesday."

Jenny tilted her head, unsure.

"And I'll bring him the paper every morning. You see there's no good looking at your whole life and trying to guess how it'll be," she said, "because it doesn't work like that. But Derek'll make me tea each afternoon, and I always know that's coming. And since the children left home, we go ballroom dancing together every Saturday, play Scrabble with friends on Monday night, and we watch our soap together on a Sunday afternoon. From our first days as a married couple, it's always been like that, our routines, taking a moment here and there to do something for one another."

Jenny and Alison listened intently as Ruby continued.

"As you get older you see that what you thought were little things, why, they were really the big things all along."

Chapter 32

Jenny

"Voila!" Maggie said as she put our coffees and some lemon drizzle cake down on the plastic table. We were back in the flea market's refreshment tent, sitting on plastic gardening chairs, surrounded by older ladies in bright dresses chatting to one another. We'd decided to leave the stall-browsing till a bit later today.

"Ali told me you're feeling a bit better now?" Maggie said, taking a seat and giving me a kind look. "Christ, I really can't believe your mum just turned up out of the blue like that! Certainly made for a pretty dramatic end to the hen do."

"Drama would seem to be her forte," I said. "But I think she's finally got the message now. And you know what, apart from her turning up I enjoyed every minute

VANESSA GREENE

of the hen, and the good bits are what I'll remember. So thanks for coming, you two."

"It was a giggle, wasn't it?" Maggie said. She picked up a forkful of cake and a mischievous smile crept onto her face. "And this reminds me," she went on, "something happened to me last week."

"Did he call?" I asked, my heart sinking. I wasn't looking forward to seeing Maggie go through a drawn-out break up, with the kind of toing and froing Jon had put Chloe through.

Maggie smiled, not giving anything away.

"I hope he's planning on making it up to you," Alison said. "What did he say? Must have been quite an apology."

"Dylan . . . ?" Maggie laughed and shook her head. "I mean yes, he did call, various times actually. But I never picked up, and now I've blocked his number. He's probably back in the States by now, and good riddance."

A wave of relief came over me, and I saw Alison's tense expression soften too.

"What then?" I asked. I was on the edge of the plastic gardening chair by now.

"Someone else," Maggie said, leaving the words dangling.

"*Who?*" Alison and I demanded in unison. A twenty-year age gap made no difference to our levels of girlish excitement.

"Well . . ." Maggie started. "It's ridiculous. And

302

reckless. And far, far too soon. Going absolutely nowhere . . ." she said.

"Who?" Alison repeated.

"But I'm enjoying myself," Maggie said, "and there's no way I'm getting close enough to get hurt this time, so while I panicked a bit at first, now I just think what have I got to lose?" She caught Alison's inquisitive glare again, and conceded at last. "He's handsome, creative . . . often pretty muddy—and a fair bit younger than me," she confessed, her cheeks glowing.

I racked my brain. Who else was on Maggie's radar? She'd been so wrapped up in Dylan I couldn't think of any other men she'd mentioned.

"Do you remember me talking about Owen?" Maggie said, after what seemed like an eternity. "The landscape gardener, the one on the Darlington Hall wedding?"

"Yes," I answered, confused. "The arrogant one, who you despise, and who is making your working life a misery?"

"Yes, him," she answered. "So it turns out we don't hate each other that much after all. In fact we nearly got caught not-hating-each-other-that-much in the woods behind Darlington Hall last week." She smiled, blushing. "We got a bit, ahem, *carried away*, plotting out a fairy-light trail for Lucy and Jack's guests, when the gardener came by."

"Maggie, that's outrageous!" Alison said, clapping her hands together. "Bravo."

"Good for you, you deserve it," I said. "So how old is he?"

"Thirty-one," Maggie said, "but I actually think he's more mature than me. In fact, I've realized I'm really not that grown up after all." Maggie certainly looked as if years had drifted away from her face. "He's relaxed with who he is, and it makes me feel like I can be the same, really be myself when I'm with him," she said.

Maggie took a sip of coffee and settled her cup back down. "I mean, granted, it was massively romantic being back with Dylan, and dreaming the dream that we could undo everything that went wrong. But all the while I had doubts. There was so much riding on things working out; we knew we had to do a better job—but then when we ended up making even more of a pig's ear of it, I realized it didn't matter at all." Maggie smiled. "I couldn't care less what other people think, because life is full of mistakes and learning, isn't it? I forgot that for a while. And this—this thing with Owen is going nowhere, it's a bit of fun and we both know that. But the *chemistry* is something else. I feel so young."

"Ooh, it sounds dreamy," Alison said, giving her a wink. "What I wouldn't give to be there again," she said, wistfully, then laughed. "I'm happy for you, Maggie. And actually, you know what, I'd be more jealous, but since Pete got his new job I almost feel like we're in a new relationship ourselves. There are days when I can't wait for him to get home so I can drag him upstairs before the girls get back from their after-school clubs."

"Ali, that's great," I said, meaning it. "If I'd known a budgeting spreadsheet would make such a difference to your sex life I'd have sent you one weeks ago."

Alison and Maggie laughed. Then a thought popped into my head. "But, Ali, hold on, back to Owen; wasn't part of the issue with him that he was refusing to cooperate over the *It Girl* deal? Did you have to give in on that?" Maggie was hardheaded when it came to Bluebelle and I couldn't believe her priorities would switch so quickly; this really was a golden opportunity for her.

"We found a way," Maggie said, with a wink. "It's astonishing what you can get a man to agree to when you're in the bath." Alison feigned a gasp and then laughed. "But, seriously," Maggie continued, "he does still feel strongly about it, and I can see his point now, so we've reached a compromise. He's agreed to work on the wedding even with the magazine exclusive going ahead, provided that I allow him to look into my proposed flower sources and find fair-trade, environmentally sound alternatives, so that his brand isn't associated with anything he doesn't agree with."

"That's sounds reasonable," Alison said. "And surely that's a good thing for your business anyway? I mean people care about the environment more than ever. Pete's obsessed with our vegetable patch."

"You're right," Maggie said. "Anna kept bringing it up, but it seemed like there was never time to look into it properly, and to be honest I didn't really know where to start. But if Owen's willing to do the legwork then who am I to argue?" She shrugged. "I've also managed to convince him that getting publicity in the right circles could open up good opportunities for him. A couple of lucrative new projects would mean he'd be able to take on some pro bono work for local community projects and charities, for example. There's one initiative he's really interested in, working with the long-term unemployed to help them build skills and confidence through gardening—I pointed out that designing one WAG's garden would give him the cash to start helping people back into work and he warmed to the idea."

"That's a good way of looking at it," Alison said.

"Absolutely," I agreed, "and you know what? With all this gossiping out the way already, I'm almost ready for a bargain hunt. What do you say?"

Both women nodded, and Alison finished her coffee. "We've done well," Maggie said, "but we are still two cups off our target."

Alison gave a gentle laugh. "I know how you and Jenny like to make your targets. So far be it from me to stand in the way of that. Let's hit the stalls, ladies." She stood up, then stopped for a moment, a pensive look on her face. "But seriously, two weeks to go and only two little teacups to find. It's amazing really, isn't it?"

"It is," Maggie agreed. And we raised our cardboard coffee cups to that, knowing that in just two weeks' time, I'd be getting married at a beautiful wedding full of vintage teacups and we'd be able to toast our success in a far more appropriate way.

We ducked out of the marquee and I squinted up into the afternoon sunshine. It had been drizzling that morning when I'd set out, but now the rain had stopped and everything—from the beads of rain on the grass to the thick green leaves in the plane trees overhead—was gleaming. Alison stretched like a happy cat next to me and retied the red headscarf she had knotted around her hair.

Behind us we heard a voice calling out, "Help me! I'm stuck."

Alison and I locked eyes, then turned around to see Maggie still at the entrance of the tent, her high heels sunk deep into the wet ground. She was a vision—sophisticated from the ankle up, in a bias-cut lilac shift and a white headscarf, but anchored to the ground in a muddy and not entirely dignified fashion. Ali and I walked back and took hold of a side of Maggie each, letting her lean on us while we tackled the issue at ground level.

We were still laughing as we made it back onto the tarmac of the car park. We stopped next to a stall and I recognized the owner at once—it was the man who'd sold us that first teaset, Ruby and Derek's neighbor. I was pretty sure a glimmer of recognition passed across his face when he caught sight of the three of us together. He gave a little nod of acknowledgment and I smiled back. Alison and Maggie hadn't noticed him and moved on to the next stall, where crockery was piled high. I lingered and picked up a brooch inlaid with green stones; it was only costume jewelry but it would be perfect for Maggie. I wanted to get her a little something to say thank you as I knew she was giving me a really good deal on our wedding flowers.

"That'll be seven pound fifty, love," the stallholder said. I handed over a tenner and he passed me the change together with the brooch in a paper bag.

"Thank you," I said, and gave him a smile before walking away.

We found the final two cups for our collection at the stall nearest to the church, which was run by a mother and daughter team. As they told us, in animated voices, about the quiet Saturday when they'd decided it was time for a major clear-out, I felt a pang. I imagined the radio on and laughter as boxes were opened and emptied, childhood treasures rediscovered.

But that feeling, of something in me being missing, was fleeting; after all, I'd not had that closeness with Mum since I was tiny, so how could I miss it? We'd never have that, even if I did let her back into my life. And while this mother was affectionate and loving, my mum had proved without a doubt that she only cared about herself.

"These will make gorgeous candles," Maggie said,

lifting two cups with silver trim and paintings of lavender on the sides.

"Done. Our final two!" I said, triumphant, as the daughter wrapped our new purchases in bubble wrap and taped them up. Maggie, Alison and I couldn't resist a high five.

I was home first, cycling past the Saturday shoppers and bolting my bike to the rail before Dan got back from football. I settled onto the sofa in front of the TV. Thirty minutes later there was a clunk as Dan opened the door, sweaty and muddy in his gym kit.

"Hey," I shouted out, leaping up in time to get a newspaper under the football boots he was about to put on our cream carpet. "Ha-ha!" I said, pleased with the rescue mission.

"See, practice really does make perfect," he said, giving me a wink. I screwed up my face into my best fishwife scowl and he kissed me like that.

"We're not having cream carpets when we move. Not with you and the new puppy, it would be a full-time job."

"When can we get him from Ali?" Dan asked.

"Three weeks still, Dad's got the kennel nearly ready." We'd gone around to see Cassie and George's new litter of puppies last week, adorable squirming brown balls of fluff scrambling over their mum on Alison's neighbors' kitchen floor. Dad, Dan and I had both fallen head over heels in love with a small pup with a pink nose. He'd waddled up to us right away and it was like he'd chosen us, rather than the other way around. Dad couldn't wait to get him home, in fact I was concerned we might end up with a custody battle on our hands when Dan and I finally got around to moving to a place with a garden and wanted to take him back.

"How was football?" I asked, like I did every Saturday.

"I scored for us," Dan said, smiling. "And we beat them 3–0."

"Well done," I said, kissing him again. I caught sight of a white envelope in his hand. "What's that?"

He passed it over and I saw it was addressed to me. "Joe from downstairs gave it to me," he said. "It went to their flat by mistake."

"Oh, fine," I said, putting it down on the dresser.

As I lifted my hand though, I caught sight of the handwriting on the envelope and felt my legs buckle.

"I'm not opening it," I said, shaking my head, as Dan took a seat next to me on the sofa. "There's no way."

"That's fine," Dan said, shrugging and putting a hand on my shoulder. "Jen, you don't have to do anything you don't want to."

I glanced over at the envelope propped on the sofa arm. The silence between Dan and me seemed to go on forever. Eventually he looked over at me but I carried on staring straight ahead, not meeting his eyes. Then he put his feet up on the coffee table and reached for the remote control.

"Dan!" I snapped.

"What?" he said, jumping a little as he turned back to me. "What have I done?"

"You can't just . . ." I huffed. "Look." I grabbed hold of the letter and thrust it at him. "You open it. Read it to me."

He raised his eyebrows as my emotions, messy as an old set of fairy lights right now, caused me to lash out.

"Please, I mean," I corrected myself, wrinkling my nose in apology. "If you don't mind. I just don't think I can do it myself."

"Sure," Dan said, as he took the envelope from me gently.

As I watched him open the letter, heard the paper ripping, the muscles across my shoulders were tight. "Jen, try and relax," Dan said, taking in my pose and giving my leg a stroke. I realized I was sitting bolt upright. I wriggled my shoulders to release the tension and tried to make myself comfortable on the sofa.

"I'm relaxed," I said, knowing I didn't sound it. "What does it say?"

"'Dear Jenny,'" Dan started, shuffling the pages of the letter to see how many there were. "God, there's loads here—who writes letters this long nowadays?" His eyes were wide and I could tell he was trying to lighten the situation, but it just made me impatient. I gave him a look and he carried on.

" 'I'm really sorry, I know I upset you when I visited.' " Dan was trying to keep his tone neutral, even though he was even crosser with my mum than I was, if that were possible. " 'I've been talking to Nige.' " Dan stopped. "Who's Nige?" he asked.

"Her boyfriend I think, go on, carry on."

Dan shrugged and continued, " 'He's made me see I didn't go about things in the right way. I shouldn't have come to your hen night.' " He nodded then. " 'Maybe I shouldn't have got in contact at all—but I just wanted to speak to you again. You're still my little girl, even after all this time.' "

Dan must have seen my eyes starting to water because he stopped.

"Do you want to read the rest yourself?"

I nodded and took the pages from him, casting an eye over the round handwriting that was so familiar to me—it might have been over ten years since I'd heard from my mum but I had looked over her old cards and notes a hundred times since then.

I've never really been that good at getting important things right, I get nervous and Nige says that sometimes I get swept up in the moment without thinking things through. But I just wanted to see you again, to try and get back to the way we were, even though I know a lot of time has passed.

Deep breaths, Nige says. This part is hard for me to write but I know I have to, because I don't want you to think that I don't care. Because I do. About you and your brother.

Dan made a sign for tea and got up to go to the kitchen and I read on.

You wanted to talk about Chris and I know I should be able to. But I find it hard, because I know I haven't been a good mum. I know that you and him are, like you put it, "a package," and I think that's great. I'm glad you look after each other. But when I spoke with you it hurt, because it reminded me of how much I let your little brother down, even more than I did you. Marriage isn't easy,

I paused for a moment. Was I really ready to hear advice about marriage from my mum, of all people? But I couldn't ignore the temptation to read on. I'd been waiting ten years to find out a little bit more about what made my mum tick.

Marriage isn't easy, but you seem like a sensible woman, Jenny, and stronger maybe than I was when I married your dad. I wish you the best for your marriage, and don't worry, I understand now that it wouldn't be right for me to be there on your big day.

Thank you, I thought to myself, for realizing that. I felt Dan's presence behind me and he touched my hair and smiled as he put down a cup of tea for me on the table. I touched his hand and held it for a second as he moved away.

Anyway, to explain it, I think I have to start at the beginning. When you were born they put you on my chest, Jenny, and I held you. I felt your little heart beat and saw your eyes. Even then they were the same as mine. You were such a gorgeous baby. We brought you home from the hospital the next day and I was with you all the time, cuddling you, holding you, and then when you were bigger, we'd play together. But when Chris was born they took him away, they told me something was wrong and they didn't know how bad it was yet. When the doctors came back they told me he might never walk, and that there could be worse things too. I'm not trying to make excuses, but I thought I'd done something wrong, Jenny. Your dad and I made him, so it must have been our fault. That was how I saw it. I thought maybe it was the wine I'd had before I realized I was pregnant, something like that, or the

time I slipped and fell over in the kitchen. But
anyway, I was thinking all this back then. They had
to do tests on Chris, so the way things happened
they didn't put him on my chest at all.

I read the rest of the letter in silence. Dan was keeping himself busy with something in the other room. Mum talked about how she had found things more and more difficult once she was able to take Chris home.

I realized that I couldn't bring the fun, good, happy
things into your lives that I wanted to, that you
needed, when my head wasn't right. When what
I felt, even looking at your little faces, was sad.
You were only kids and I knew you'd be soaking
everything up like little sponges, the bad with the
good, the arguments, my moods, the way both me
and your dad felt as we started to grow apart.
I loved you and I loved Chris. But I couldn't stop
feeling like a failure for not knowing how to support
Chris, for worrying that I might not be able to care
for him the right way. I thought you'd be better off
without me. I suppose I ended up taking it out
on your dad a bit too; maybe I blamed him. But
I just didn't know how to cope. I cared about
your brother, and I still care now. I've written to him
too. If he reads his letter, hopefully he'll start to

*understand what I did a bit better. But I love him
just like I love you.*

I read the final lines of Mum's letter.

*I'll understand, Jenny, if you never want to hear from
me again. But if you and Chris are willing to give
me a chance, I'd really like to get to know you, as
the adults you are now, and have you be part of my
life again.*

Tears were falling down my cheeks. I rubbed them
away with the back of my hand.

Chapter 33

Maggie

No, this couldn't be happening. Maggie was in the back room of the shop, diary in hand. And her head was spinning.

After the flea market she'd gone back to the florist's, and Anna had been out front arranging the flowers for a memorial service later that week. Maggie could see she was handling quite complex work with ease, and was clearly enjoying having a project of her own. Maggie was reminded of the enthusiasm she'd felt when she'd first been learning the trade.

"You're doing a wonderful job on that," Maggie had said, as Anna finished off one of the wreaths.

A thought had struck her then. People had always given her chances, hadn't they?

"Anna," she said. "How would you feel about looking

after the shop on your own when I go on holiday in September? With a big pay increase, of course."

Anna's eyes had lit up. "I'd like that."

"Great," Maggie said. "Give me a minute and I'll get the details."

Out in the back room, Maggie found the event schedule and got her diary out.

Kesha had called her last week and asked if she'd be free to join her family on their Italian holiday. It was all very last minute, but her sister had dropped out of the trip, so there was a place going in the Tuscan villa they'd rented. Maggie's first instinct had been to dismiss the idea, but in fact, with Anna so much more confident and capable now, taking a holiday was becoming a real possibility for the first time in years. The idea of catching up with her old school friend over a leisurely pasta lunch by the pool was almost irresistible. The kids would be splashing around, yes, so it wouldn't be quite the same as the carefree, G'n'T-fueled holidays they'd enjoyed when they were younger. But Oscar and Evie were gorgeous, Dave was pretty laid-back, and it would be good to spend some time with them all.

She opened her diary and checked—10–18 September, Kesha had said. Still far enough away for her to train Anna up in a few things. She'd flicked back to the calendar section at the start of the diary and counted—six, seven, just over seven weeks and it would be olives, pizza, good wine and days filled with nothing to do. Bliss. She'd have to brush up on her Italian a little bit before that, but she'd get some CDs out of the library and listen to them when she was cooking. Yes, she'd been having fun with Owen, but Kesha was a friend for life and she was keen to get their friendship back on track.

It was then that she'd noticed the circled days on her diary calendar; neat, regular, clusters of five blue rings, appearing through the year right up till—June. Her skin prickled and she felt sick to her stomach. There were no rings in July and it was nearly over.

Her period was late.

Chapter 34

Jenny

It didn't feel real until I was out in the garden by my dad's workshop, telling him all about it.

"Are you sure, love? It is definite?" he asked.

"It seems pretty certain, yes." A wide grin was spreading across my face.

"My little girl," he said, enveloping me in a huge hug. He looked like he might actually jump up and down. "I always knew you were a star. Can I have a look, have you got a copy?"

"I've got the original here actually," I said. "Do you want to have a look?"

"Of course I do, Jen. This kind of thing doesn't happen every day."

I went into the kitchen and took the pages of my

children's book out of my bag and brought them out into the yard.

Dad smiled at the first page and carefully turned it over. I still couldn't really believe everything that had happened. Since reading the email from Alison's publisher friend, JoJo, it felt as if my life had been running in fast-forward. JoJo's note had been brief but very positive, she'd said she really liked the book, and asked me to call her up to discuss it.

Dad let out a little chuckle at one of the images I'd painted and carried on reading.

I'd snuck out of the office to call JoJo the moment I finished reading her message. I resisted the temptation to tell anyone before speaking to her, as I didn't want to jinx things. JoJo was bubbly and enthusiastic and said that at Parakeet Press they'd been looking for new titles for the 4–6 age group and they thought *Charlie, Carlitos and Me* was going to be a great fit. "There are a few changes I'd like to suggest," JoJo had said, slipping into a more businesslike tone. "And some of the illustrations need a bit of tidying up." That was definitely true, I thought, feeling a little sheepish and hoping Alison had explained that it wasn't a polished version. "But if you're prepared to do some further work, we'd like to make you an offer. We'd be very proud to have you and the chinchilla boys on board."

I'd been so dizzy with excitement when I put down

the phone I didn't know what to do with myself. It was really happening! I had to share the good news with someone, and it was Dad who first came to mind.

Dad was pointing at the picture of Jake, holding Carlitos and singing a little song in Spanish with him.

"That's just like Chris and the guinea pigs, isn't it? Do you remember how he used to sing to them all the time? Horribly off-key it was, but they seemed to like it."

I laughed. "Of course, Dad. How could I forget Chris and those furry Queen fans? Who do you think gave me the idea?"

"Galileo, Galileo," Dad said, as he held up two imaginary guinea pigs and swiveled his head between them.

"Figaro, Magnifico!" I joined him, laughing. He put the invisible pets down.

"I hope I'm not the inspiration for Jake's parents." Dad said, his tone a little more serious. "I mean, his dad never believes a word he says, does he? Poor chap's carrying this secret with him and feels like he's talking to a brick wall. And as for his mum . . ." Dad's sentence drifted off, and he looked a little awkward.

"Yes," I said, putting my hand on Dad's leg. "Safe to say she was definitely from my imagination." The muscles in Dad's face seemed to relax.

"Have you heard any more from your mum since the hen night?" he asked tentatively.

"Yes," I said, thinking back to what she'd written to me. "She wrote me a letter."

Dad looked at me, trying to gauge my expression I think.

"I haven't replied." I shrugged, a lump forming in my throat. "I don't really know how I feel about it, Dad."

"She did sound pretty sorry when she called, love," Dad said. "It's your decision, but I wonder if she might finally be starting to understand what she's done."

I raised my eyebrows, so Dad could see just how skeptical I was about that. But then, maybe, just maybe, she had meant some of what she said . . .

"I'm not saying you should give her another chance," Dad said. "What I mean is, I don't want you, or Chris for that matter, to think that having a relationship with her would be betraying me." From the creases in his brow, it was clear that Dad had been carrying a huge burden, and it pained me to see that.

"I know that, Dad," I said. "But thank you." I gave him a cuddle. "Anyway, you're my number one parent. Rest assured that it's you I'll be buying a mansion for when *Charlie* sells a million."

"You never know, Jenny," Dad said, deadly serious. "It might do. I always knew you were good at drawing." I thought back to the amateurish caricatures in the kitchen, the fingerprint paintings Chris and I had done that Dad still had Blu-tacked up in the living room. He really wasn't the most objective of judges. "And you know that woman, she did quite well out of children's books, didn't she, whatsername, you know, the ones about the boy magician . . ."

"Oh, Dad," I said. "I love you. You poor deluded man." He gave me a confused look as I kissed him on the cheek. "So are we ready for the grand unveiling, or what?" I asked, nudging him.

Dad had been hard at work for weeks designing a bar for us to serve drinks from during the evening wedding do, but he'd been really secretive about it. He'd wanted it to be a surprise but had finally given in to the demands of my inner control freak and agreed to let me have a sneak peek ahead of the party.

He led me through into the glorified shed where he did all his carpentry, and we stepped over the bits of timber left over from the kennel he was making for our new puppy. There, against the wall, stood a stunning wide curved bar, with poles at the side and a banner made out of thin wood overhead, with A TOAST TO THE NEWLYWEDS! written on it. He'd painted the bar in sunshine yellow to match one of the colors in our theme.

I clapped my hands and then brought them up to my face. "It's beautiful, Dad."

He moved forward and bent down, pointing to one of the wooden joints. "The really ingenious bit is this," he said animatedly. "It all comes apart, you see. So it'll be easy to transport to the venue—then we can just put it all back together once we get inside." He then pulled up the pole that held on the banner section, showing me, his eyes lighting up.

I held out my arms for a hug. "Thank you, Dad," I said.

He hugged me back, then pulled away. "I wanted . . . I wanted to get it right for you, Jen," he said.

I realized when he looked away that there must be tears in his eyes, and seeing the bar he'd gone to so much trouble making had brought some to mine too.

"You've always got it right for me, Dad," I said.

Chapter 35

Maggie

Maggie must have been lying there for about half an hour before the doorbell rang, startling her. Getting up and glancing in the mirror, she tidied her hair and went downstairs to answer it.

Alison was on her front step, with a big smile on her face, in the denim dungarees and red headscarf she'd been wearing earlier.

"Hi, again," Alison said. "Sorry to drop by unannounced, but you're on my way home. You know I told you about the Blitz Spirit launch party tomorrow, Jamie's new café on the high street?" Maggie nodded. "He asked me to give you and Jenny these ages ago and I'm afraid I completely forgot." Alison passed her a stylish square card invite with lettering that looked like it had been made with old printing blocks.

Maggie nodded and took it. "Nice," she said, admiring it.

"Free cocktails," Alison said, smiling and tilting her head to try and gauge the expression on her friend's face. "Are you OK, Maggie? You look really pale."

"I'm not feeling that great actually, no," Maggie said. "Have you got a minute to come in?"

"Sure, sure—of course," Alison said, following Maggie through to the living room.

Mork meowed from his spot on the white sofa, then leapt down onto the carpet, arching his back. The two women sat down and Alison waited for Maggie to break the silence. She didn't.

"What's up, Maggie?" she prompted. "You seemed fine earlier . . . do you think it was something we ate at the flea market?"

"No," Maggie shook her head. "It definitely wasn't anything I ate."

"What then? You look gray," Alison asked, putting her hand up to Maggie's forehead.

"I don't have a temperature, Ali," Maggie said. "I think I might be pregnant."

"What?" Alison's eyes were wide.

"I know," Maggie said, furrowing her brow. "My period's late. I'm never late."

"And what, are you just planning on sitting here?" Alison said. "Or are we going to find out for sure?"

*

Maggie and Alison had got to the chemist just before it closed and bought a pack of three pregnancy tests.

"Will you wait with me?" Maggie asked, back home, her voice unsteady. "I feel like I might faint any moment."

"Of course," Alison replied, passing her the box.

Maggie took a test out, unwrapped it, and they went together to the bathroom. Alison perched on the side of the bath.

When Maggie had peed on the end, she put the cap on and put it by the sink. "Can you look?" she asked. "I don't think I can face it."

They waited a moment and then Alison said, "It's a yes, Maggie."

Maggie picked up the stick, saw the positive blue icon had appeared in the window and nausea flooded back.

She was meant to be a grown-up. How had she let this happen?

Ten minutes later Maggie and Alison were on the sofa, with sugary cups of tea in their hands.

"Oh God," Maggie said, slumping back and letting the sofa cushions take her weight. "I'm old enough to know better, aren't I?"

"Well, you're certainly in good company," Alison said. "Sophie may have been planned, but Holly is our favorite mistake, a mini-break on the Isle of Wight when I'd left my pills at home." She smiled.

"But at least you're in a relationship," Maggie said. "I really should have been more careful."

"What's happened has happened," Alison said. "There's not much point dwelling on it now. And anyway, last time I checked it took two to make a baby—the responsibility doesn't all rest with you, you know."

"Thanks," Maggie said. "You're right."

"Is it Dylan's?" Alison asked, gently.

"No," Maggie replied. "It can't be, we were always really careful. I think he was probably terrified at the idea of an accident happening, in retrospect. But with Owen the moment swept us up, more than once. Plus I think it's really early, just a couple of weeks, so that ties in too."

Maggie lifted her feet up and hugged her knees to her. "Oh God, Ali. I hardly know Owen . . . and he's all, you know, all *free*."

"OK," Alison said. "Forget about Owen for a second. How do you feel about it?"

Maggie hesitated. "Sick."

Alison raised an eyebrow.

"OK," Maggie continued, "I suppose after Dylan and I got divorced I just resigned myself to the fact I wasn't going to be a mother. And I really am fine with that. I mean I *was* fine with that. I don't know, Ali." She gestured to her immaculate living room, taking in the white carpets, the orchids, fragile glass ornaments on every surface. "I don't have my life right for a baby."

"Does anybody?" Alison said, with a shrug.

"I suppose not," Maggie said, her feelings searching for space among the practicalities. "But the business, I have all these plans for it. To set up in London . . . I can't just give up on everything I've achieved to have a baby."

"It doesn't have to be either/or, Maggie," Alison said. "Lots of mothers work."

"But I'll be . . . I'm going to be a single mum, aren't I?" She started to chew on a manicured nail.

"You don't know anything for sure," Alison said, her voice calming.

"I will be," Maggie said. "I'll be on my own trying to work out how to do up a nappy and remember the words to lullabies, and deciding what to do when it gets ill . . . God, Ali, I don't know if I can do it." Adrenaline rushed through her veins as she pictured it. Alone. With a *baby*.

"I've only known Owen five minutes, Ali. He's not going to sign up for this, and to be honest I can't blame him."

"But let's get back to what I said," Alison said, taking Maggie's hand. "Do *you* want to sign up for this?"

The answer came to Maggie more quickly than she'd expected. She stopped chewing on her nail and looked up at Alison. "It's completely and utterly terrifying." She took a deep breath. "But yes, I think I do."

"There you go," Alison said, with a smile. "So there's a start." She put her arm around Maggie's shoulders. "But before you make any decisions you need to speak to Owen. Call him. He needs to know."

*

Maggie felt sick to her stomach. Here she was, meeting Owen for lunch at the Queen's Head, a cozy, quiet pub hidden round the back of Charlesworth train station. This would normally have made for a dreamy escape from the shop—but not today. How was she supposed to handle a conversation like this? Would Owen be reasonable, or bolt for the door?

When they'd kissed hello, Maggie had felt a rush of happiness; being in Owen's arms felt right and for a fleeting moment she almost forgot the reason she'd asked to meet him. But as he let her go, reality hit. If she kept the baby, she was going to lose this good man she'd found.

The pub was empty apart from one other couple in the far corner, a pretty red-haired woman about Maggie's age and a man in a dark suit with his back to them. Maggie and Owen ordered their food and then settled in a booth by the window.

"How's the Japanese garden going?" Maggie asked Owen, feigning calm.

"Oh, fine," he replied, "but I've been looking forward to seeing you so much that it's been hard to focus on the bonsais." He reached over and gave her a kiss.

"By the way," Owen said. "I called Lucy and reassured her that everything is going fine with the wedding plans. She was a bit concerned she hadn't heard from either of us for a while."

"Ah, yes, thanks for that." The wedding was getting

closer but keeping the bride-to-be updated seemed to have slipped down both of their priority lists.

"It's great to see you," Owen said. The top buttons of his shirt were open and Maggie couldn't stop her eyes drifting down to his chest. "And I'm absolutely not complaining," he continued, "but I thought you were normally too busy for a proper lunch?"

"I made time today," Maggie said, then paused for a moment. "It's important."

"OK," Owen said, a curious smile playing on his lips.

"Owen, look," Maggie said, sitting up straight. "I'll get to the point. I didn't see this coming, and you won't have either." She bit her lip. "I'm pregnant."

"Woah," Owen said, sitting back in his seat, his face registering the shock.

"Yes, I know," Maggie said, breathing out. "That's how I felt too."

"I suppose I just assumed you were on the pill," he said, after a long silence.

"I wasn't, and I should have discussed it with you," Maggie said, her voice a little tighter than normal.

"It's only been a few weeks—"

"I know, I know. We hardly know each other." Maggie felt alone all of a sudden. "And I'm not sure yet how I feel about all this. But, I'm thirty-six, and while I didn't expect this to happen I just don't think I could face—I mean, I wouldn't expect . . ."

Maggie's sentence trailed off as at that moment the

food arrived. "One jacket with chili and cheese, one chicken caesar salad," the stocky, middle-aged barman said as he arrived at their table.

"The salad's for me, please," Maggie said, taking it swiftly and putting it down in front of her. As she looked up, she saw the couple at the back of the pub get up to leave, and realized that the man was Alison's husband, Pete. He caught Maggie's eye, but looked startled, a rabbit caught in headlights. Maggie smiled hello, distracted, as he led his attractive female companion to the door.

Owen waited for the barman to walk away and then put his plate to the side, taking Maggie's hands in his again.

"Impeccable timing," he said, nodding towards the barman's back and smiling. "Anyway, Maggie, what I was about to say is I know it's only been a few weeks, but strange as it sounds, I'm already pretty sure how I feel about you."

A lump formed in Maggie's throat as Owen continued.

"And I don't imagine that's going to change. I know I'm younger, but I've lived a bit, and I know what I want. I want to be with you, Maggie. And while I didn't expect it—the idea of having a baby together makes me happy. I think we should do it."

Looking into his face, so open and earnest, Maggie felt tears start and rushed to brush them away. "Good," she said quietly, her voice cracking, "because I didn't realize until now how very much I want this too."

Owen smiled, and reached across the table to kiss her. "Don't cry," he said, catching a stray teardrop with his finger. "It's good news, Maggie."

"But seriously," he said, slumping back and putting both hands to his head. "Seriously." Then he started to laugh. "It's a lot to get your head around, isn't it?"

"Yes," Maggie said, gathering her strength again, "and it certainly shouldn't be done on an empty stomach." She pushed Owen's food towards him and took a bite of chicken from her salad.

"Woah," Owen continued, cutting a chunk of his baked potato. "You're going to be a *mum*," he whispered, trying out the word, "and I'm going to be a *dad*. We're going to have to pretend we know what we're doing, aren't we?"

"I think so," Maggie said, then shrugged. "But I reckon we can do it."

Owen was beaming. "I've always wanted to have kids," he said. "Obviously I didn't think it would happen like this, but I feel ready, I think. Do you?"

Maggie tucked a strand of hair behind her ear and thought about it before answering.

"As ready as I'll ever be."

Chapter 36

Alison

"Cheers!" Alison clinked her cocktail glass with Jamie's. The launch party was buzzing, people were wandering around, chatting, drinks in hand, admiring the café interior and the vintage furniture. "Here's to Blitz Spirit," she said. Jamie's eyes were bright with pride.

Jamie had worked tirelessly on the café over the last few weeks, with Alison helping out whenever she could, but the person by his side throughout had been Adam. While Jamie had clearly been holding back at first, the two of them were now virtually inseparable.

The café's backyard, once just a plain square of concrete with rubbish strewn across it, had been transformed. Adam had brought some railway sleepers and created flowerbeds that Maggie had filled with lavender plants and wild flowers. Tiny lights nestled in holes in the wood, brightening the mural on the back wall—a Bovril ad that Alison had painted, giving it a faded look, as if it had been there all along.

The fringed standard lamps, glass-fronted cabinets and wall-mounted flying ducks the Spencers had donated gave the place a genuine wartime feel, and with 1940s tunes playing out from a gramophone the scene was perfectly set. Alison's favorite feature was the dummy by the window, dressed in an original cinema usherette's uniform and presiding authoritatively over the party. She was carrying a wooden tray with a strap that, for one night only, was laden with Manhattans. Authentic blitz cocktails they might not be, but they were certainly doing a great job of livening up the crowd. Union Jack–themed bunches of poppies, cornflowers and sweet peas were in glass vases on the tables, put together by Anna.

Pete came back in from having a cigarette, and as he and Jamie started talking, Alison leaned in towards Adam.

"So," she said, conspiratorially. "Looks like you're doing something right." She nodded her head in Jamie's direction. "You really have put the smile back on his face."

Adam laughed warmly. He was younger than Jamie, maybe mid-thirties, and was handsome in a rugged way, but with a style that was sleek and retro: hair cut short at the sides, with a longer, styled quiff. Tonight he was dressed in a checked shirt and indigo jeans.

"You don't meet a man like Jamie every day, do you?"

Adam said with a smile. "I'm just lucky he let me snap him up."

Alison saw Jamie glance over Pete's shoulder and catch Adam's eye.

"Will we be seeing you in Charlesworth a bit more often now?" Alison asked.

"Maybe," Adam said, teasing, "although I can't see myself moving here." He mimed an extravagant yawn. "Too sleepy. And I hear the burlesque scene is pretty dead too." He gave Alison a cheeky smile. "Brighton's the place for me," he said. "But happily it's close enough that Jamie and I can see each other as often as we like. While he's getting this café off the ground we'll spend more time here, but hopefully when there are staff on board we'll get more time by the sea." He took a sip of his cocktail.

"Sounds good," Alison said. "And, like I say, it's great to see Jamie so happy again."

Alison spotted Jenny and Dan then, weaving their way through the crowd towards her. Jenny had her hair styled into big blonde curls and was wearing a sailor-style dress in navy and cream paired with red heels. Her makeup was normally muted, but the bright red lipstick and thick eyeliner she had on tonight really suited her. She made a perfect pair with Dan, who was dressed in jeans with a khaki forage cap on at a jaunty angle.

"Alison," Jenny said, breathless from squeezing through people. Alison introduced Jenny and Dan to Adam and they kissed their hellos.

"Nice hat," Adam said to Dan. As they started to chat, Jenny swept around to Alison's side.

"Alison, you'll never guess what's happened," she said, a huge grin on her face.

"It's not . . . Did you hear . . . ?" Alison started, hardly daring to hope.

"Yes! Your friend JoJo contacted me about *Charlie, Carlitos and Me* and she loves it! They want me to make a couple of changes but she's gone ahead and made me an offer."

"That's fantastic," Alison congratulated her. "I *knew* there was something there. I'm glad JoJo was smart enough to see it too."

"Jenny!" Jamie snuck in between the two women, putting his arms around them both and looking Jenny up and down. "You look hot, dear girl. But where's your cocktail? And Dan's without a drink too? Ah, a new café-owner's work is never done!" He reached behind him to the usherette's tray and passed them both glasses.

"Jamie, congratulations. This place is fantastic," Jenny said.

"Quite a transformation, isn't it?" Jamie said, sweeping his arm from the front door to the back garden. "I was sad to leave the hospice shop behind, but it was time to move on. The ladies have been right behind me actually." He pointed with a nod of his head at the group of older ladies standing by the gramophone. "I think they're excited to have a place to come for tea that isn't Joey's," he said.

"Aren't we all?" Jenny added, laughing.

"That's what I'm hoping," Jamie said, then added in a stage whisper. "On another note, have you seen those two?" he said, pointing out into the garden where Maggie and Owen had snuck out and were kissing up against the wall. "I nearly had to wrench them apart to get a hello," Jamie said, laughing. "They're really into each other, aren't they?"

"Oh yes. Something tells me they might be in this for the long haul," Alison said, smiling.

"Jamie," Pete said, turning to face them, "Dan was just asking about . . ."

As the men got caught up in conversation, Jenny whispered in Alison's ear, "Maggie told me her news. It's crazy, isn't it?" Alison nodded. "But amazing. She seems happy."

"I think she really is," Alison whispered back.

They'd all toasted to congratulate Jenny on her publishing deal, and then Alison had gone to greet the Spencers, who were standing by the doorway.

"You made it," she said, delighted to see them.

"Oh we wouldn't have missed it," Derek replied, looking around the room. "Our things look rather nice in here don't they?"

"Much more room for them here," Ruby said. "I brought along some of the lavender furniture polish we used to put on the cabinet, I thought your friend Jamie might be able to use it." She patted her bag.

"Oh, I'm sure he will," Alison said. "Can I get you a drink? Will you have a cocktail? Or there's lemon barley water and orange squash. There are a few sausage rolls and things up on the counter, so you can just help yourself."

"Two squashes would be nice," Derek replied. "We don't drink much really, leave that to you young people," he said, smiling, looking around the room where couples were starting to sway to the wartime tunes.

"Come with me," Alison said, leading them by the arm over to the other side of the room, "I'd like you to meet my mother, and some other friends."

By the time she'd brought the Spencers their glasses of squash, they were deep in conversation with Alison's mother, Cecily, her neighbor June, and two of the ladies from the hospice shop, Muriel and Anne.

"Oh, we won't stay long," Cecily said, although in truth they'd already been there over two hours and had shown no signs of wanting to leave. "June will want to drive back soon, I'm sure." June was smiling from ear to ear, starting to bop along to a new tune. "But this is quite nice, isn't it?" Cecily said.

"It certainly takes me back," Ruby joined in. "This music, when you hear it, it could almost be yesterday, couldn't it?" she smiled. "Do you remember the evacuees arriving? I was just telling Alison, the other day, about when they came. Those startled little faces, more used to smog than fresh air."

"You're looking at one," Muriel laughed, pointing to her friend Anne.

"Oh really? Is that right?" Ruby said. Alison kept quiet, enjoying listening to the ladies talk, and above all seeing her mum so animated, looking healthier than she had been in weeks.

"Yes, it is," Anne said. "Arrived here from London in 1943 and then after the war I came right back," she laughed. "The family where I was housed made me feel right at home. I'd never been away before, but they really looked after me. Anyway, we stayed in touch and I'd come back from time to time to visit, with my parents. Andrew, their son, used to tease me and pull my hair—he was all freckles and grazed knees, always getting into scrapes. But one day when I came back he was all grown up, and pretty handsome with it. He asked me out dancing, and the rest was history. Seven grandchildren the two of us have got now." Anne's eyes were bright as she told the story.

"Oh my," Ruby said, "I've heard about you two, local legends you are. How nice to finally meet you."

"Wonderful," Cecily added. "They were different times back then, weren't they? Simpler. I remember when I met Alison's father Gerry . . ."

"That was fun, wasn't it, sweetheart?" Pete said as he pulled out of the parking space.

"Absolutely," Alison replied. "It's great to see the café

up and running, and Mum was on good form, wasn't she?" Pete nodded.

"And to be honest," Alison said, "it's nice to get out without the kids once in a while, just us, isn't it?"

Pete took his attention off the dark road for a moment and caught her eye. "Yes, it is."

Alison put on Fleetwood Mac's *Greatest Hits* and the two of them sang along to "Everywhere" as they wound down the country lanes back to the house.

When they got back home Alison walked up the moon-lit gravel path, still singing, a bit tipsily. She tripped and leaned on Pete for support. He laughed at her wobbliness but then took her in his arms. "I love you so much, Pete," she said, kissing him. He kissed her back in answer.

When they got inside it was just before midnight and the house was completely silent. "Pete, before we go to bed there's something I want to show you," Alison said.

"OK, sounds intriguing . . ." Pete replied, as his wife led him back through to her workshop. She opened the door slowly and the first thing they both saw were the shafts of moonlight, slightly dappled by shapes of leaves, casting silvery beams across the studio.

"My," said Pete, as he took in the full picture. Alison's entire set of shelves was stacked with teacups; blue, pink, yellow, gold, decorated with flowers of every shape and size.

"They make a pretty impressive collection, don't they?" Alison said.

"I'll say," Pete replied. "I mean I knew you three had been busy, but what a hoard this is. How many do you have here?" he asked, walking towards the shelf and picking up one of the blue and white cups that were Alison's favorites.

"A hundred cups and saucers," Alison said, waving her hand to point them out, "twelve creamers and sugar bowls, ten teapots, four cake stands and a couple of other things that took our fancy along the way. It should all be boxed up, but I couldn't resist taking them all out to have a look."

"They look terrific," Pete said. "It's a shame to see them go really—but they'll be making us our fortune, won't they?"

Alison smiled. "Something like that, yes," she said, putting her arms around Pete's waist. "Their first stop is Jenny and Dan's wedding next week."

"Ah, yes," said Pete.

Alison narrowed her eyes at him. "You did remember it was Jenny's wedding next week, didn't you?"

"Yes, I mean, yes, of course I did."

"Anyway, enjoy them now, because I'm going to box everything up tomorrow and drive them over to the old schoolhouse so that they're ready for Jenny and Dan's big day."

Pete gave his wife a squeeze. They turned around and walked out of the studio, and as Alison closed the door behind them she kissed Pete again, her kisses deeper this time. "It's about time we went up to bed, don't you think?"

*

"Pete, what time is it?" Alison stirred and then, seeing the sunlight coming in through the window, groaned and covered her face with a pillow.

"It's six-thirty, sweetheart. Sorry, I've got an earlier start today. I made you a cup of tea and put it on the side. I didn't want to wake you."

"Urgh, Pete, I feel dreadful."

He sat down beside her on the bed and kissed the top of her head. "You'll live. Look, I've got to run, but let's speak at lunchtime. I'll be back late tonight—it's manic at the office at the moment I'm afraid—so don't worry about dinner."

"OK, darling. Have a good day at work."

A few minutes later, as Alison heard his car start up, she slipped on her kimono and silk slippers, clipped her hair up and took the tea Pete had made her downstairs to her workshop. She had an inbox full of emails that needed responding to and no one ever said you had to get dressed properly to do that. George cornered her in the kitchen, whining to be taken out for a walk, so she let him out into the garden to buy herself a little time. She watched him now through her window as he darted towards a squirrel. It only seemed like yesterday they'd brought him home as a puppy, the girls squabbling over who could play with him first—and now he was a dad himself.

Hearing a sound in the hallway, Alison turned and

caught a glimpse of Sophie coming down the stairs, another figure tiptoeing behind her.

"Morning," she called out. "You're up early, girls."

"Er, yes, Mum," Sophie said, before adding more quietly, "couldn't sleep."

Alison craned her neck to see better through the doorway, and clocked right away that the person behind Sophie wasn't Holly.

"Sophie," Alison said, raising her voice. "Get in here this instant."

Alison caught a glimpse of a teenage boy in a military-style jacket as her daughter shooed him out of the front door. Once the door was shut behind him, she walked over into her mum's workshop, dragging her heels, her head slightly bowed.

"What just happened there?" Alison said, standing up and fixing her daughter with a stern look. "Did I just see you let a boy out the front door?"

"Yes. It was Matt," Sophie replied, rolling her eyes to the ceiling.

"Sophie. Look at me." Alison took her daughter's chin in her hand, and Sophie's eyes dropped down to meet her mum's. "So Matt *stayed* last night?"

"Yes," Sophie retorted.

Her daughter's betrayal hit Alison like a jolt.

"Your dad and I go out for the evening, *one evening*, Sophie, and trust you and Holly to look after yourselves, and this is what you do? You sneak your boyfriend—who incidentally we haven't even met yet—in to stay the night?"

Sophie sighed audibly. "We didn't *do it*, Mum, if that's what you're thinking."

Alison took a deep breath. "Well I won't pretend I'm not relieved to hear that. But it's about more than sex, Sophie, and you know that." Sophie visibly cringed at the word. "You've betrayed our trust," Alison continued. "We thought you were grown-up enough to leave in charge of the house alone—that you were enough of an adult to look after yourself and set a good example for Holly—but it looks like we got that very wrong."

"What do you expect, Mum?" Sophie's expression was stony. "You say it's the first time you've left us alone, but it feels like Hol and I are by ourselves here all the time. Since Dad started the new job it's like we hardly see him, he's working so much—and you're hardly around either, what with your business and this stupid teacup obsession." Sophie waved a hand at the laden shelves behind her mother. "It's like neither you or Dad even care about us anymore."

"Sophie—that's not fair and you know it," Alison said. "We explained that things would change a bit when your father went back to work and you and Holly said you were fine with that."

"You know what, Mum, we aren't. You've neglected us. Holly thinks so too. And it started when you met your new friends." Sophie had a vicious look in her eye. "All you care about is hanging out with them and pretending you're young again. It's like you don't even want to be a mum anymore."

Alison's jaw dropped. "How dare you. I work hard for this family." Alison thought of the late nights she'd stayed up with the sewing machine, over the last few months, just to bring in a few more pennies. How many times had she dropped everything for Sophie? And she saw her kids far more often than other working mums she knew. "I don't have to listen to this. There's no excuse for what you've done and you know it. You're grounded, for a month."

"You can't." Sophie's eyes were wide and her bottom lip quivered. "What about Matt?"

"I certainly can. And I don't care, Sophie. You forfeited your freedom last night when you let us down."

"You're horrible, Mum." Sophie said, shaking her head at the perceived injustice. "You are a total, utter COW."

With that, Sophie turned on her DM-clad heel. On her way out she grabbed hold of the studio door, slamming it shut behind her with such force that the windows in the room rattled. George jumped up at the window outside and let out a loud bark. Alison looked towards the window and froze. Then it was as if she was watching everything in slow motion.

The blue and white cup Pete had held in his hand last night clattered to the floor, shattering to pieces on the bare wooden floorboards. One of the precious forget-me-not set followed, knocking the creamer next to it and dropping to the floor, crashing. The bracket holding up the middle shelf strained and snapped so that the entire shelf slid down to the right; the cups, like little china lemmings, fell to the floor and shattered one by one. Alison's hands went to her mouth. She rushed to the shelves and tried to rescue the cups, catching two but watching at close range as others clattered to the floor, smashing one after another. When the last one on the middle shelf had fallen, silence descended.

The door creaked open again and Sophie's face appeared. She surveyed the room, taking in the damage she'd caused and her eyes filled with tears.

"Oh God, Mum. This is all my fault. I'm so, so sorry."

Chapter 37

Jenny

I was sitting on a bench on the green by the fountain, where today two toddlers were dipping their toes in the sparkling water and giggling. I opened up my new Rough Guide to Ireland and underlined a couple of pubs on the east coast that they recommended for live music. It might not be the Maldives, but the closer our honeymoon got, the more excited I was about spending it there, driving between cozy B&Bs and going for walks in the country-side. I picked up a California roll from my sushi set and guided it into my mouth as I turned the page.

Chloe had been off sick today and things were quiet in the office, so I'd flown through most of my tasks before lunch. I only had a week left at work and was feeling quite relaxed for a change, mainly because I was glowing with my new secret. Yesterday JoJo had emailed over some rough cover ideas for me to see; the visuals were using one of my illustrations of Jake and the designer had used a selection of different fonts that all matched the playful feel of the story. They looked terrific and it was really starting to sink in, for the first time I was able to picture my book up there on the shelves.

As I dipped a tuna and avocado roll in soy sauce, my mobile beeped with a text. Putting the sushi to one side I got my phone out—Maggie.

> Jen, Ali has some news. It's urgent. Call me or her when you have a min? x

I flicked to Maggie's number and called her right away. "Hi, Jen," she said, and I heard her disappear into what must have been the back room, away from the noise of the shop floor.

"Thanks for calling back," Maggie said, her voice giving nothing away. "I'm afraid it's not good news. This morning there was an accident in Alison's studio—"

"What is it?" I jumped in, nearly choking on an avocado roll. "What's happened? Is Ali OK?"

"Yes, she's fine, it's nothing like that," Maggie said, and I let out a relieved sigh. "The thing is," she continued, "she had the teacups out on her shelves, she wanted to look at everything before packing it all up. But she and Sophie had a row and Sophie ended up slamming the door shut really hard."

"No," I said, my heart in my mouth. Our cups—all our work. My wedding. Oh God. *My wedding.* I forced myself to ask her, "What . . . I mean, how many, how bad is it?"

Maggie paused before continuing, and I bit my lip. Images flooded my mind of the delicate china smashing. "Almost half of the cups have been broken, Jenny."

"They can't be," I said, panic making my heart race. "Please tell me you're winding me up."

"I'm afraid I'm not. I'm so sorry," Maggie said, trying to console me.

There was one week to go until my wedding.

Ali was even more upset than me, if that was possible. It wasn't her fault, I tried to reassure her—after all, it had been a joint decision to store the cups at her house, and no one could have predicted how things would turn out. Sophie had made a card for all three of us and had left it in the studio for her mum to find.

On the front were three women, a collage of magazine images—one tall lady with green eyes and red hair, a little one with blonde hair and a bike, and one in the center, with dark curls, red lipstick and a frilly 1950s apron. Inside she'd written a message in purple pen:

To the Vintage Teacup Club. I'm so sorry I ruined everything. I didn't mean to. I thought the cups were really cool and I never meant to break them. Sorry. Sophie x

The Vintage Teacup Club. I smiled, in spite of everything. I liked that.

"I spent the morning clearing up," Alison said. We'd settled down at the kitchen table and she was pouring out Earl Grey for us. "There were some larger pieces, but I can't see that we'd be able to repair any of the cups with them. I've kept the bits in a box and I thought maybe we could use them—Maggie, they might work to decorate a flower bed or something? I don't know. It seemed a shame to throw them away."

Alison looked crestfallen. I couldn't even bring myself to think about those broken pieces of our precious teasets. There were still forty-odd cups on the shelf, and most of the saucers, but it was nowhere near what we'd need for the two weddings.

"All that time . . ." Alison said. Maggie and I hugged her as her voice started to crack. "And nothing to show for it."

I pulled back from the hug. Yes, this was a disaster, but as Alison said those words I realized how far they were from being true.

I looked at her. "Nothing to show for it. Are you sure?" I asked, a smile forming on my lips.

"OK, so I suppose when you look at it that way," Alison said, wiping away the tears that had started to form and letting out a gentle laugh instead.

"You're right, Jen," Maggie said. "We're strong, ladies. And it'll take more than a few broken teacups to break us."

"Look," Alison said, the familiar matter-of-fact tone returning to her voice. "I know it's absolutely not the same, but I do have a stash of other cups that might work for your wedding, Jen. I bought them a while ago to make candles, but they weren't right. I mean they're fine, but they're just IKEA-type ones."

"Oh, OK, great," I said, ignoring the lump in my throat. Cups were cups, after all. Weren't they?

"And Maggie, you've got a bit longer until the Darlington Hall wedding, haven't you? We should be able to find replacements before then," Alison said.

"Oh, don't worry about me," Maggie said. "I'm sure I'll find some more—and with Owen's research the flowers are now coming in under budget so there's still a bit of cash to play with." Maggie really did seem *a lot* more relaxed about her work nowadays.

"I'll tell Jamie and Adam to keep an eye out," Alison said, "and there's still one Saturday left before the wedding—shall we give it one last go driving around the local flea markets and see what we can find? We might just get lucky."

"Yes, sure, let's do that," I said, trying my best to stay positive.

"Are things all right with Sophie now?" I asked, changing the subject. "I mean, from the card it does look like she's genuinely sorry."

"I think she is," Alison said. "Sorry that she broke the cups, I mean. But I'm not sure she feels the same about what she did in the first place. Can you believe it? Sneaking a boy in here for the night? I would never, ever, have done that at her age."

"No comment," Maggie said with a wink.

"Have you talked to Pete about it?" I asked.

"No, actually, I haven't had a chance," Alison said. "I didn't want to call him at work, they've been so busy lately, and it sounds as if he's really been thrown in the deep end. He's enjoying the work, but says he never gets time to take lunch, and he's working late quite a lot too."

"Oh, I see," I said.

I was sure I could see something flicker across Maggie's face.

"Let's meet first thing on Saturday then, shall we?" Maggie said, quickly changing the subject. "And why don't you ask Sophie if she wants to join us?"

"What was that all about?" I said to Maggie, my voice hushed, as soon as Ali's front door was safely closed behind us.

"What was all what about?" she replied, buttoning up her jacket and not breaking her stride.

"That," I said, catching her elbow as we reached the gate. "The way you were just then when Alison was talking about Pete working late. Why were you being weird?"

"No reason," she said, pulling away and giving me a tight smile before walking off to her car. "I mean, I wasn't being weird."

"You—"

"Want a lift home?" she interrupted, her face blank. "We can stick your bike in the back."

"Sure," I said, shaking my head a little. I couldn't have been imagining it. I could read Maggie like a book, and there was definitely something she'd wanted to say but hadn't.

In silence we put my bike across the back seat of her car and then got inside, strapping ourselves in. Maggie turned the key in the ignition and we set off down the country lane.

"Look," she said, once the tension between us got intolerable. "I didn't want to say anything, because I've probably got entirely the wrong end of the stick."

Right, so I wasn't going mad here.

"I've been totally wrong about this sort of thing before, and I'm sure it's just my own paranoia."

"What is it?" I asked. "Maybe if you tell me we can work out if you're barking up the wrong tree or not."

She shook her head, not taking her eyes off the road. "I'm sure I've got this one wrong."

I waited until she eventually spoke.

"It's Alison. She said Pete never takes his lunch break—that since he started his new job he's been too busy. You heard her say that, didn't you?"

I nodded. Then, realizing she couldn't see me as she kept her eye on the road, I said, "Sorry, yes, I heard that. And?"

"It's just that I saw him, Jenny. The other day, in the Queen's Head—I was there for lunch with Owen and Pete was there with another woman. I mean not doing anything, but he was certainly out for lunch with someone else."

I shrugged it off, relieved that it wasn't anything more serious Maggie had been hiding. I was sure that Alison would think it was sweet, actually, that Maggie cared so much about her to worry unnecessarily. "Pete's completely devoted to Ali. I'm sure he didn't mean he never, ever takes lunch, he was probably just saying that as a general thing, you know, how—"

A memory caught me then, and I felt a heaviness in the pit of my stomach. The window at the auction hall, Pete's face as he walked by. Alison had been so upset that day she'd hardly looked at him, but through the glass panes I'd seen that he was with someone else.

"Maggie," I said, staying calm but a cold chill running through me. "Just out of curiosity, what was the woman's hair like?"

"Red," she said, not missing a beat, but more relaxed now. "But not like mine. That kind of dark chestnutty-red that comes from a bottle."

Chapter 38

Maggie

Maggie had stayed at Owen's place almost every night since she'd told him about the baby. She liked waking up there, in his quiet attic room, and it felt like a world away from everything—although she was one down on her list of stresses anyway now that Jenny had dismissed her worry about Pete.

Owen had the top flat of a cottage by the converted stables where his workshop was, overlooking the cobbled courtyard, and in the evenings they'd make dinner together there. The flat was a real little hideaway, miles from her home and the little traces of Dylan that lingered—she wasn't ready to make her house anybody else's just yet, and eight months was long enough to get her head around that idea, she'd decided.

Mork had started to complain about Maggie's neglect,

meowing endlessly when she swung by her house to give him his food and collect a change of clothes after closing up at the shop. But for so many years the shoe had been on the other foot—her fickle Burmese had been out for the night tormenting the neighborhood females when Maggie could have done with some company on the sofa. So she shrugged off the pet-owner's guilt.

It was still early on a warm Friday evening and Maggie and Owen were lying tangled up in his bedsheets, plates of food half eaten on the dining table. Owen moved his hand down to her bare stomach and then leaned down to kiss it, and Maggie laughed and stroked his hair. He came back, leaned down to kiss her on the mouth and then lay his head next to hers on the pillow.

"I spoke to Anna this week," she said, her mind switching back into work mode, not entirely free of the week yet.

"Mmm-hmm," Owen said, his hand idly stroking her shoulder.

"And she's fine about covering my holiday to Italy," Maggie said. "But I'm thinking—seeing as I'm training her up to run the shop anyway, maybe I can start handing over more responsibility to her, before the baby comes, I mean."

"Relinquishing control," Owen said, smiling. "Is this the same Maggie I fell in love with?"

"Maybe things have changed a little bit," Maggie said, narrowing her eyes at him playfully. "You know, I think it's about time I let someone else take the reins for a bit. In the long term, I'd like to be able to focus on the events side of things, have someone else handle the shop."

"But what about the London branch?" Owen asked, propping himself up on his elbow. "I thought that was your big dream?"

"I thought it was too," Maggie said. "But I just wanted to prove myself to someone who wouldn't even be here to see it." Owen furrowed his brow, confused.

"My dad," she said. "Long story, but he thought I was throwing my education away by setting up on my own. He loved me, but we never saw eye to eye about the business. Expanding to London felt like, I don't know, like enough to prove I was right. Anyway, I've realized it's pretty unlikely I'm going to convince him beyond the grave, so I'm going to go my own way, instead."

Owen put his arm around her and pulled her closer. "Good for you," he said. "And I'll be with you every step of the way."

Maggie had fallen into a doze, and when she woke up, Owen was gone.

Tired from the pregnancy and a week of work, she had closed her eyes and let herself be lulled to sleep by the heat of the summer's evening.

An hour later, bleary-eyed, she was faced with an empty pillow next to her. Almost empty; where Owen's head had been there lay a brown card luggage tag. She propped herself up, looking around the room and through into the bathroom, but saw that they were both empty, and the flat was silent apart from the hum of a solitary trapped bee.

She picked up the card tag and looked at it. There was writing in black pen on the underside:

"*Oh my ears and whiskers,*" she read to herself, "*how late it's getting.*"

There was a hand-drawn picture of a white rabbit next to it.

Maggie got out of bed, rubbing her eyes, and slipped her flowery maxi dress back on. Still dazed, she wandered through to the kitchen to get a glass of water and drank it down in one. It *was* getting late, she thought, looking out the Velux window at the sun setting. How had she fallen asleep like that?

She filled her glass again and looked over at the kitchen wall clock—nine-thirty. Then she spotted it; there, tied on with string, was another note, the same as the last.

Who dares to taint
with vulgar paint
the royal flower bed?

This time she recognized the words right away: of course, the red queen from *Alice in Wonderland! Off with their heads*, she recalled. Maggie slipped on her sandals and, with the clues in her hand, rushed down the stairs and out of Owen's cottage into the courtyard. Across it, over at the stables, she could see that the door to Owen's workshop was slightly open; she smiled as she realized he must be over there waiting for her.

She closed the cottage door behind her, and saw that to the side of it was a child's wooden writing desk. On it was a violet-colored glass, with a label around the base. "Drink me," it said. She flipped the lable over, and as she read the other side she smiled: "(I'm non-alcoholic, by the way)." She took a sip of the drink, cooling elderflower cordial.

Maggie took the glass with her as she crossed the courtyard. As she reached the door to Owen's workshop she remembered how she'd once slammed it in fury, on a day that already seemed a lifetime ago. This time she pushed it open gently, and felt something flutter down onto her shoulder, then another soft touch against her face, her arms, against her head. She looked down at the ground where a rain of diamonds, clubs, spades and hearts had fallen all around her. *You're nothing but a pack of cards*, she thought to herself, picking up an ace.

Owen's workshop was empty, but the back door was open and she could hear the soothing sounds of jazz playing in the garden. Maggie put her empty glass down on the side and walked over towards the music, knowing exactly where she was heading. At the back of Owen's walled garden was a sprawling white rose bush. She made straight for it, nearly tripping up on a loose paving stone.

She looked at each of the flowers and then crouched down to check the ones closer to the ground. It was then she saw the single red rose hidden low; next to it was a small pot of red paint and an abandoned paintbrush with another tag round it. On the card were the words: "*Who's been painting my roses red?*"

Maggie looked back at the red rose and saw that the paint was still wet. There, hung around one of the leaves on the stem, something was shining. Reaching for it, she saw it was a bracelet, inlaid with polished pieces of amber, a perfect match for the necklace her grandmother had given her, the one she was wearing right now.

She turned around and there, sitting on the driftwood bench, was Owen.

In the drawing room at Darlington Hall, pictures of bouquets were spread out on the table between Jack and Maggie. Lucy had left to get some more water and Jack leaned towards Maggie, a mischievous glint in his eye.

"I know it's early days," he said. "But I think it's great about you and Owen getting together." He gave her a wink.

"Thanks, Jack," Maggie said, feeling her cheeks color. "It's been a bit of a whirlwind to be honest."

"I can promise you, Maggie, you've picked a good one there," Jack said, more seriously now. "Owen's a good friend and a really nice guy, through and through. I'd marry my sister off to him if I had one."

"Well, I'm glad you don't. And that's what I thought, well, hoped," Maggie said. "I've not had great luck this year, but he does seem different. And he doesn't seem to think I'm past it yet."

Jack laughed. "Of course not. You're a total catch." He gave her a cheeky smile and Maggie was reminded of how much she'd warmed to him from their first meeting. "Anyway, Owen's always been pretty grown-up, and I think working for himself has made him a lot more responsible too."

"Does Lucy . . ." Maggie asked.

"Nah, I haven't told her anything yet," Owen said. "We don't want her leaking it to *It Girl*, do we? God, you'd end up seeing a picture of you and Owen as a box-out feature in the wedding exclusive," Jack drew the imaginary box in the air with his hand, "HOW WE FOUND LOVE AT WONDERLAND WEDDING."

Maggie laughed. "We'll tell her soon, though," she said. "Should put her mind at rest about the two of us getting on at any rate."

"Yes," Jack said, "and you know she's going to be thrilled. She'll claim the credit for matchmaking you is the only thing."

Lucy came back into the room with a jug of water. "Did I hear someone say *It Girl*?"

"It's nothing, darling," Jack said. "Just talking about some of the feedback we had from the magazine over features they want to include."

Lucy settled herself on the sofa close to Jack. "They're big on the croquet," she said. "Although I said a definite no on using live hedgehogs as balls for the shots they wanted." Maggie smiled.

"I mean honestly," Lucy said. "I know they said we'd just be posing, but I got enough hassle just for wearing a mink fur to that premiere, didn't I, Jack? I don't want all those animal rights people on to me again. It took the dry cleaners forever to get the fake blood out of it, and it still looks a bit pink."

Jack gave Lucy's leg a little squeeze. "So is everything OK, Maggie?" Lucy asked. "It looks like you and Owen have got it all in hand now."

Maggie tried not to get distracted as Jack leaned back on the sofa, making kissy-faces at Maggie that his wife-to-be couldn't see.

"Yes, everything's going perfectly, Lucy. Your wedding is going to be truly spectacular."

"Well hooray for that!" Lucy said, bringing her manicured hands together. "I can hardly wait now, you know. It's not easy finding the man of your dreams, is it?" She looked at Maggie with pity in her eyes. "But I tell you, I can't wait to get that ring on my finger." With that she cupped Jack's face in her hands and gave him a big kiss on the cheek.

Chapter 39

Jenny

"Surprise!"

Zoe, wearing a strapless black and silver dress and looking somehow even more fearsome than she did in her suit, handed me a glass of fizz the moment I stepped through the door of the Fox and Pheasant.

I looked around the pub, taking in the scene. Oh my lord. Today had been my last day at the office, and it had felt much like any other, just with a bit more to do to ensure everything went smoothly while I was away on my honeymoon. My last week had passed in a blur, with my mind very much on the wedding. Dan kept telling me that everything would be OK, but while it was true we'd worked past other hitches, a tea party wedding with cheap blue cups just wasn't the picture I wanted framed on my mantelpiece. There were only three days to go until Dan and I tied the knot, and I was really having a hard time letting go of the day I'd dreamed of.

Chloe had coaxed me out for drinks after work though, and when I said I was feeling antisocial, she insisted that I needed to take my mind off the wedding. I looked over at her now and gave her a discreet glare as I saw that most of the office had turned out for my celebration drinks, party poppers firing at me from all angles.

After my second glass of Cava I'd started to get in the swing of things, and I was touched by the giant card everyone had bought me, filled with signatures and nice notes wishing me luck for the wedding. There really were some lovely people in the office and I felt bad for having been grouchy earlier about celebrating with them. Zoe had even got me a present, a voucher for tea for two at a four-star country hotel nearby. She watched intently as I opened the envelope, trying hard not to stare at the serious amount of cleavage she'd got out for the occasion. "I thought you and Dan could go after the wedding sometime, when all the excitement's died down. And you know what," she said with a wink, "it wasn't even a freebie."

Chloe and I found a nook away from the crowd to catch up a bit in peace.

"You don't need to worry," Chloe said. "It's the people who make a wedding, Jen, everyone knows that. We'll all be there, your family and friends, and we'll make sure it's special."

"And don't forget," she continued, "you've organized loads of other things. You managed to book that all-female swing band, didn't you?"

I nodded. I'd heard them at the summer festival on the green last year, and watched in awe as couples from the swing-dancing group twisted and spun across the grass. Alison and Jamie would probably have been among them.

"I know you're right, Chlo. Of course it's all about the people," I said, snapping out of my sulk properly at last.

"Chloe," I said, taking a sip of my drink. "If you thought something was going on, between Dan and me, if you saw him with someone else . . ."

"What?" Chloe said, spluttering out her drink in a decidedly unladylike way.

"No," I said, passing her a tissue which she used to dab at the damp patches on her top. "Sorry, I mean hypo-thetically speaking. If you saw Dan with another woman, not kissing, but just together—would you tell me?"

"Oh, thank God," Chloe said. "You had me worried there for a minute. Don't do that to me, Jen," she said, putting a hand to her forehead. "Anyway, so, right, if I saw Dan with someone else—I'd think, Dan is generally a fantastic guy who has proven his loyalty time and again. It is highly unlikely that he would cheat on you, and if he did you'd hope he'd be smarter than to do it round here where someone like me would be bound to spot him. I'd assume there was a rational explanation."

She tilted her head, thinking. "And then if it happened again I'd talk to him about it, I think."

"OK," I replied. "You're right."

"Am I?" Chloe said. "Oh good. Do I get another drink? Or do I get to find out who you're on about, at least?"

"You've earned your next drink, yes, Chlo. But no, I'm not saying anything as I'm sure now there's nothing to say." I felt bad now for ever doubting Pete, it was none of my or Maggie's business who he was friends with and after our talk Maggie had quickly rejected her concerns, putting them down to post-fallout paranoia after Dylan's betrayal.

"Anyway, talking of couples," I changed course to deflect Chloe's interest, "are you OK about coming to the wedding on your own? Do you want to invite someone else as your plus one, now that Jon's out of the picture?"

"Oh no, don't worry, Jen. I'll be fine." Chloe was attracting more admiring glances than ever this evening, so I didn't doubt it. She was dressed down, in loose black trousers and a coral blouse, her hair up in a French braid, and she looked radiant. The initial shell-shock of breaking up with Jon had worn off completely and she had bounced back better than ever. Ben, the feisty reporter who'd been on her case for months—more smarm than charm, in my view—really couldn't take his eyes off her tonight.

"Anyway, enough about the wedding—I thought you were supposed to be distracting me from it?" I said, teasing. "So tell me, how are things going at work?"

"Gary's finally giving me a break, can you believe it?" Chloe said, her face lighting up. "I pitched two feature ideas to him—one on boutique hotels, the other on budget interior decorating, and he's letting me write both. Seeing as Alan left to go traveling and there's the recruitment freeze still on, I think he's realized he'll need me to work on more features, so he's sending me on some journalism courses too."

"That's fantastic," I said. Then as we spoke something caught my eye, a flash of silver and black at the bar. Woah. Was that . . . ?

"Oh. My. God. Have you seen that?" I said to Chloe, nodding over towards the bar as I gradually took in the full picture. "Do you think there's another reason Gary might have chilled out a bit?" Chloe stared openmouthed and I let out a snort of laughter as we clocked Zoe's hands creeping onto Gary's bum as he kissed her up against the bar.

Chapter 40

Jenny

"Here we go, one last trawl for the Vintage Teacup Club—and our honorary member," Alison said.

They'd met just outside the gates by the local flea market, where Alison had pulled up in Pete's Volvo with Sophie in the passenger seat.

"I'm pretty good at bargain hunting," Sophie said, once she'd got out of the car, looking down at the floor and pulling her sleeves down over her hands, then peeking up with a hesitant smile.

We were going to need all the help we could get. I'd spent a couple of hours looking online on Thursday, but while there were still plenty of teacups up there they were either out of our price range or delivery wouldn't be possible until after the weekend—and after our wedding.

Jamie had found one at the hospice shop, but it was tatty and chipped.

"OK, let's get to it," I said. "We've got three more flea markets to hit before one o'clock, so we're going to have to be quick."

"Not a sausage," Alison said, disappointed, as the five of us reassembled by the gates twenty minutes later. "Gareth, the guy who sold us the original tea set, said they'd had a few cups out this morning, but they got snapped up really early."

"I couldn't find any either. But this place is brilliant," Sophie said, holding up a 1980s framed Madonna print. "One pound fifty this cost. And he chucked in a CD too." She was beaming.

"Sophie," Alison said, "aren't we meant to be looking for crockery, not CDs?" She opened the back door of the car.

"I know," Sophie said, then reached into a plastic bag she had hooked over her arm. "And while I couldn't find any cups, I did get these." She propped the framed poster up against the car and unwrapped one of the newspaper parcels she'd pulled from her bag. From the black-and-white newsprint she brought out an antique medicine bottle in pale green glass. The sunlight glinted off it. "I got twelve of them, all different colors and sizes. I thought we could use them to put some of the flowers in on each of the tables at your wedding, Jenny." She looked uncertain as she waited for our reaction, hurriedly unwrapping another one to show us.

A smile spread across my face—the second bottle was even more beautiful, larger and a paler green with letters in raised glass spelling out the manufacturer's name. They would add a pretty vintage touch to the tables. "They're gorgeous, Sophie," I said, taking one from her for a closer look and touching her arm in thanks.

"Anyway, onwards and upwards, ladies," Alison said, returning to her usual businesslike manner. "Jump in."

We all piled into the car and strapped on our seatbelts. Sophie put her new CD in the stereo and we drove out of town singing along to "Borderline." Sophie complained that she didn't know Madonna's early stuff, but we drowned her out with our off-key voices. Or rather me and Alison singing off-key and Maggie singing surprisingly well.

By lunchtime, though, when we'd stopped for sandwiches in a tea house on the outskirts of town, our spirits were beginning to sink. Our morning's search had resulted in nothing but a little white sugar bowl with primroses on it.

"It looks like we should have got up even earlier," Alison said. "A couple of the stall-holders said that they'd had things but they'd already been sold before we arrived."

"We did what we could," I said, my heart heavy. "And I refuse to complain about it. I'm getting married tomorrow! Actually," I glanced down at my watch, "I'd better start getting the show on the road, Chloe's coming around in an hour to pick up her bridesmaid's dress."

As Chloe buttoned up my wedding dress she looked over my shoulder into the mirror. Yes, it had been a stretch financially, but somehow Dan and I had made enough money to cover it and the dress had been worth every penny. Chloe smiled and as we both took in the full picture, I knew she was thinking the same thing. The dress fit me perfectly, the corset underneath nipping in my waist to fit the fifties silhouette, and the sweetheart neckline setting off the string of pearls Alison had lent me. I felt like a film star.

I'd found ivory silk shoes with pearl buckles to match and wore long vintage gloves. Chloe had practiced styling my hair so that it fell in soft curls onto my shoulders, the way the hairdresser was going to do it tomorrow morning, and had added a sparkly clip of Grandma Jilly's to pin back the front on one side.

I did a curtsey for Chloe, the petticoat rustling, and she whistled appreciatively.

"Not bad," she said, biting her lip as I saw her eyes start to well up. "Not at all bad, Jen."

I turned to look at Chloe and wondered again at the wisdom of picking such a totally hot bridesmaid. I think it probably makes me a bigger person, or something. We'd picked out a red dress for her together, with a full skirt to match mine and the same short sleeves, but without the lace overlay. The color was gorgeous with her pale skin and there was a naughty flash of cleavage that upped the glamour element. I'd had a go at styling her hair but her ringlets had frizzed out, and the result was more Kate Bush on a bad day then sleek silver-screen actress. Together we'd decided that hair like hers was best left to the professionals.

"Where's Dan tonight?" Chloe asked, looking around as if he might suddenly pop out of the bathroom even though I'd told her he was out.

"He's gone round to Chris's. Chris had a couple of new ideas about tunes for his DJ set and wanted to run them by him first."

"Oh, I see," she said, fiddling with her silver bracelet. "Well it's great to have a sneak preview of what you're going to look like tomorrow."

"Thank you," I said as I gathered up the skirt of my dress and sat back on the sofa. "You've made me feel way better." Chloe took a seat opposite me. She furrowed her brow in concern.

I knew it was written all over my face that I wasn't a hundred percent glowing bride-to-be, no matter what I said. This morning's failure to replace the cups had been a real disappointment, and there was no hiding that. I was slowly facing up to the fact that my wedding was never going to be quite the day I'd hoped for.

"It is all going to be all right, isn't it, Chlo?" I asked her, longing for her to tell me it was.

"Of course," she said, taking my hands in hers and giving me a warm smile. "Look, let's get out of these," she said, pointing to our dresses. "Ali and Maggie will be round in a minute." She was struggling to undo her zip and I got up to help her. "I'm sorry I can't help you set up the hall, but I promised Chris I'd help him print out the table plan. The files he designed and sent me to print corrupted somehow, so I said I'd take a look," Chloe said, as I slipped my jeans back on and she wrestled to get her hair back in control by tying it back.

"What is it with my brother?" I responded, wondering for a moment why she was looking increasingly panicked as her hair refused to lie flat. "He seems to be doing more for my wedding than I am. And you're always round there," I laughed.

"He just wants to make sure you both have a great day, that's all," she said, doing up the buttons on her cardigan. Was I imagining it, or was she blushing?

My thoughts were interrupted by a car horn tooting in the road outside. Chloe and I opened my living-room window and leaned out, taking in the scene in the street. Maggie and Alison had the top down on Maggie's Beetle and it was draped in pastel-colored cloth bunting. We whooped from the window and Maggie tooted back again.

"Come on," Maggie called up from the car. "We've got a wedding hall to decorate!"

I was crammed into the back seat of Maggie's car, next to some of the boxes. "You all right back there?" Alison asked, turning around to face me as we drove out of town. "Yes, fine," I said, rearranging some bunting that my foot had got tangled up in. As I sat back I looked at Alison and Maggie chatting in the front, talking loudly so that their voices carried over the music.

They both had their hair loose today and the wind had messed it up so that there were more untidy strands than neat ones. I'd noticed when they'd arrived that, like me, they were in jeans and trainers, ready to get down to work setting up. Alison was in one of Pete's shirts, Maggie in a faded Blondie T-shirt. Laughing with each other now, they both looked more relaxed that I'd ever seen them.

"I've been thinking," Maggie said, turning to Alison. "Do you think Sophie would like a bit of work experience at the shop?"

Alison smiled, but furrowed her brows, questioning. "Of course she would. But are you sure you know what you'd be letting yourself in for?"

Maggie laughed. "Yes, maybe. But I also think she could be great—she's got a good eye, Ali. Anna'll be covering the shop for me when I'm away in Italy and she could use another pair of hands. Might give Sophie something to keep her occupied during the holidays?"

"I'm sure she'd love that," Alison said. "I'll talk to her about it."

As I watched Ali and Maggie talking, I thought back to the start of the summer and the moment we'd met, how little we'd known each other then. Step by step we'd let each other in, and now it was hard to imagine that we hadn't always been there for each other. These women were both so strong, had bounced back from life's knocks and come out better for it. But then I suppose, somehow, with their help, I had done the same.

The sky behind the old schoolhouse was streaked with pink, and as we approached it we all went quiet for a moment. It was as if the little Victorian building was suspended in time; the sunset cast it in a warm reddish light and the weathervane swung in the breeze. Fields lay all around, making it seem farther away from town, and modern life, than it really was.

Maggie parked just outside. "This place really is gorgeous," she said. "Jen—you've got the key, haven't you?" she asked.

I felt for it in my pocket, "Yes." I'd asked the caretaker if I could borrow it so we could start setting up early.

"OK," Maggie continued. "Why don't you open the place up, and Ali and I will unpack and bring the things in."

"Sure," I said, opening the car door. "See you in a sec."

The lock in the big wooden door was a little stiff—not surprising really as it had been years since the building was used regularly. A better-equipped primary school had opened up in Easton, our neighboring village, and the kids, including Alison's daughter Holly, had been transferred over there. The schoolhouse was such a local landmark however, that the community had come together to insist it wasn't sold off, and it had become a center for plays, concerts and the occasional private party. It hadn't been used for a wedding reception before though, and as a venue it was still pretty rough around the edges—there was nowhere proper to serve drinks (hence Dad's handmade bar) and on our first visit we saw they'd even left a few freestanding chalk boards around. Alison had spotted and fallen in love with them; so one of our plans for tonight was to make big colored chalk signposts to the cloakroom and toilets.

As the heavy wooden door creaked open, warm light spilled out from inside. Alison and Maggie were laughing together over at the car as they unpacked the boxes, but the schoolhouse itself was silent. Why was there light coming from inside? Had Dad come by earlier with another key? Surely not, he'd promised me he'd wait until I called him to say we'd arrived, so that we could all set up together.

I opened the door all the way and looked inside. It took a moment for my eyes to adjust, but when they did I saw that each side of the room was lit with tealights, leading up to a central wooden table. The first surprise was seeing

Dan, the second was registering that the table was laden with dozens of delicate, colorful teacups.

"Dan, what the . . . How?" I said, taking in the whole scene, from Dan's beaming face to the cups and saucers that surrounded him, a smile spreading across my face.

"Jen," Dan said, walking over to stand in front of me. I felt a rush of love for this man I was about to marry. "You've been working so hard organizing everything; and I know I haven't always done as much as I could. When the teacups got smashed I could see how upset you were, even though, in true Jen style, you tried to play it down. I wanted to help make everything perfect." He reached up to stroke my hair.

I could hear the school door opening behind us, and Alison and Maggie's voices as they stepped inside. As I looked over my shoulder at them they fell silent, staring openmouthed at the laden table. "Oh," said Dan. "And by the way, while I'm here taking all the glory, Owen and Pete actually did quite a lot to help." Dan motioned for the two men to step out of the shadows, which they did, taking theatrical bows.

Maggie and Alison had already hurried over to the teacups to take a closer look, and Dan and I went to join them.

"But where did you find them all?" I asked, picking up just one of the tiny cups to hold it, checking that all this was real. Dan looked more gorgeous than ever today, a modest smile on his face and his eyes crinkling a little.

"Dan had us all up at five this morning," Owen said, feigning a yawn and giving Maggie a little wink. "Trawling the flea markets, charity shops, everywhere. Pete gave Adam a ring and he'd found quite a few in Brighton for us so we drove down to collect those too."

"It was *you*—you were the early birds," I said, putting two and two together.

"After today, I tell you," Pete said, "we started to understand how you three ended up such close friends. We bonded a little ourselves. I guess you might call us the Teacup Widowers."

I laughed, and hugged Dan close.

"Dan, thank you," I whispered in his ear. He reached down to kiss me.

The hall filled with wolf whistles as he swept me up into his arms.

Epilogue

Jenny

Dear Alison and Maggie,
Hello ladies. Here I am in a cozy little Irish B&B, in
an enormous squishy bed with a view out over a
beautiful lake . . .

I looked out of the window at the sun on the water, taking in the beauty and calm of the green hills behind it, and put another pillow behind me to get comfy. Dan was snoring softly by my side.

Yes, it really was all true. Who needed five-star hotels? I was in heaven. I went back to the letter and continued writing.

It's a pretty perfect start to the honeymoon,
although the less romantic bit is that Dan is out for

the count. After a few pints of Guinness watching a band in the pub down the road, he's now snoozing away. So I thought I'd take the opportunity to write to you, the old-fashioned way.

When we left, the wedding party was still in full swing and I didn't get a chance to say goodbye properly (you know how I hate to leave a party early).

The schoolhouse looked beautiful, and I have you both to thank for that. Ali, everyone loved the handmade bunting, and the teacups added something very special to the proceedings. Sophie and Holly did a sterling job as waitresses, too.

But back to the party, and the dancing . . . Well. As much as I enjoyed my first dance with Dan, Ali, I don't think it can match the moment I saw Pete lead you up to the dance floor when the swing band came on. The look of shock on your face was a picture as you two started to dance and you clicked that rather than stepping on your toes, Pete could step and twirl you with the best of them. He is such a fantastic dancer—who knew? In that sunshine-yellow dress and red shoes you looked stunning as he spun you around.

While you were up there Jamie confessed to me that for the past few weeks he had been giving Pete and your neighbor Sally some private dance lessons

*together, in secret, so that Pete could surprise you
with his skills. How lovely is that? Jamie said Pete
had really thrown himself into it, fitting classes
around the new job in any spare time he could find.
He needed a female partner to practice with and
apparently Sally's always wanted to learn, so they
paired up. I hope you and Pete keep it going. You
looked great up there.*

*Maggie, thank you so much for your song—I
couldn't believe it when you got up on stage to join
the band. How come you never let on that you had
such a spectacular voice? "Say a Little Prayer"
was the perfect song to choose. I know you said
afterwards that you were nervous, but it didn't show
at all—you're a true professional. Owen looked really
proud to see you up there. He said you'd found
another local band to sing with regularly, is that
right?*

*It was incredible to have everyone we care about
there in one room.*

I put my pen down for a moment and glanced over at
the card on the windowsill. I'd brought the lone pink
envelope with me to Ireland, the only wedding card still
untouched. When I finally opened it, I found a card with
a happy cartoon couple standing on a wedding cake.
Inside, in big, round handwriting, it said: *Happy Wedding*

Day. I smiled, despite myself. *With love from Mum and Nigel.* At the start of the summer I could never have imagined receiving it, much less feeling the way I felt now, not angry anymore, not sad, perhaps even a bit *warm.* I hadn't spoken to Chris properly yet about Mum, but it was time. Dad has forgiven her and now that Chris and I were adults, perhaps we should give her the chance to put things right too.

I went back to the letter, feeling lighter somehow. With Chris on my mind, a memory came back to me and I continued writing:

> And did you <u>see</u> what was going on behind the DJ booth? I'm surprised Chris could even get through his set with Chloe snogging his face off like that. Hilarious. How did I not see that coming? I nearly dropped my champagne. My dad gave me a nudge, that sly old dog obviously knew all along. Anyway, they both seem smitten, and while I'm at a loss as to how someone could fancy my little brother, they're actually a pretty good match, aren't they?
>
> Dan and I have two long, blissful weeks ahead and we're planning on doing absolutely nothing. After all the, er, <u>excitement</u> of the past few weeks I'm looking forward to relaxing. But the stress was absolutely worth it—it was the best day of our lives by far.

Anyway, I can't wait to see you both when I get back. I'm looking forward to your first Stitch "n" Blitz session out in the café garden, Ali. Maggie, I'm sending a kiss to your still-secret bump.

All my love,
Your friend in teacup fondness,
Jenny XX

Readers Guide

The Vintage Teacup Club

Discussion Questions

1. Jenny, Maggie and Alison meet at the beginning of the summer and bond over their shared love of a vintage tea set. Other than teacups, what brings the three women together and allows their friendship to blossom?

2. Each member of the Teacup Club is at a different stage in her life. What do you think the women gain from each other as a result of being in different places in life? And what role—if any—does timing play in a friendship forming? What role does timing play in one ending?

3. Mother-daughter relationships are a recurring theme in the book. Although Jenny is looking forward to her upcoming wedding, she feels emptiness because of her estrangement from her mother. Meanwhile, teenage Sophie continues to rebel, causing Alison to feel that the daughter she knew is now gone. Discuss how complicated this relationship can be and the hold that mothers have on their daughters.

4. Aside from mother-daughter relationships, what are other recurring themes in this book? Discuss.

5. When Jenny is in her childhood bedroom, she finds sketches and pages of a book that she wrote when she was younger. While looking at the book she had hoped to see published one day, she realizes that she allowed the nagging voice of doubt to get in the way of pursuing her dream. Who else in the novel puts her dreams on hold or gets in her own way? What ultimately helps these same people confidently move forward?

6. Maggie is stunned when she first sees an email from Dylan, but eventually replies and agrees to meet up with him. What do you think of their reunion—their initial meet-up and how things progress?

7. Ultimately, Maggie feels that she and Dylan have grown over their four years apart and that they now know what it takes to make their relationship work. In the meantime, we see Alison and Pete struggle a bit in their marriage—they each feel taken for granted. Finally, we see Ruby and Derek discuss the highs and lows of their years together. What do you think it seems to take to make a relationship work?

8. Jenny's mother reaches out to her after walking out on the family two decades earlier. Consider both women,

their varied perspectives, and discuss what is right or wrong in what she wants and in how she handles the situation.

9. Both Maggie and Jenny are forced to confront the past, when their ex-husband and mother, respectively, reenter their lives. When is it too little, too late? Is it ever too late to forgive and start over?

10. What character do you identify with the most? What friendships have you unexpectedly formed and what allowed the friendship to form?

NOTES